abouttheauthor

John Reed was the kind of man who, one instant, might touch you to your very core—send a symphony into the marrow of your bones. But he was also the type who, the next instant, might prove exasperatingly shallow. Such was his sad contradiction. There he'd be reciting something truly something—but reciting it at the exclusive room of the trendiest possible of-the-second club to an audience of those beautiful and ambitious New Yorkers who, though not always successful at it, were the most *willing*, in the name of glory, to lead lives unexamined and vapid.

His tragic and untimely demise unfolded at a juncture when I was most disgusted with him—for not a month earlier, his reprehensible behavior had ended our relationship. One that had seemed riddled . . . well, with potential.

He could be a boy sometimes, standing as he would have in 1977, a child of the Manhattan wasteland—a body filthy and lean, and trying to discover for itself honor in the void. This aspect of his work had been of interest to me. And since, during the course of our romance, we discussed our writing with each other, I became quite familiar with his proposal for *Duh Whole*—the tale of a girl gone awry, and a great big hole. Hence, it was not unexpectedly (the prospect of finishing the unfinished works of expired authors ever-tempting) that I was approached the very minute John first coughed (with luck, it'd be a foreshadowing of consumption and doom). His outline proved surprisingly complete, and having no book deal of my own, I was soon secured in the effort—and with John's institutionalization and rapid decline, I was given the green light. If you like my work, you might look for other novels ostensibly by Reed, such as *Snowball's Chance* and *A Still Small Voice,* which, incidentally, I also wrote.

foreword

Jake Hoye, that finest of editorial representatives from that finest of institutions of fine letters, sat at his favorite table at Zen Palate, jingling the coins in his pocket as John explained that he had never had much of a hand for journalism (just look at that Orwell fiasco) and doubted his usefulness. *Why,* Jake suggested, *we can call it fiction.* And dipping his summer roll, the editor inquired—

"So, you don't mind writing a tell-all book about a former lover?"

Well, John ventured weakly, she was a celebrity. And presumably that meant someone would have to expose her eventually, and if he was the one who had to do it—then, do it he would. And thus, John sighed heavily and resigned himself to the betrayal of Thing, a woman who, at that moment in his life, he didn't think he ever liked that much anyway. Still, it'd be no mean feat giving his literary agency their thriller, and Jake his exposé, and some film/television agent, yet to be named, God knows what. It wasn't really that hard to write a good novel—but to write a good novel and get it published, and make money—it took a sinister mastermind. Well, there was always his brother. In fact, the whole family being something of an evil empire, John hoped he might draw on it. Alas. What did he expect? No one had sat him down when he was three years old and said—

John Reed, what the world needs now is another novelist.

It was all his own dumb idea. The alphabet, the words, the sentences—all of it. He couldn't blame his parents either, they discouraged reading. Actually, he believed it to be when he first showed signs of the rotten habit that his mother had a second son—and this one, at her insistence, was brought up properly. Agent at birth, modeling—and already a producer at . . .

"Well yes," said John, slumping, "I do know all about the whole."

the

WHOLE

johnreed

POCKET
BOOKS

NEW YORK   LONDON TORONTO   SYDNEY

POCKET BOOKS, a division of Simon & Schuster, Inc.
1230 Avenue of the Americas, New York, NY 10020

MTV Music Television and all related titles, logos, and
characters are trademarks of MTV Networks, a division of
Viacom International Inc.

Library of Congress Cataloging-in-Publication Data

Reed, John, 1969–
   The whole / John Reed.
     p. cm.
     ISBN 0-7434-8501-7
     I. Title.

   PS3568.E366447W47 2005
   813'.6—dc22

                            2004059233
First MTV Books/Pocket Books trade paperback printing January 2005

10 9 8 7 6 5 4 3 2 1

Interior design by Ruth Lee-Mui

Art direction by Jeffrey Keyton & Deklah Polansky
Cover design by Christopher Truch
Cover illustration by Dover Publications, Dover Pictorial Series

For information regarding special discounts for bulk purchases,
please contact Simon & Schuster Special Sales at
1-800-456-6798 or business@simonandschuster.com

Manufactured in the United States of America

the

WH●LE

It happened in the heartland.

Little Bobby Peterson was digging a hole. A deep hole, for he was an ambitious boy.

He pushed his shovel into the sand, and edged it out—full. He emptied the load into the sandbox—a six-by-six-foot hole that his father had dug and bordered with wood, and filled with sand purchased from Home Depot. Beyond, in the green grass, the boy's toy dump trucks, cement mixers, cranes and tractors were parked in neat rows, awaiting their use—as if the child meant to reconstruct the worksite just as faithfully as the toy makers had reconstructed the rigs. He pushed the earthmover into his deepening hole, and with a load of damp sand, circled the truck in the air—and blew through his lips in an engine sound.

"Brrrgghhrhuuummmmm."

And, it was then that he looked down, and replaced the rig, and picked up his red, plastic shovel, and prodded at his hole, because, it seemed, the hole was growing—*all by itself*. The sand funneling inwards, Bobby peered puzzledly at the depression. It was a peculiar hole—this hole. And rising from his crossed legs onto his bent knees, Bobby leaned back, lifted his eyebrows and tilted his head. *What chicanery is this?* And he had meant to simply look up, to call his mother, to question her on this bizarre and possibly frightening development. And yet, instead, his head jerked upwards and he saw the sun, and when he opened his mouth it was to scream—for the hole had suddenly enlarged, taking him. It engulfed him—sucked him down like a spider down the drain. And Bobby's dog, Rupert, he saw it, and he barked—and because he was a loyal dog (a Benji mutt rescued from the pound), he ran to the boy who screamed, whose arms flimmered in the air, shovel in hand. And then the dog, he went too—for that hole had grown. Yawping, crying, he scrabbled at the sink-

johnreed

ing ground—trying to pull away from a circumference that was ever increasing.

And so, as the dog barked and the boy screamed in the sinking sand of the sandbox, Bobby's mother, Jane, she abandoned her wicker basket. On the laundry line, bed linens remained—white and crackling in the summer sun and summer breeze. One damp sheet slid out from under its clothespins and fell to the springy grass—as the mother walked, then ran towards her child. From the sideyard to the backyard, she rounded the corner.

And there was the hole. And there was Bobby, in the middle of it—half in, half out. His arms waved. And as his mother ran, she saw her son slide from view, and the wooden borders of the sandbox slide in over him. She screamed, as the lawn joined the sandbox in the hole. And still, the hole widening, she ran towards her child. And then the hole took her too. And all trace of them disappeared. The three. Boy, dog, mom. And there followed a moment of silence, as dad, in the workshop, looked up from the lumber on his saw table. And he wondered if maybe he had heard something through the sawing. And he took the pencil out from behind his ear and placed it on the counter. And he walked out of the workshop, calling—

"Jane? Jane? Bobby? Rupert? Jane?"

And just as he closed the door to the workshop—the hole took him, and it. And they were gone.

And as the hole neared the house, sister Bethany listened to bubbly rock music and talked on the phone. She lay on the bed, her legs lilting behind her as she lolled this way and that—until she felt a shudder. Then she stood and went to the window. And she saw it. And she dropped the phone, and screaming, just as her brother and mother had screamed, she fled her room— teenage legs hurling her down the hall. On either side of her, framed pictures and flower vases were falling—shattering. And the house was tipping-like, onto its side—and she ran towards the front door, to get there before . . . before . . .

She didn't understand it—

But Jeez, before the house sinks into the ground!

So, still screaming, she bounded down the stairs, through the living room—and into the foyer. And she reached for the door handle. And she turned, pushed the brass lever. And the front door opened—

the**WH**●**LE**

And she stood there on the threshold as the house bucked and rolled—and she clutched at the coat pegs fixed to the wall. And the front door, which once opened onto a green lawn and a red Chevy and a yellow Ford Explorer, now, as the house pitched back, opened onto blue sky and a few scattered clouds. And then, that open door slammed shut—yanked by an angry gravity. A vengeful gravity—that took the girl and the house with it.

And finally . . . after the driveway and what remained of the landscaped yards, the white picket fence, it too crumbled—and succumbed. And there was, then, a welling up around the fringe of the hole—and the Earth, it seemed to burp. And where there had once been a family and a house, there was now no more than a pit. A pit of churned, brownish-red earth—and only the occasional tree branch, brick, or strip of vinyl siding. Uniformly nothing.

And a few minutes later, the summer songs of birds returned, but a sadness imbued them, for a sadness imbued all. To see the ribbons of dust that spired up to the white sun was to know that this was no hour of serenade. Just lamentation. *Paa-uu-eeeee, paa-uu-eeeee*, whistled the black-bellied plover—

Paa-uu-eeeee. . . .

Now, several years ago, the lass who would become our girl, Thing, disembarked from her New Jersey homestead, waving forever good-bye to the strangers she called parents. One hour later, opting for a room in the city over the rigors of college, the lone eighteen-year-old stepped out of her U-Haul, and into her East Village share.[1]

With those rather small features that some might associate with fashion models (others, fetal alcohol syndrome) and that straight blonde hair and baby fatt[2] that belies flavored lip gloss and Wonder bread, the girl was attractivish, in an at-one-with-Middle-America kind of way. And thus, it was then, in her first incarnation—a young stylist who had chanced into regularity at MTV—that John Reed (just stylish, a poet and chess player) took up cohabitation with the plump wage earner.

Some time later, there was acrimony. And, as she had continued to gain weight, upon greeting her at some stranger's party, John gleefully puffed up his cheeks, as if to say—

My, aren't we a blowfish?

---

[1] At the risk that this digression be confused with the egoistic juvenilia that dots contemporary fiction in the form of foot and margin notes, I must interrupt, nevertheless, to address an issue that Jake strongly discouraged me from broaching—citing the writerly tendency to paranoia as an ongoing unpleasantness of publishing. Yet, I will tell you—all this really did transpire. And it is due to a conspiracy far beyond the reaches of a mere writer that, unfortunately, none of you remember it. Make no mistake—despite the fact that I was forced to accept the categorization of "novel," the account herein is entirely faithful to the events *as they happened.* This is how it was. What you remember is the fiction.

[2] While the author refused to explain to readers this misspelling of "fat," I find the reference too obscure to let go without addressing. According to the author, to Thing, "fat" is a "four letter word." Hence: "fatt."—Jake Hoye, Senior Editor, MTV Books.

johnreed

But to John's disgust, she rented out that second bedroom (his erstwhile office) to someone who paid his share of the rent—and, flush with this windfall, she went to fatt camp, and underwent liposuction, and breast augmentation, and bought an entirely new wardrobe. And although she had no friends or lovers, she was admired intensely by the guys at the deli. And as she lost weight—fatt camp taught her to survive on a diet of radishes—even more so. Yes, perhaps she was alone. Yes, perhaps she was lonely. Yes, perhaps she did lead a sad miserly life, which, for that matter, she experienced only partially—as the radish diet, while it subtracted the pounds, added a permanent state of bewilderment. But, despite the mistakes she made as a result of malnutrition, she worked hard in the way that only the deeply lonely can work hard. And, because of the goofy, malnourished, lonely things she said, she was funny. And, with all that malnourishment, and all that lonely time in front of the mirror with a make-up kit, and all that time under the knife—she looked damn good. So Viacom (MTV) hired her more and more. And in that capacity, she was enlisted to play a part in the MTV Spring Break festivities in South Beach. And, tanning for a week before she left, the lonely, malnourished girl showed all she could of her freshly formed figure—sporting a thong bikini upon arrival. And when the fourth Thing for a Day contestant dropped out of the newt-eating challenge, a cameraman named Otto asked if that stylist girl wouldn't do, as she was a pretty good white girl, and that was what they needed. And when word came down that the freelancer *was* eligible to enter the contest, our young, thonged prospect was consulted. And she readily agreed to do her part with the amphibian (or so it would seem), and then they were live—nationwide.

Verne, a blond linebacker from Tulane University, swallowed his newt easily, and thereupon, burped. Cora, from Puerto Rico via Brooklyn, had more trouble—but she did get the critter down, and make an awfully funny face in the process. Jerome, a black, red-haired, dreadlocked surfer, reveled in the procedure—he chewed, opened his mouth, and stuck out his tongue.

Objectively, Jerome looked like he'd be hard to beat, and when our petite, pink stylist came to the microphone, the few screaming collegiates in the crowd courageous enough to bankroll the unlikely aspirant were getting odds of 20 to 1.

the**WH●LE**

Frankly, few were surprised when the stylist begged off partaking of the live snack.

"I'm sorry, I thought you meant a little piece of paper—maybe with some writing on it."

All were confused, until Otto, cameraman, called out from behind his camera—

"A note! She thought it was a note!"

Boos followed. A splash of beer arched across the contest area. Our stylist's bikini top was dampened. Her chest heaved—expanded with the cool shock of the Amstel. The crowd quieted. The contest announcer coaxed—

"C'mon, just hold the little guy. I know you can eat'im."

Our stylist took the squirming hors d'oeuvre by the midsection, between her thumb and forefinger. The contest announcer turned to the crowd—

"They all want you to eat it. Don't they?"

The crowd chanted, "Eat it."

Our girl eyeballed the striped newt, dangled it above her dainty nosetip, lowered the struggler into her open mouth, closed her mouth, swallowed—and then the gag reflex kicked in. And, seeing as how that gag reflex had been well practiced since fatt camp (a weakness for BLTs left few alternatives), that newt went flying into the crowd as if it had been shot from a canon. And one of our stylist's breasts, packed so tightly into its bikini triangle—it too blasted off, leaving that baby-faced blondie scrambling for coverage, and the crowd in an enraptured apoplexy. Someone squealed—

"The newt broke in half!"

The contest announcer turned to the judges—

"Does that count?"

The judges conferred, reviewed the rules—there was nothing to say that once you swallowed the newt you weren't allowed to projectile vomit it. The question was—did newt hit bottom? That is, had it been, however briefly, stomached?

"Let's go," said the announcer, "to the videotape!"

The videotape was gone too, and it sure looked as if that newt

johnreed

had made it all the way down. And our girl's newt swallow was declared good. And the Applause-O-Meter measured applause levels for each of the contestants—and our girl was triumphant. She was MTV's Thing of the Day, and had won the right to star in several spots that would help to promote the conglomerate's exhaustive coverage of people drinking on the beach.

"You're the Thing, girl," the contest announcer told her.

And it was not ten minutes later that, right there and then, in thong, microphone in hand, our girl interviewed a pair of reckless fashion models (desperate—no surgery, noses too big) who had composed a little ditty about the youth bonanza—

> *Woodstock was hip and Lollapalooza was hot,*
> *But here at South Beach, MTV rocks!*

This was accompanied by some swagger and shaking of their own thonged bodies. And thus did the world see the birth of the Singa-Thinga-Thong spot—which fed and grew to include every genus of singing, shaking maniac. Exalted by glorious resurrection in broadcasts from Boston (St. Patrick's Day) and New Orleans (Mardi Gras), the Singa-Thinga-Thong spot became something of a staple for the network. A dependable dalliance, they called it. And thus, also, was the birth of "Thing" herself.

Like many artists, great and slight, Thing's sense of direction was not navigated so much by map as by intuition. Sometimes she'd have the whimsy to get out of a taxi four blocks too early, only to discover that she was standing in front of that shop where she had seen that dress she had thought of buying at the end of last month, when unhappily, her ten thousand dollars a month had run out. (And look, coincidence of coincidences, now she had the money!) Strictly speaking, Thing was so very sensitive that it did not take a thought at all, but the mere echo of a thought to inspire her to action. Her wants were virtually preverbal—an infant's craving for that stuff out of reach. And as for her discovery by MTV, it was quite fitting—as, ever since grade school, she had wanted to be a star. And not—no, no—just any star. Not just some Hepburn or Monroe. She had to be more. She had to be the most. That was all she wanted. The only little thing. And aside from that, she had no particular loyalty to anything—not this ethic or that revolution.

To her, all these cultures and identities, which the world so treasured, they were no more than eggshells—while we ourselves were more prone to scrambling. Indeed, it was by attempting to preserve the eggshell (culture, identity) that world suffering was brought about—for the eggshell was a refuge inherently doomed. As a species, we were overly sentimental about language and religion, and all those other trappings of life that we found so extraordinary—which were really just rote and mundane. Honestly, nobody cared one whit for any of these allegiances, except in the respect that if it was all they knew, why then, it *had* to be good. But Thing, she sensed the truth—that assimilation was our friend, and that humankind had to embrace the leveling of tradition. And yes, it was nice that it so happened that it was precisely her own cultural milieu that was the most powerful—and the one doing the leveling. But even if that circumstance was a relief (which had, possibly, saved her, on the way to stardom, a little time and effort here and there), she was nonetheless convinced that had she been an Ethiopian, or any other ilk of underprivileged person, she would have found a way to be leading exactly the same life she was leading now. It was simply inconceivable that her good fortune could have anything to do with luck—as anyone would tell you that you made your own luck. Why, that was a medical fact! Her psychiatrist had told her. And her psychiatrist would know, as her psychiatrist was rather lucky, well, quite fortunate herself. By willpower alone—the sheer force of positive thinking—had Thing achieved the correct socialization and taste. No, no, no, not by chance, but by hard work was she in perfect sync with the global standard—which might even be an intergalactic standard, as she had often heard it called "universal." And by that, this guiding principle of the universal (and yes, she was absolutely self-assured in this conviction), anything deemed weird or abnormal, or even just weak or secondary—well, it would have to be forgotten. She knew (and she knew she was right too) that only if we were to aspire to utter homogeny might we expect peace and harmony—and that conversely, to aspire to individualism, we might expect trouble.

Suffice it to say, Thing understood television.

Not to be misconstrued—Thing didn't consciously understand it, and television was terrific, and none of that homogenization was to create any unity, or movement, or any such dark and foreboding thing, but rather, a crowd, an audience—a happy-go-lucky assortment of good scrambled eggs. A world of swaying spectators. Of course, to avoid any variety of unfortunate melee, they'd have to be just different and isolated enough to, somewhat, resent each other's company. A certain level of autonomy (if not actual individualism, which was fine, in groups) had to be encouraged. Nothing too genuine, obviously (authentic emotions tended people towards outbursts of emotion), but just bits and pieces from so many sources that it could never add up to a whole—just a confused kind of medley that might mask as a whole, and be insecure and envious enough to be threatened by other confused kind of medleys—thereby preventing any ill-advised *collusion*. The ideal thing was to promote autonomy without identity, to make people just separate enough to have their own separate "interests" that kept them from assembling—that kept them, for the most part, alone, suspended in a state of perpetual yearning in front of their own separate computers or televisions. And even then, when they did get together (and they would too, because, like so many of God's creatures, they had that irrepressible drive to flock, herd and swarm), it'd be over something delightfully peripheral—like music, or sports. Nothing that could really matter, to any sane person, one way or the other. . . .

There were high points.

Among the 162 minutes of Thing's sixty-two spots (thirty-seven aired), there were moments when she attained, if not true perfection in the sublime, true perfection in the burlesque—

These were the good things, and dubbed so, "the good things," by her editors and producers. Here were the five shiningest examples of Thing's accomplishments. These five things. Largely, with an accompaniment of maudlin Muzak, the quintet made up the best-of selects in Thing's year-end, farewell tribute.

1. Swiss Alps, X-Games—April

Freezing with snowboarders, Thing and her crew attempted to improve their ratings.

As it broke down, over Thing's year on the air, she'd wear three thongs, one pair of pants (a mistake), and thirty-seven bikini tops. . . .

And it was on this occasion in the Swiss Alps that Thing's fiddling with her top reached a peak. It was as if, to her, the slippage of a strap or cup represented her flagging on-air popularity. Of all the types of bikini tops there were . . . well, she tried everything. And throughout, she commented, asked the camera—

"Strap?"

"No strap?"

"Stripes?"

"Pad?"

"No pad?"

"Polka dots?"

"Push in?"

"Push up?"

"Print?"

"Or . . . lift and separate?"

The permutations were endless, and the team had not yet discovered the delicate balance—though this was to be that world-rocking instant when that balance was first struck, and Thing and her producers discovered what *it* was all about. For though she was right—the Thing was the cleavage—it was not merely the cleavage, nor even primarily the cleavage. It was, rather . . .

Thing in her thong bikini in the cold, well . . . her anatomy had the expected reaction. That is—her nipples hardened. And, in her silky white top (after this, all her tops were silky, and nearly all, white), the situation was apparent. It mattered little what up, over, in or out Thing applied to herself, or indeed what wretched rhyme the poor snowboarders were attempting to execute—Thing's stiffness was mesmerizing. At last, the ratings would soar.

Upon their first viewing of this triumph, Thing's producers would forge a couplet of their own—

Herein, herein, herein's the tip—
Stiffen those, stiffen those, stiffen those nips!

As far as what lengths those producers would go to do just that—well, they'd go to great lengths. Extreme lengths . . . Any lengths.

2. Cancún, Cinco de Mayo—May

Sand, litter, blue ocean, and the roasted hides of mealy fraternity brothers. And Thing, on the beach—doused in beer.

The emptied buckets clunked, tipped in the sand—and suds ran down her body as she squeezed her breasts together with her forearms. And the wet, white bikini top, it stuck—clung to her.

"Ewww—it's chilly!" she shrieked.

Laughing their belly laughs, the beer boys nodded, delivered each other claps of congratulations, and thumped their meaty shoulders into other meaty shoulders.

And Thing was thrilled. Her wild, cold eyes apertures—rapturous of those enraptured. The zoom lens delivered her goose bumps to all of America. Shivering, giggling, this young Thing found herself surprised—elated by the dependability of her own physiology. She was just so fortunate, she thought (her eyes glowed with the blessing), so very fortunate that her plastic surgeon hadn't severed any of those nerves that had turned out to be so crucial!

So, smiley, Thing's glance fell to her own chest—while, likewise, beside her, equally smiley, and awed, the beer boys who had immersed her, they too watched, and waited. . . .

3. The Grammys—May

Thing was setting the scene—

"Fame, wealth, beauty, extraordinary talent—the atmosphere here is positively intoxic!"

This said, Thing's breathy phrases abruptly expired—and the VJ took a moment to meditate not only on her own perplexity (for something, somewhere in what she'd said, she suspected, was amiss), but on her fascination with her own perplexity. Her own stupidity, well, at times, it was riveting—shaded by deeper meanings, perhaps, or even genius. And though the specifics of that genius, in this incidence, as in most others, were just slippery enough to elude her, nevertheless, she decided—it was impressive. Thus, she looked down to check that her nipples were still there. They were. Impressed with herself in that too, she resumed—

john**reed**

"Here we be! The red carpet. Oh look, it's Hugh!"

The aging publisher wore satin pajamas and dark glasses. A short hop behind him were six of his bunnies, and Thing primped and pursed her lips with rivalry. (The camera loved her collagen pout.) And behind the sextette of fleshy midwesterners (just moved to California!), there stumbled the target of Thing's interview. Lecherous and impaired, Tommy Lee bobbled a cocktail in the crook of his claw.

Thing thrust up her microphoned hand like he was the teacher and she had to pee, "Ew, ew." She panted—

"There he is! There he is!"

Startled by her own voice, Thing raised her eyebrows, looked to the camera lens, and remembered her dignity.

"His music is better than it sounds."

Then she cleared her throat.

"Ehem, so, yes, there he is. That daaaarrling of drummers, adored, mostly, for his trouble with the three Ls—love, law, and Lee."

Having successfully read the cue card, Thing checked to see what she was wearing (a white thong bikini), and adjusted the little there was of it—although to do so was to risk toppling over. In fact, any sudden movement raised that risk, as Thing, having chosen for the occasion extraordinarily high platform sneakers, was forced to take a rather unstable and suggestive posture—just to stand up. And, it being a windy, chilly afternoon, her bikini top (like her posture) commanded attention—and the tattooed and greasy rocker lowered his sunglasses, reached into his pocket, and offered Thing a lollipop. Through her 800-watt tan, she blushed with the attention, accepted the Blow Pop, and immediately regressed to five years old—sucking on the lolly so raptly that a stain of cherry-red juice fringed her lips.

"I'm musical too," she offered, shyly—

"I've always wanted to play the strumpet."

With that, Tommy Lee commandeered her microphone—and nudged her to a position very nearly beyond "title safety," or, in other words, to an inauspicious location at the periphery of the frame. Even so, Thing, puddingified, wasn't about to stop him. And just as if it were a serenade, she remained transfixed, as Tommy, who knew more or less what he was supposed to do, belted out his four lines—

> *You're as hot*
> *As a Malibu snot!*
> *Sweet for the pickin',*
> *And salty, for lickin'.*

Then he retrieved the gift sucker (which evacuated Thing's lips with a kerplop), and advanced on his next conquest, while Thing managed little more than a limp, damp look . . . and a sigh. . . .

4. Los Angeles Courthouse—September

Sadly, the anatomical formula was an unforgiving one, and after a few dozen spots, it was rather a tax on the imagination to find novel approaches to exploit that aspect of human physiology. *How much swimming? How many pools and beach showers? How much cold water?*

Accordingly, as the result of a dearth of ideas (and shaky ratings in the key consumer category "had four-plus pieces of chewing gum in the past week"), it was decided to divert attention to Thing's backside, the rationale being that this might prove as bounteous as her frontside—or, if not that, a divergence amusing enough to buy some time. And though they'd fairish success with the recipe (Howard, for example), interest was rapidly exhausted, and the backlash of the experiment was to put Thing in pants (she retained her bikini top) in an effort to classen things up.

And so, in pants, outside the Los Angeles courthouse, amid throngs of newscasters, in that primordial war with ratings, Thing faced an unfamiliar challenge—to battle with all the other media flunkies for a few mortgage-paying words from an alleged child molester.

johnreed

Thing reported from the courthouse steps—

"At any moment, we expect pop star Michael Jackson, who most believe isn't so bad after all."

The pedophilia, the pants. Thing knew it was a break, but she also knew it'd be a long bloody march from here to the news desk, and she elbowed her way to the front lines with Kong-like self-importance. She'd get something off that chalky Sambonochio if she had to kill someone to do it.

Still . . . it was almost too much to ask when Jackson bounded down the steps and leapt into the media frenzy, hollering—

"Where's Thing? I've got a song for Thing!"

And yet—despite her gleeful squeaks—Thing somehow knew that this was not how it was supposed to be. It was not that she was experienced in such matters, but when that barrel-chested Peter Pan hopped onto the roof of his personal ice-cream truck, which began to issue forth that candy, welcome-to-the-carnival tune—she had the sense that her peers at CNN would be unforthcoming with that key to the clubroom.

> We get sweaty riding rides.
> We cuddle in our tighty whites.
> It's natural that boys get stinky.
> We scratch our pits and sniff our pinkies.

For verse two, Jackson reached for Thing—to pull her up beside him on the roof of the ice-cream truck. She resisted—at first quite casually, and then quite pronouncedly, with flailing desperation. She was sure that he was going to say something he shouldn't say—not on television—and she could already feel the weight of Public Opinion. But the other reporters, palms and probing fingers on derrière, they pushed her aloft—and, flashbulbs flashing, cameras humming, jingle music jingling, Jackson piped his second verse.

We giggle when we drink our juice.
We like it sweet and 90 proof.
Bear cubs wrestle, bear cubs grunt.
You think it's wrong, you're ignorant.

Helpless to his charm, Thing tapped her foot, for even if it wasn't, dead-on, the beginning of something she wanted, it was the beginning, dead-on, of something.

5. Death Row—December

Though unrehearsed (no cue card), Thing knew very well to look directly into the camera, and to stress at least one word per sentence as she made her introduction—

"Talking about justice in America," she said, by way of clarity—

"Here, in the United States, we aspire to a justice of integrity, one above reproach, of absolute purity and purity of intentions. And . . . we don't care if we have to get our hands a little dirty to do it! If we want law and order, we're gonna have to kick a few people around! Like . . . the lady with the scales, how's she gonna know anyway?"

Thing muffled her microphone and leaned around the lens to the cameraman. Her voice still audible, she asked—

"I mean, Otto, justice is blind, right?"

Thing, for this misadventure in crime journalism (MJ had yielded the numbers), was back in her thong. She stood in front of a wall of ceramic-tiled bricks. And after some out-of-range discussion with her cameraman, Thing readjusted her microphone (and bikini strap), and delivered her lead-in—

"Capital punishment—cruel and fruitable, or, the ultimate in criminal detergent?" Turning her head, from a three-quarter view to full on, Thing proceeded gravely—

"Today we interview three men on death row. Three men who are here, in this maximum-security facility, because they never had a chance! Or, dad-burned it, because they never pulled themselves up by their own bootstraps! These are men who are sentenced to die because they were never loved enough—or good enough—or hardworking enough to make anything of themselves! And . . . or . . . er . . . rather . . . these are savage and sociopathic men who never had the capital to form their own corporations!"

Thing scrunched up her eyes and mouth—because that didn't quite seem to capture the mood of what she was saying, even if it did sort of sum up what she meant.

She looked to Otto for encouragement, or, maybe, reproach. But Otto, a long-haired, bearded and bellied type, tended to think everything was okay—always.

"Cool, cool," he rasped.

Thing tilted her head, utterly baffled. She struggled for clarity. She knew that it was really just a question of mind over patter. And then . . . she suddenly gave up, or succeeded—and after sighing miserably at the confusion of it all, jiggled her breasts, widened her eyes and smiled her porcelain-capped smile (a recent procedure).

That was the cut.

Then, Thing, her crew, the warden and his guards walked down one of the cement and glazed-brick hallways. Speaking into the microphone, which Thing held for him, the warden explained the preparations that he and his staff had made for her visit—

"We got'ar boys set up for'ya down'na wreck'all. It's ushu'lly no more than four at'a time down thair—but we maid'an e'ception today."

The warden was a roly-poly Texan (at home in his own state of the electric chair and good ol' American barbeques) and he grinned from ear to ear—satisfied with his command of the situation. Soon, the procession turned a corner through two steel doors—entering a darkened room.

the**WH●LE**

"I can't see anything," whispered Thing gleefully, into her crackling microphone—

"It's way spooky in here."

At that, an inmate ignited—swinging about a dozen flash-lights this way and that. After a bit, the beams settled, illuminating the faces of individual prisoners—every one of them hard and mean.

Although Thing was unfazed by the dangerous detainees (she knew greater anxiety from the calorie count of a milkshake), the patriarchal warden assumed she was a shrinking violet—

"Oh," he laughed, "honay, honay—don'chu worra. Tha's jus' fo' 'fect. We got ova' a hun'red ahmed g'ards in heah."

As if on cue, the show began.

"Wee-*haa*!" exclaimed the warden—

"Jus' like Elvis in *Jailhouse Rock*!"

And Thing bestowed on him an empty smile, because he was yammering to her about some really ancient stuff that didn't mean anything at all.

Elvis? Jailhouse what? Should someone look that up?

A single spotlight circled the room, coming to rest on an old man sitting on a balcony. He held a guitar pick, and lifted a worn acoustic onto his lap—and then, he began to rock, that is, *to rock out*. It was plugged in, that guitar, and the old man had his Fender *weeping with Rock & Roll blues.*

Thing was ebullient, and over the din, for the camera, she made her introduction of the prisoner—

"That shriveled guy, he must be Uni the Pepperuni, convicted for criminal conspiracy and the murder of six bookbinders, or, I mean, uh . . ." Thing read her cue card, ". . . bookmakers. He's been battling his sentence, death by elocution in the electrolysis chair, for over thirty years."

Drums, bass, the rec room came alive with music, as the old man crooned his croon—

Bein' rich gets all da larks,
Like suits made from da skin a sharks!
And bein' poor gets all de lumps,
Like one-eyed broads who's gots two stumps.
No wonder, as a caused by dat, I grows up ta be a rat.

A broader spotlight assumed duty, and behind Uni, a group of old men playing dominoes arose, and, barbershop quartetish, the four codgers leaned together to harmonize the chorus—

A rat, a rat, a caused by dat, I grows up ta be a rat.

The beam of the flashlights then abandoned the geriatric songsters, and located a lank, young prisoner, surrounded by lawyers and reporters and other hangers-on.

Quickly, Thing ducked her face in front of the camera—

"Oh, that must be Little Stevie, who, after his Middle-America crime spree of two years ago, has been waging his own battle in the courts—to have his death sentence carried out."

By the time Thing had finished her introduction, Little Stevie was singing—

Myself, I have no reservations,
For in a swap of situations,
I'd have no cause for hesitation.
(No remorse or contemplation.)
I'd gas you till asphyxiation—
And, revel in your fibrillations!

Several prisoners, made up to look like lawyers and reporters, shook their pens and pencils—and provided the chorus.

Your fibrillations, fibrillations,
Revel in your fibrillations!

The spotlights dropped. And Otto turned to Thing, who informed her television audience—

"I'm presuming that we'll next hear from The Smiler, the final subject of our death row interviews. He killed a bunch of nuns."

A soft luminosity diffused a balcony cell, where a spongy middle-aged man with a Prince Charming haircut frolicked with a feminine black man in his early twenties. They were sharing some drugs. When a spotlight brightened the spongy white man, he began his song with a shrug of the shoulders—

Death row isn't really bad,
If you're one of us junkie fags.
We happen to like a little kick in the pants.
We happen to like a little tragic romance.

And then the spotlight was down again . . . until a group of bathing-suited drag queens appeared—all reclining in outdoor lounge chairs. The chorus, abruptly set aglow under the blue haze of tanning lamps, lowered sunglasses and gay porn magazines to versify—

Happen to like a little kick in the pants.
Happen to like a little tragic romance.

With the fading of the ultraviolet lamps and the slowing beat of the drum, Thing was right on time with her wrap-up—looking into the camera, she awkwardly snapped her fingers, and bopped her hairy blonde head.

Now . . .

Let me be the first to admit that as a result of my various entanglements with Thing (John Reed), not only do I deeply identify with

john**reed**

her—I totally despise her. And while perhaps my attitudes may seem magnified by my own peculiar associations with her, I firmly believe that nearly all of us, to some degree, share in that emotional macropsia. She was our girl on TV. A girl we knew, and a girl we did not know. A famous woman, and a not-so-famous woman. An enthralling and likable woman, and an insipid and detestable woman. An attractive woman, and unattractive woman. That was her appeal. Any man might look at her and say—*she's good enough.* And any woman might look at her and say—*I can be better.* She was all things. And nothing. The smartest of the dumb people and the dumbest of the smart. The prettiest of the homely and the homeliest of the pretty. The commonest of the glamorous and the glamorest of the common. And that was her, the girl on the Singa-Thinga-Thong spots—the best among the worst asses, and the worst among the best. She was all question, and no future. A potential with no prospects. She was our own forever baby girl. Big-eyed and smiling, and adored and whining, and petulant and annoying. That was her, on the television—just as she had been when she was two years old, sitting on her rump, too young to stand on her own, and reaching out to us, up to us, to lift her . . . to carry her away.

It was a perfect, perfect world, and Thing loved it. That is, until her ratings plummeted, her show was dropped, and her thriving turned to starving. One karaoke night at Junno's, there was that ghastly incident when someone asked her if she was *that model* on *that feminine hygiene commercial.* Shortly thereafter, not to let suffering get the better of her, or go unapplied, Thing began to take herself seriously, and she stopped wearing her thong to nightclubs and parties (she'd always been tasteful about it, enlisting the services of a cloak, if the situation so warranted), and started introducing herself as a video journalist. She'd point out—

"You know, it's an interesting thing, as a matter for the record, that I've always been a journalist, and that I'm working on some freelance projects, and I expect to have a holiday special quite soon, and, and . . ."

the**WH●LE**

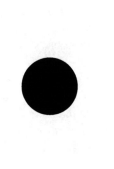

"I don't think I've ever been unhappy about anything," said Thing, fondling her thigh with a nervousness that bordered on excitement.

"Indeed," she giggled, swirling with her finger at the sugar which had precipitated out of her pink cocktail, "mine is a life of fabulous wealth and privilege, and I'm going to loaf and meander and dawdle right here at the top."

Doubtless—she thought she was kidding, though her ambition was no joke. She had a dim awareness that she should rule the world—and maybe the universe. Oh, she accepted that famous people were just like everyone else—aside from the fact that only famous people mattered, and that in terms of how much a person mattered, the only other thing that mattered was how famous a person was. After all, it was the natural order, like Darwin said, "survival of the famous." Fame, Thing knew, was the single achievement. And virtue too. It was the measure that made somebodies somebody, and nobodies nobody. And for anyone that was smart, or nation that was civilized, well, therein was the operating principle. True, Thing realized that a handful of people did exist who were more famous than herself, but she had what she deemed a rather simple rationale for looking at that—anyone below her she had beaten out fair and square, and anyone above her had benefited from some unjust, contemptible and probably illegal advantage. . . .

Amid the air of disgust which emanates from arrogant people among other arrogant people with whom they are unacquainted, Thing sat at the bar of Eugene, the swankiest of the trendsettyish variety of night joint, sipping a strange cocktail provided to her by the increasingly available Black Rabbit. Having originally been led to the VIP section of the VIP section, Thing's hostess, alerted by signal, had, instead, detoured her to the mere VIP section. Madonna, evidently, didn't like *any* young women at the table. And though it would not have been long ago that someone important, a producer of some

johnreed

breed, would have championed Thing, that day was done. Still, our girl was not dejected, for it was just a little setback, and she was positive she could overcome it.

Besides, the talk was scintillating enough, as the Black Rabbit was an entertaining varmint. And aside from that look of menace he seemed to hold in common with her own species, he appeared honorable enough. There was that he was a rabbit, or rather, had a rabbit's head, or rather, had a rabbit's head, which a man might have—were he a rabbit. Regardless, he was dressed impeccably (aside from the cowboy boots), and seemed to have no trouble negotiating his cigarillos and pink cocktail with his paws. And even if he was a trifle oddish, he was handsomish in a way, with his long whiskers, jet-black fur and the very pink skin of his upstanding ears. His eyes were delicate yet intense— large and brown but almost almond shaped. Asian. And Thing, of all the things she was, she was sure she was no racist, and she accepted the Black Rabbit as he was (Negroid, Asian), as did, it seemed, everyone else.

"Well," resumed the bunny, upending his pink cocktail and swishing the juice throughout his mouth, "a girl like you—you're one of the few people who have the resources to make a difference."

"Which is why," replied Thing, still joking, "I have no need to."

Then, suddenly unsure if she really was joking, she laughed, and to assuage the Black Rabbit, who was suspicious of the quip himself, she offered—

"Oh, but I do want to be famous, or, I guess, stay famous."

Clearly possessed with an uncommon common sense, the Black Rabbit shrugged—

Well, obviously.

Thing considered, "We all create our own realities."

"That's true," nodded the Rabbit.

"And," Thing sulked, "I really did earn it."

"Indubitably," affirmed the Rabbit, clicking his glass against hers. "But . . ." he hesitated.

"Yes?"

"If I might be so bold—to be top dog is not . . . Well, did you know

the**WH●LE**

that the alpha dog, that is, the top dog, does not mate nearly so often as the beta dog, that is, the second top dog?"

"Really?" Thing inquired.

"Yes," said the Rabbit, "and the bottom line is, well—everyone roots for the underdog anyway. Nobody wants to see the top dog win. So you, because you're by nature the top dog, that means that everybody's always rooting for the other dog—which, in some way, sort of makes you the underdog. So, if I might say so, you're really the under upperdog. Or in other words, the upper underdog."

"Which means they might root for me?"

"Exactly," and they clacked glasses.

"But, I suppose, that means that once I'm favored, that makes the other dog the underdog, and they root for him."

"Well yes, but that makes *you* the underdog."

And they clacked glasses again.

"Here's to your success in the dog-eat-dog world of video jockeys!"

To this toast, however, Thing faltered—lowered her glass unsteadily.

"Uhh," asked the Rabbit, dropping his chin and wrinkling his furry forehead in mock bewilderment.

"You are Thing—the video jockey Thing?"

"Oh yes, that's me. I mean, it's not me. I mean, it's me but it's not. I mean, I'm not really a video jockey. VJ doesn't stand for video jockey—or, it doesn't always. VJ, in my case—it stands for video journalist."

"Excellently phrased."

"Thank you. I mean, it's sometimes hard to explain myself—especially since . . ."

"Since they yanked your spots?"

"Yes, since then, I've been feeling not really myself—so, to explain myself, it poses a challenge."

"I could see how it might."

"But . . . it's not as if I don't know who I *want to be*, or, who I *should have been*—even if I *might have been* someone else."

john**reed**

"So then," deduced the Rabbit, the long padtips of his paws stroking his whiskers, "I imagine you have some . . . ambition."

"Why yes! As I was saying, to be a *serious* video journalist . . . or, I don't know . . . to get married. . . . Or, maybe both."

"Enterprising."

"I think so. . . . And, it's not as if it's just some passing fancy—it's just that . . . that . . . that I want to."

"Yes," nodded the Black Rabbit, mulling that one over, and, ultimately, agreeing wholeheartedly, "that would be it—the only pure pleasure in life—to lend oneself to a purpose greater than oneself—and to dedicate all of one's energies to that selfless thing, rather than let those energies molder and go to waste—to be a force to reckon with, rather than a hot lump of greed, whining that the world is not so good as to dedicate itself to your whims."

Thing, hearing this, straightened up, stunned, for that's not what she'd meant at all. Still, she was soon nodding her own head. And she toasted, "Exactly," for she couldn't have phrased it better herself—that is, what she knew she didn't mean—and following their toast, during which she drained her martini glass, she limped through a winding, roughish sentence which implied that she was working on several ideas—

"Along those . . . uh . . . those selfless kind of lines."

"Ah yes," asked the Black Rabbit, somewhat distractedly, for he was draining his own cocktail, "like what?"

This was a surprise. Thing had never come so far in her formulations, and she recognized that the intellectual terrain, it could prove not only unfamiliar, but treacherous. There was the Black Rabbit, lying in wait—ready to pounce. A predator. And she lying as limp and vulnerable as a leaf of lettuce. She'd have to come up with something quickly! Something brilliant! Earthshaking! She felt remarkably on the spot, actually, for if she didn't produce something Einsteinian that very moment—something worthy of a Nobu Prize at least—well, it would be catastrophic.

Thing wrung her hands and looked around—maniacally. Nearby, someone had managed to secure a side order of mashed potatoes and was prodding at them with a spoon. The potatoes were so incongruous there, amidst

the**WH●LE**

the booze and cigarettes, that Thing resolved there must be a significant significance to them.

Mechanical but kooky, the spoon handler's actions reminded her of something. Some actor, some movie. Oh, she remembered, it was that movie, *Third Enclosure of the Kind Count,* and that creepy little Dreyfuss guy who built a mountain out of his food. (Thing had an appreciation for those early Hollywood films.) And then, that crater the potato spooner was shaping—it made Thing realize. Why, why . . . she wanted to find . . . to search for . . .

"The middle!" she said, "I want to find the middle."

"Ah," considered the Black Rabbit, now looking at the potatoes himself, as Thing had stared at them so protractedly, "the middle. I suppose it would miss the point to ask the middle of what?"

"Why yes," she replied, "it would."

"Well . . . I know some people at Viacom, I'll run it by them."

"Oh," said Thing, accustomed to the helpful inhabitants of this easy, easy world, "that would be . . . nice."

The Black Rabbit had procured two more of the neon cocktails—

"Another drink?" he asked.

It dawned on her that though she had been consuming amply of these Molotovs, not only their origins, but their contents remained suspicious. (And, come to think of it, since the application of this particular brand of cocktail had commenced, she had been feeling somewhat funny.) Why, these things were so pink, so very, very pink, that she couldn't help but ask—

"Those aren't, uh, nuclear, are they?"

"Why no," said the Black Rabbit, taken aback, "heavens no, what would give you that idea?"

"What are they," she asked, "I mean, precisely?"

"Precisely? Hmmm," the Black Rabbit pondered—

"Well, this is a drink with something in it."

"I see," she said, though for some reason she couldn't pin down, that answer wasn't wholly satisfactory to her—

"Are they free-range?"

"Excuse me?"

john**reed**

"Are they organic? You know, like, overseen by hippies."

"Oh yes," said the Black Rabbit defensively, "absolutely."

And then, assenting, Thing reached out her pink little hand to accept her very pink cocktail from the fuzzy paw of the Black Rabbit. And thus began a steady stream of the stuff for many moons to come. . . .

Not unrelatedly, it was less than an hour before Eugene started to spin, and Thing found herself drooping on her stool. She listened intently as the Black Rabbit advised her that she might as well fall flat on her face as lean over too far forward. Virtually boneless, Thing rolled from one impossible angle to another, until, finally, she did take the plunge—whereupon, the Black Rabbit was available to assist her from the floor.

In response to the Rabbit's inquiries after her health, she assured him that the fall was of no consequence, as she screwed up her brow and wondered—

Great consequence, no consequence, great consequence, no consequence . . . which sounds better?

Later yet, she and the Black Rabbit parted ways, and she was followed about by a tabloid cameraman searching for the fallen. There were a few nice shots (soon-to-be voiced-over "VEE JAY'S BREAKDOWN!") of Thing huddled behind chairs and under tables—a frightened gremlin. ("HAUNTED BY SPIRIT OF E.T.!") But eventually, as terrified Thing was of the camera, the chase grew tiresome, and she and the cameraman decided to collaborate. They went here and there and Thing kissed anyone who'd agree to a kiss—men, women, transsexuals alike. ("HUNDREDS OF LOVERS!") She had a sore appear the day after the next, and she tried over the weeks to ignore it, but she couldn't ignore it—no more than she could ignore the terrible longing in her chest and abdomen that manifested itself whenever she was forced to be alone, for even an instant. And that sore (for she couldn't be seen like that!) it meant *alone*, for weeks and weeks. . . .

the**WH●LE**

Though she was no longer on TV, what followed was, to Thing's mind, all very TVish. No doubt, her way of seeing was influenced by her continuous intake of cocktails, as supplied by the Black Rabbit. Always, he was standing in the shadows, like some cocktail party Deep Throat. Consequently, Thing's cerebral cortex was sluggish. Now, one might think that would result in a world slowed down—a crank film cranked by a sloth. But no, that would be the famed hyperconsciousness attained by some athletes ("the zone"), which was not at all indicative of Thing's temper. To Thing, consciousness was a long stream of static interrupted by brief flashes of data. Clarity ever-fleeting, whole days, weeks and months would transpire. It was as if, not a sloth, but a hyperactive marmoset had gotten hold of that crank—and the film of her life had been, for comic intentions, speeded up. Sometimes she felt as if it was a DVD she'd rented, which she was forced to watch (with a broken remote control) on only two settings—fast forward, and pause.

Thing had joined the party. The never-ending party of New York City. A soirée forever on the drift from here to there—and sometimes, back. Beginning with CK One's sponsorship of a rainforest fundraiser, Thing's nights were an aimless progression of products and benefits. Starbucks for Schoolbooks, Diesel Jeans for Brechtian Cinema, Lucky Strike Massive Music Night. In due time, a sort of group had formed—one which Thing was a part of. And, following Stolichnaya's nightclub rendition of Alaska (the Snowy Owl was endangered!), the group changed course, forsaking the charity circuit for a cycle of big lofts. One to the next. And Thing was happy, as she always was with anyone who would help her to combat the loneliness (and, anyone who needed her to combat their own loneliness). And after about a month of this (not going home, but just shopping and borrowing from her new friends, who were also just shopping and borrowing), she flew down to Barbados with some director

johnreed

she kept telling, "No. Never. No." Of course, he said, if he got her to Barbados it'd be otherwise—and he was right. Then, the next day, he was exceptionally cold to her—neglectful and nasty. (And he was bald, too!) It was so humiliating. And there was nothing she could do about it, as, without him, she'd have to figure out how to fly home by herself, which was so daunting as to be virtually impossible. She'd almost rather have sex with him again than go through such an ordeal—and that's exactly what she did. And she liked him again. And everything was great. But then he was cold again. And they flew back to New York. And without pause, she went right back to the loft (the most recent loft) to find that the group had not only not advanced—they had hardly stirred.

Several hours later, the listless assembly was joined by a newcomer—a director friend of her ex-director. And because the scene at the loft was a trifle dull, and, moreover, with all the cocktails delivered by the Black Rabbit, life was both very fast and very slow, she was, shortly, on a plane to Aruba with director *numéro deux*.

Then she went home and changed clothes—and upon her return to the loft, the clustered idlers consisted of new people that she didn't recognize—all except for this little guy, Pancho, who she'd barely noticed before. Well, it wasn't really that she hadn't *noticed* him (as he was covered from head to foot in tattoos and piercings, and his earlobes were stretched out to the point where they could accommodate dishware), it was just that she had chosen not to pay attention to that shrimpy Mexican. (Or was he Italian?) In any event, one night, he was there at the loft, and he was *going out* somewhere—so Thing chose to go with him. (They took a taxi to the wrong location, then walked.)

People sometimes laughed at Thing when she started shaking at the prospect of being alone. She, however, didn't think it was funny, and more than once, tears streaming down her face, she screamed, "It's not funny!" For to be without someone else, that is, someone else with whom to flirt and generally entertain oneself—well, it was dastardly. Indeed, that was what was so tantalizing about boys—they provided stimulation. And especially in the beginning—then, they were so thrilling. So vigilant and responsive. *Could he be the boy who will always pay this much attention to me?* The problem was that, sooner or later, every one of those boys did seem to have something else he wanted to

the**WH●LE**

think about—whether it be a job, or looking at another woman, or even just checking his e-mail. But this Pancho, he seemed different—and as they walked the streets, they drank the Rabbit's cocktails (amazingly solicitous, that bunny, to provide them cocktails in the thoroughfares) and goofed around together.

As it turned out, at the gala, Pancho wasn't on the guest list, but Thing was (plus one!). After switching a few place cards around, Thing and Pancho took their places at table five, with Martha Stewart, Mr. T and four Osmonds. It was an awards dinner—fame, riches. Stars, fashion. And awards to rich and famous stars of fashion. Mildly amusing, though lapses in the presentation were strained, as Thing's ex-director was also there—seated at table six. And later, when Thing, Pancho, Thing's ex-director and several other members of their group (who'd also managed invites) made an after-foray to the right restaurant, the strain began to swell. Thing knew she looked good, as she hadn't eaten at all in Aruba (with her second ex-director), and thus, the agony of her first ex-director was particularly delectable to her. Loudly, delightedly, she discussed with Pancho his penile pierces, and gave him a few deep kisses on his pierced lips.

And even if the deep kisses did not make her ex-director wild with jealousy, as had been intended, they did do something, for back at the big loft, the director suggested something called a *manage à trois*. Thing didn't know what that was, however—and neither did Pancho. The director assured them it was French, whereupon the two agreed that it had to be good. But when the director provided details, Thing wasn't entirely won over. (Pancho was.) And yet, with the loss of her show, and, well, the loss of a whole bunch of money, Thing's state of mind, as of late, was something akin to that of a whacked mole. (She had trusted that untrustable psychic! If only she had known!) And, whack-a-moles apt to indulge their imprudent urges, it was nary a pink cocktail that led to the VJ feeling a tad lightheaded. And, whether by this lightheadedness or sheer temerity, a certitude had soon been fostered, that she could meet her ex-director on his chosen field of battle—and defeat him. She would use her wiles—and she had this idea that if she went along with him . . . well then . . .

Well then . . . she was sure it would work out to her advantage!

john**reed**

And, that schema schematized, inspiration struck, and Thing came up with her very first, very own rhyme—over which she grew whoppingly puffed up.

> Love is splendorous—orgies are sick.
> But an orgy ain't too bad, once in a bit.

And, afterwards, she felt as if somehow she really had enjoyed a glorious victory over her ex-director, as well as everyone else who was there at the party—sitting around watching.

A genuine triumph!

Through the rest of the night, and the sleeping and waking of the next day, she and Pancho remained together on a distant, out-of-the-action couch. Even though she had done *that thing* with him (and her ex-director), she was unscintillated by Mr. Pancho Ponzini, the tattooist, who didn't go in to open his shop that afternoon. But on the other hand, he never did stop paying attention to her, and after countless pink cocktails, and days of his waiting her out, she began to weaken—to change her mind. Yes, he was round, and short, and homely—but he was *so beautiful.* And the way he held her when they slept (which was most of the time), it was so superb, and deprived—and all around, just what she liked.

When at long last the pair did venture out from the loft, he lured her to his apartment. He purchased a bag of Reese's Pieces, which he held out one by one in his hand—through the subway, out to Brooklyn, and down the stairs to his basement apartment. (*Why, if heaven meant radishes—to hell with it!*) And, following the crunchy-chocolaty-peanut-buttery path, Thing realized that the way to hell *was* a trail of Reese's Pieces. And this, she saw, was the safe way to hell—an easy decline down a soft carpet. A way without abrupt starts, or stops, or landmarks or even road signs. (Just some parking placards which she'd soon see in Pancho's bedroom.) No speeding, no weaving—here was a clean, four-lane highway, and a pace of sixty minutes an hour. (When, at Pancho's bedside, they ran out of Reese's, Pancho reached into his pocket, and there were Gummy Bears.) And yes—*the way to hell was a trail of candy.* And

the**WH●LE**

hell itself was the land of sweets. Salt too. It was snack central. Yes, surprisingly, hell was full of candy. And chips.

Pancho's apartment was loaded with goodies—soda, chocolate, candied orange peels. It was to be a two-month stay—Thing returning home but once for a change of clothing. (And that pilgrimage she only made as it neatly flanked Pancho's visit to the loan shark.) True, Pancho's entourage tended to need new underwear, and delousing—but Thing was a girl with a boundless propensity for denial and self-deception. No matter how minor and paltry her life and the players in it had become—she deemed them the penultimate echelon of the mighty. She enlarged DJs and bouncers to international players—everyone could help her. (And Pancho wasn't really fatt at all, he was just short for his size.) To Thing, even if it appeared to be a falling off, this Dekalb Avenue lifestyle would ultimately prove to be what pushed her over the top—right into superstardom. (Street cred. Now she had it.) And it was this very power of exaggeration and self-deception that allowed Thing to lend Pancho a great deal of money (a great, great deal) to pay off the loan shark. Like any respectable entrepreneur, Pancho had gotten into debt to go into business, and it all had been going along famously—payments and so forth—until he met Thing, and he quit going to work, quit opening his store and quit paying his employees to go to work to open the store. Therefore, the store was closed, his cash intake was nil, and his clientele was fast diminishing. (The likes of a tattooing/piercing enterprise demanded that one constantly coddle and *relate* to the patronage.) This downward trajectory depressed Pancho, and sent him into his own process of denial, which discouraged him from working, which, in turn, discouraged the business, which once again discouraged him from working . . . and on and on.

Still, the fact that Thing had liquidated her stock portfolio to save Pancho and his business didn't worry her—for Pancho was planning to pay her back. And besides that, all he had to do was go into work and pull a few all-day/all-nighters and everything would be okay. Not only his bills, but hers too. They could just kind of live in the store for a few weeks—and then, like, they'd buy the stocks back. But that didn't happen, and instead, they lay in bed, flattened by cocktails (ever-pink, ever-willing, ever-cold) while Thing thought how marvelous it was to have Pancho hold her. She had never been *held* like that.

john**reed**

There were the threats of eviction, as the rent on Pancho's store hadn't been paid in months—but this worry was alleviated by the constant offers from Pancho's various competitors, who wanted to buy Pancho out. It seemed that everyone wanted to help Pancho, and it was hard to even entertain the idea that someone wasn't going to march right in and take care of his problems. Unforeseeably, when Pancho was evicted from his store (the couple didn't find out until nearly a week after it happened) the offers dried up—and that was that.

Thing however, she retained faith in Pancho (and that her money would be returned), for he was clearly an individual of profound personal and professional depth.

At any rate, they were happy where they were. In Pancho's bedroom with the lights off—drinking cocktails, spinning records and watching television. It was what they dubbed Eden, and only extraordinary circumstance expelled them from the gates. No one was to blame—it was simply bad luck—but the situation of the squalor had become . . . untenable. One had to pick a path from here to there, attempting only to step on step-on-able things. When Indian food spilled—it was left where it was. Similarly, a bowl of cereal had tipped over near the corner of the bed, and the milk, which had stunk for so long, no longer stunk, though it had left a ring, as well as a large quantity of white dust—all of which served as an unpleasant reminder. Still, no one did anything about it. Once something went into that bedroom—pizza box, bag of Snickers, comic book, seafood salad, *Star* magazine—it never went out. It was archeological. Food, clothing, food, clothing. Everything was around—everything that had ever happened in that bedroom. It all just coalesced into this mass of memory that got denser and heavier. Half-eaten ice-cream pints melted in corners—and in time, became cheese. Occasionally, Thing had to shake a cockroach out of her hair.

Meanwhile . . . the situation back at her own apartment had improved to the degree that the place might be called *orderly*. This, because Thing had not one, but two cleaning women. Her original reasoning had been that if she had two, each would independently think that she was fairly neat (appreciating the other's work), and thereby be inspired to higher levels of sanitation. It was a method that had achieved little in the time that Thing had lived in her apartment, as she was so messy that each cleaning woman, independently, thought her employer merely disgusting, as opposed to inhuman. But with Thing gone, between the two cleaning women, the place had gradually gotten ship-shape—tip-top. So, having discovered this development (upon Thing's field trip home to change clothes for month two), Thing and Pancho packed up a few belongings, dug their way out of their burrow, and migrated to Thing's apartment, which, between the two cleaning women and its vast square footage, would probably take much longer to befoul. Maybe forever. . . .

Thing's East Village lair (no roommate now) had long ago been reconfigured to conform less to the East Village of old (junkies and poets and artists and such), and more to the East Village of new (real-estate brokers, lawyers and assorted urban professionals). Near about that time MTV had discovered her, Thing's tenement building had been deregulated and luxurized, and her rent had skyrocketed—and thus, the two bedroom overpriced enough, the VJ had stayed. Postremodeling, amenities included—

- An eentsy-weensty office with a slam-bang T1 connection that she couldn't figure out how to hook up to her slam-bang computer that she couldn't figure out how to plug in.
- A big kitchen with a powerful microwave oven & a gigantic (empty) refrigerator & an oversize dishwasher (in which she stored plastic utensils and paper plates).
- A big bedroom with a four-poster, queen-size bed under a gauzy big top of mosquito netting.
- A huge living room with a huge couch & huge coffee table & huge flat-screen television.

It was her mindset. And loath to do anything that might jeopardize that mindset, she preferred not to venture beyond the confines of this paradise—to venture, to put it plainly, *outside*. Oh, now and again she slipped into a thong, strapped on a pair of high heels and toppled into the street. But the cold hard truth of the matter was that Thing had good reason to stay inside, as, outside, the unwashed masses were laying siege to her castle. Or at least, one unwashed mass was. During the time Thing and Pancho had been in Brooklyn, a derelict woman had moved into the crawl space under the front stoop of Thing's building. Because a good part of the neighborhood's appeal was formulated upon a few colorful types (be they creative or indigent), who still lingered here and there, Thing, like everyone else in her building, was forced to tolerate this scourge, uh, make that *homeless woman.* Day and night—soliciting offerings from luxury apartment dwellers who thought they were politically correct— the wrinkled stinker sat in her pit under the stairs. Indeed, for the first few weeks, Thing herself made several charitable forays to pass along whatever old sushi that she and Pancho hadn't managed to finish. But after the time the woman expressed her gratitude by throwing up for three days, Thing decided to forego the personal bestowal of such endowments—and, instead, sent Pancho down to throw the witch the scraps.

Thus, as a convenient coupling to this errand, did it become Pancho's duty, and exclusively so, to sally forth into the world to secure provisions. And perhaps this duty was not indiscriminately appointed, as Thing (by cash advance and pawn shop) was footing the bill, whether for guacamole or double-chocolate cookies or soymilk. Furthermore, that miserable old woman (what was she, Russian?) had begun to recognize Thing specifically. She'd say—

"Vat's wrong honey? You hold head so high, you nose block sun."

But that hag, she was always smiling at Thing—like she loved her. Like she was saying something nice. *Crazy-like.* And, equally unpleasant, the woman had started confusing Pancho with all the other boys that Thing had taken home. "You different," she'd say to him—

"You short now."

Tattooed, pierced and carved as he was, it was as if, to that old woman, Pancho was just another middle-class boy from the suburbs. (Nothing could be wronger—for Pancho had come a long, long way from his Cranston, Rhode Island upbringing.) It was as if, to her, they all looked the same—as if American people were as hard to tell apart as the other races. Needless to say, Thing knew that these incongruities *were* crazy—sure signs of insanity. But insanity, as much if not more so than poverty, made our heroine somewhat nervous. One screaming match with the woman had proved particularly trying, and had ended with Thing repeatedly exclaiming—

"Immigration is the highest form of flattery!"

So, rather than have to deal with the woman, Thing stopped leaving the apartment altogether. It'd just be Pancho. This did not mean, however, that Thing's life was sedentary, given that her fear of boredom, or, not of boredom, but of spending a moment *in thought*, was so encompassing as to prevent her from lying still for even an instant. She'd always been floppy, yet, living indoors 24/7, she became exaggeratedly so—flouncing around the couch into contortions bizarrely situated towards the television screen. Be that as it was, she did occasionally cogitate, and her cogitations went something like this—

My life is running in circles. No, not circles. Downward spirals. No, not spirals. I'm a Slinky. Going down a stairwell.

She'd ask Pancho about her money, and he'd promise he was going to pay her back. He wasn't like that. He began to prefer oral sex to genital sex. That is, to be the recipient of oral sex.

And worse—Pancho began to venture out, not just for stuff, but to *do* things. Record spinning, meeting friends—and most daunting, feeding and changing the tanks of the turtles of his ex-girlfriend, who was out of town, or so he said. For long stretches he'd disappear, and attribute his time to that—the turtles. Thing grew suspicious. In a test of not only her determination, but her skills as an investigative journalist, she located Pancho's address book (under an oily mound of moldy cheese fries), looked up Pancho's ex's phone number, and called to see if Pancho was there, and/or, if his ex was really out of town. Well, she wasn't out of town—but neither did it seem that Pancho was there. The ex, by her own representation, wanted nothing to do with Pancho—nor would she ever trust that yo-yo with her turtles, who required a quality of care far beyond anything that wetback was capable of providing.

"So typical," she said, and hung up.

Still, Thing knew that the woman had split her tongue down the middle—and how deeply Pancho appreciated that sort of demonstration. Thing had once heard Pancho say, "C'mon, ya put two twats in fron'of a guy, one wit'a clit pierce and one wit'it not, de guy'll go fer'da pierce." But Thing wouldn't pierce

john**reed**

it. And now, she imagined, Pancho was back with that scag, who would, or, rather, who had. A forked tongue and a pierced clit—Thing feared the worst.

This fear, however, did not bear out, as several days later, when Thing cabbed it to Brooklyn and clambered down into the alley to peek into Pancho's window, he wasn't with his ex-girlfriend, but a totally brand-new eighteen-year-old. Thing, twenty-two, couldn't stand the thought of Pancho with a younger woman. What followed was mayhem.

After that, Pancho was under house arrest, and Thing forced him to sit with her all day in bed—watching television and shelling her pistachios and lychee nuts.

Unfortunately, she couldn't blame him nearly as much as she wanted to—because whenever she looked in the mirror she realized that, in fairness to him, she had gotten kind of fatt. The cheating, the love, the loyalty—it was all a matter of weight. Long ago, Thing had decided that hers was one of those faces that didn't look good with a few extra pounds. It did something to it. Something unseemly. And Pancho, he had just responded to that. It was to be expected—he'd succumbed to a thin girl, a young thin girl. So, well . . . Thing had to get him back, to make him love her, to make herself feel thin again, to make herself feel young again—so she could dump him and have her revenge. She had to have the upper hand if this whole thing was to end. Forgive, forget, even grovel if she had to—it was simply a matter of pride. She would show him how selfless, how adoring she was—and then she'd drop the hammer!

Alas, this logic backfired, for not only did Pancho manage to cheat again (which made Thing more desperate to stay with him, to get the upper hand that held the hammer), it would turn out that *he was* cheating with his ex-girlfriend (forked tongue, et cetera) who was not actually his ex-girlfriend—but his wife! He was married. But separated, he told Thing. Then it turned out that he was also married in another state, where he had a child. A bigamist with a child. Well, thought Thing, at least he ignored the kid. (*And a man that ignored his kid couldn't be all bad.*) And that he'd abandoned the wives, well, that was good too—Thing had to hold that in his favor. She wasn't biased. . . .

Fatt. Fatt. Fatt.

Thing thought about it constantly. Fatt people didn't lead revolutions, or even gather into angry mobs. Never. It was the lean and hungry who were the heroic rebels. They were the rock stars.

And so, as by Thing's way of thinking she'd become fatt as a house (and wouldn't leave the house as a result of it), she stopped eating, or, to be more exact, digesting. Erstwhile, Pancho, who remained under house arrest (fatt house arrest), was growing a bit abdominous himself. But since he was basically spending all of his time with her again, well, soon enough, she was back in love—though home life got worse. Pancho began to like to masturbate without help, and often in private—which was no fun at all. By Jove—it wasn't even disagreeable! It was just boring—which was worse than anything.

In a daring attempt to shift the attention back to her own body, Thing agreed to let Pancho pierce her nipples. It went okay, and Thing seemed to think they were pretty. Then came the tongue pierce. Pancho'd had one too many cocktails, and didn't get the stud into the middle of Thing's licker. And it was a lick crooked. He assured her that when the swelling went down she'd see that it really was right in the middle. But when it did, it wasn't. And it remained crooked. Still, he assured her that if she ever wanted to take it out, because of the way he'd done it, it wouldn't leave a scar, and she was satisfied with that—though of course, it would leave a scar. An unusually globular and hideous one.

Sometimes, Pancho spoke of the forces that were holding him down. He was so competent, and generally superhuman that only something vast and sinister could be the cause of his travails. He detailed involved conspiracies—his theories and arguments so tedious that, for sheer restlessness, Thing began to listen to them. To the point where she was interested. Now, as far as JFK—well, that was a cover-up, she had to admit. And the moon, it was true that it wasn't in an elliptical orbit but a circular one—which meant, indisputably, that it was put there by aliens. And, listening to Pancho and his analysis, she could see that he was right, as there were so many reasons, well . . . to think, well . . . she need hardly elaborate. . . . And there were so many people that . . . well . . . it was perfectly obvious. . . . And there was so very much evidence. . . . And all that was out there, well . . . everyone knew. . . .

For the infidelity, Thing would often find herself enraged—and to alleviate this, she would arbitrarily levy fines against Pancho. He agreed to pay. Thirty-seven dollars and twelve cents. Eighteen dollars. Fifty-six dollars. And Thing, she took these fines seriously—although, well, he already owed her oodles of money . . . and . . . well . . . She paid for the movies and food, and puked later. It was usually a disturbance to the movie—but inasmuch as she was picking up the check, Pancho wasn't difficult about it. If he was permitted to metabolize his bacon cheeseburger, he was willing to accept that, for Thing, the only foodstuffs unnecessitous of a finger down the throat were carob-coated raisins and Starbursts. Indeed, he was willing to accept that Thing's primary source of sustenance was a continuous chain of Virginia Slim Luxury Light Menthol 120s.

And so it was that finally, in this gravitational collapse of smoke and candy and love and hate, and all the other phenomenon manifested by the approach of infinite density, there came the hole itself—

Lying in bed, Thing and Pancho sucked the froth off the tops of a batch of superlatively foamy pink cocktails. It was an MTV affiliate the frothed duo were watching, or, not so much watching as adhering to—as stuck to the screen as gum to a bedpost.

Resolving to interrupt this dull futz, Pancho took it upon himself, during a commercial, to deliver Thing a little tickling—

"Are ya dair? Ya dair yet?"

The game was that Pancho would torture Thing until she confessed that she was "there," an admission liable to be long in the coming—and not without suffering and undue humiliation. The procedure tonight was far from atypical—Pancho sat on a pillow on Thing's face as she struggled, tickled mercilessly. It was so awful and confusing to be laughing and tormented all at once. And in this degraded posture, under a pillow under Pancho, life was especially unpleasant, as Thing was having trouble breathing. It wasn't just the laughter—but the fact that even when she did gasp for air, the pillow was smothering her.

She shook and writhed, while Pancho demanded to know if she was "dair." That is, she shook and writhed until she stopped, and Pancho guffawed that she wasn't going to fool him—and, meantime, Thing's lips went blue, and she whirled and enlarged into something pleasant and light—

Why she . . . why she . . .

She woke to Pancho's beaming face.

"Chump!" she screamed, "You almost killed me!"

Pancho snorted and resumed the tickling, still thinking she was joking—and Thing became irate. He really was doing this way too much. It made her feel . . . alone.

"It's not funny! It's not funny!"

But he didn't stop. . . .

And, tears in her eyes, she watched television through the agony.

And it was then that she saw a spot for an upcoming spot, featuring the winner of a recent Greek Islands, fish-guts-eating challenge—a pretty boy named Hal.

Hal, boasted the VO, was on his search for *the middle*.

This, Thing knew, was important, and she again yelled at Pancho to stop—but he didn't.

She howled—

"It's my career! It's my career."

And as she wept, her spirit was so crushed that Pancho ceased his assault. Furiously shaking, she wiped her eyes—

"I told you to stop. I told you."

"Oh," said Pancho irritably, "you were havin' fun. It's jus' dat Hal guy. 'E replaced you—an'ya feel competitive."

"No, that's not it. And I'm not competitive. But life . . . life . . . life's just a game!"

Thing, her lungs finally full of air, had been able to achieve maxi-

john**reed**

mum volume on that holler of hers—and afterwards, as she took a breath and soughed pathetically, she wondered why she was with this lowlife.

"I mean," said Thing sincerely, "I'm not competitive with . . . Hal. I mean, I'm happy for him. I mean, I really, really, really am. I mean, I am, really."

The couple quieted—and after the skin commercial, and the soda commercial and the fast food commercial, Hal appeared. Broadcasting from a helicopter, he enticed the viewer—

"Today, we're headed into America's heartland, to look into . . . the hole!"

The camera revealed the one-and-a-half-acre hole of the Peterson lot below. Hal, preparing to jump into action, ran his fingers through his spiky, stippled hair—

"Join me, on my search for the middle."

With that, the helicopter began its descent—and up came a banner for another show that would come on even later, and another commercial for fried food, and Thing and Pancho discussed this development of the hole, and more important, *the middle*.

"You see," said Thing, "I told you it was a good idea."

Pancho nodded—

"Yeah, I knew it was, totally—dey stole our idea."

Thing pondered—

"Have you, uh . . . heard anything about a hole?"

"No," said Pancho, suddenly curious, "I mean, whadaya think it is? Duh hole, I mean."

And with that, i.e., Pancho's Brooklyn accent (*he was from Rhode Island!*) Thing became enraged—

"Duh duh duh! It's not *duh*. It's *the!*"

And then Thing sat up in bed and crossed her arms and scowled, just as she had seen actresses do on TV—

He doesn't understand. He doesn't understand how important this is. And as much as I love to be with him . . . well, this is a case of unrequired love!

"Pancho," she said, "it's just—it's just that it was love at first sight, and now I've taken a second look."

the**WH●LE**

"Huh?" he asked.

"Duh? Huh? Duh? Huh?" She was disgusted—

"D'oh!" she said, mimicking Homer Simpson. "Maybe you'll understand that!"

He did. It hurt. It meant, get lost. His face slack, he sat up, looking so pitiable that Thing felt a twitch of sympathy—

"I mean, I *really* do love you. I mean, as a friend. I mean, we *really* can respect each other."

"Wha?"

"Like, what you do, I *really* respect it."

"Oh yeah, really?"

"Yes," she said, "really," and she put her hand on his cheek, to comfort him, and to hustle him out of bed—

"I really, really do respect you," she assured him, and began to think about taking out that tongue pierce, and, what's more, the nipple pierces. (*How could she have done that to her livelihood?*) All of which she would do, or rather, undo, within four minutes of his walking out the door.

"I'm sorry but—stealing parking signs isn't fun anymore."

Poor Pancho, he took the sign with him, as she wondered—*Why does he like it so much, anyway?* She remembered how he had unscrewed the school-crossing hexagon while they were sitting outside a subway stop in Brooklyn. Without makeup. *She'd been sitting there without makeup!* Her eyes went big like empty wells. *She hadn't worn makeup in months! What was she doing?* She went to the bathroom to see what she had in the way of supplies. And as she did so, she heard Pancho packing his belongings into garbage bags. (Videogames, piercing magazines, dirty clothing, toothbrush.) And then, as she returned to the television, she heard her apartment door open, and, slowly, close. And as much as she felt a pang of guilt, and as much as she didn't trust that Mexican to keep his filthy mitts off her stuff, she didn't go after Pancho, to say good-bye, or search his bags, as the commercials were over.

Hal, hopping out of the helicopter, described a recent suburban disaster. He explained—

"This is Seven Country Cross Road. Here, midmorning yesterday, without warning, the Peterson family disappeared. But the Petersons—they didn't disappear into thin air. The truth is, everyone knows where they went— right into the earth. We don't yet know the death toll, and the entire area is—"

As Hal was gesturing out into the road and the farm (swarming with police officers, firemen and rescue workers), he received some breaking information. A faint transmission, so it seemed. He held the earpiece to his head as he spoke—

"We have a survivor!"

Hal indicated a large crane over the site—

"As you can see, a crane is situated on the edge of the hole. Can we get an overhead of that?"

Hal flopped his skateboard onto the road and skated closer to the hole (his cameraman running, heaving and awkward, in pursuit) as a helicopter cam furnished a view of the spectacle.

The hole gigantic, only a tiny corner of the house was visible. A cherry picker and a crane had lowered EMS workers and their hardware onto the protruding pyramid of rooftop, where they endeavored to saw through the shingles—to rescue the girl.

"Bethany Peterson," reported Hal, "fourteen years old, is signaling rescue workers from inside the house. Reportedly, she's blasting Destiny's Child through a battery-powered boom box. We don't know what kind of condition she's in."

The crane lifted away a section of roofing, and to the cheer of onlookers, the scraped and dirty but otherwise healthy teen was helped from the wreckage. The boom box provided musical accompaniment.

I'm a survivor,
I'm gonna make it.
I'm a survivor,
Keep on survivin'.

"Yes," Hal exclaimed, "that's right, Bethany Peterson! You are a survivor! And no, no, no, you didn't give up!"

the**WH●LE**

Hal set the scene.

"Two hours ago, after a countywide evacuation, a geological team assessed that there was no further danger. And now, a great many of the local residents have returned, and gathered here—"

Hal was again interrupted—

"Oh my . . . my . . ."

But Hal, holding his earpiece to his ear, didn't know what to say, for the hole had just enlarged—and the girl, the house and the rescue workers . . . were consumed.

He looked back to the camera—

"What we have here, right here, live on national—"

There was a crash. The camera turned. The crane, on shifting ground, fell into the hole. A man screamed from within the cab. Then the cherry picker fell—onto the crane. Another crash. Another scream. All sank.

Then the ground underfoot, it too shifted, and Hal cried to his cameraman—

"Get, get—"

The cameraman fell, as did the camera—and from the helicopter above, Thing and all of America watched Hal throw down his skateboard. As the rescue workers and fire trucks and cranes and ambulances slid into the hole (glass broke, metal clashed), Hal skated for his life. The ground rolling behind him, he skated on. Gathering speed, he passed fleeing pedestrians. . . .

And then, the ground ahead began to rock—to tilt.

First, the pedestrians plummeted—and then, scared and fast and heroic, Hal ollied his board over an onrushing trash can, and rail-slid along a curb as the blacktop of the street fell away.

And then the sidewalk went too, and Hal was gone—and from the helicopter there was nothing to see but an immense pit of upturned earth. And there was nothing to hear, save the whir of helicopter blades. . . .

There was a lag of almost two seconds before Thing's phone rang. She was rehired. "That swine's cooked, but your bacon's saved," said her henceforth producer, Matthew, who had climbed the ranks of his affiliate with a deft use of cologne and an uncanny, unflagging ability to sport the worst haircut known to man (even as they spoke, Thing could not have imagined that his brown tufts were entangled in hair curlers). She panicked about beautification, and as a car would collect her in fifteen minutes, maybe twenty, she promptly went to the bathroom to throw up those carob-coated raisins. Live coverage was to resume immediately. No, said Matthew, there would be no time for a facial, or a thong wax, or a massage, or a seaweed wrap, or a manicure, or a pedicure, or four hours in the sauna. No—no time to get her hair done, or go shopping, or flush her system with purified, superoxygenated water. Makeup was ready. Wardrobe was ready. (Her thong had been retired.) When the car arrived, she was to be there, sober and waiting—and wearing no more than slippers and a robe.

These strict orders given, Thing showered, scrubbed, squeezed a pimple, donned her terrycloth and flip flops, and curled up on the couch, worrying about how pale and fatt she had become. And then, the smell of stale Chinese food a-wafting from her bedroom, she retched. And as she was discarding the Empire Szechwan (packed into a bag that she flung out the window), she happened upon a fortune cookie. And though the very thought of Chinese food made her sick, and she knew that, besides, white sugar and white flour were unequivocally no good for you, her intuition told her that at this unique instant, really, they were. She had this undeniable inkling that, yes, right then, exactly then, a fortune cookie was precisely what she needed. Probably in some complicated scientific way. So—she devoured that fortune cookie! And because the cookie had come at such an auspicious moment (when only a fortune cookie could provide her the restorative energy she would need to resume her stardom), she read the fortune with particular attention—

> You have the key.

And since, in addition, she was feeling a smidge anxious about her appearance (she was unsure that wardrobe and makeup would help, as what she needed was a week of hydrotherapy and reflexology and rose petal massages and herbal wraps and yoga and aromatherapy and every, every thing), she decided that if she had the key—well, it might be the key that unlocked the secret to looking less fatt, less pale, and having a smaller pimple.

And if that was the key she had, well then—

She had to find it!

And she knew that there (in that one drawer in the dresser in the office) were hundreds of keys from former lovers and, and . . . who knows from where else. . . .

So . . .

She marched right back to that drawer to find that key!

But, although she had been absolutely certain *that key* would be among those hundreds of other keys, and that she would know *it* when she found it—well, *it* wasn't, and she didn't. *You have the key. You have the key.* It all began to rankle her. She searched her trunk, then the closet, and the other closet, and the last closet too. (*Hurry up, you only have six minutes. Hurry up, you only have three minutes.*) She searched the kitchen drawer, and the toolbox and the bathroom cabinet.

What key? And where?

She huffed—she stubbed her toe.

You have the key. Well . . .

No! She didn't!

And, connipting (she'd dug and rooted around enough!), she tossed that miserable rayon dress (that one stained with grape juice!) right out from under the bed—and right into the next room!! Then she went to the bathroom to refix her hair, and look at herself in the mirror. And, as she was flushed, she *was* looking a little better, and she thought—

See, that key, it did have a purpose! And besides, the maids'll clean up all that stuff anyway. And, that key! I really did have it myself all along. "The key" was just to get my heart beating—to pinken up! And even if there is a real, in-the-flesh key, well then, still, it might turn up. . . .

She knew there was a simple answer.

The thing that nagged at her nagged at the world. They were one and the same.

There was an ache in her—that pain we all have. That pain that sometimes bleeds from every pore in our skin. That pain that resides between each pair of ribs—in the cavity of the pelvis, and the bone marrow of the thighs. This is the pain made more acute by longing. The one that takes us in its grasp when we close our eyes on the beach—or on a windy day. It is that pain only alleviated by adoration, or standing in the rain.

Thing's question was one that nagged her when she walked, and shook her when she slept—

What?

What?

What?

And the answer—it was the pain. It was the pain of knowing and not knowing. It was the pain of everything put together, or taken apart. And sometimes, it was just pain. An anguish that made her scream for no reason— or because her hair wouldn't do what she wanted. She would smell the burning locks, and throw the curling iron and scream.

To Thing, there were three topics of thought. Number one and two being love/sex and career/money—and number three, suicide. Despite a mulish belief in the power of thositive pinking, when her ear touched the pillow, the *first* notion that popped into her head was to kill herself. The only thing in her life that could ever, that had ever, been a lithium to this coiling anxiety within her, was fame. However marginally it had touched her, that had been the one salve. Fame brought everything one needed—whether it be a week retreat to the Rancho La Puerta spa, or just someone's undivided attention. Too fleetingly, fame had licked her, and now she yearned for its lick again. Without it, she thought, she might as well die—and, the truth was, it sometimes seemed that only death could bring fame back. She worried that maybe she was too old. Twenty-three. But then she thought that the media might be kind (they were fickle, that lot), and for her bringing about her own doom (suicide, that is), grant her . . . well, tragedy. (*Like Marilyn Monroe*, they could say. *We all loved her. America's sweetheart. America's lost sweetheart and wayward child*.) At times, it struck her as so very appealing. The flashbulb of the day after—enshrining for eternity a broken martini glass, an emptied pill bottle, a tousled sheet and a stiff blue body. Of course, the rub was, it could well be no fun to be famous if you were dead.

That, primarily, was what held her back—that and the fact that it was kind of a one-shot deal, and if it didn't work, one had no recourse to change one's image by dint of a shopping spree, or suing a tabloid, or finding some disappearing bird that was wanting a spokesperson. She had an inkling that death was one of those big things, like AT&T, or Microsoft or Con Edison. There'd be no opportunity to lodge a remark with the complaint department. That would be it. The last cookie. And she was ready for more cookies. For kudos. She was ready for greatness—so ready, that to fail in suicide . . . well, she didn't know what she could do to herself if she was already dead, but it would be bad.

As birthed from her mother, the infant Thing had been far from perfect. She was a child who had been subject to suffering for the cause of "others." Being seen by them, being judged by them. Thing had been born with a slight harelip, though no one would ever know, as this was speedily corrected by plastic surgery. Also, Thing had been born with bowlegs, though these as well would remain secret—straightened by braces. Her ears too, which stuck out, had long since been remodeled—pinned back. As for the attendance of her massive overbite—orthodontia. And thus did this entirety (not without torment) make up the first stage of the young monster's overhaul—the second, which she had underwent at the ripe old age of twenty, being the liposuction, laserbrasion and boob job. Luckily, her surgeon (more or less a constant) happened to be a sadist, so he was really quite good. And, over time, he and the acquiescent Thing suppressed the beast, and strengthened in her that which they believed to be divine—helping her to join the Earthbound Gods. And all that toil and agony, it had taught her endurance—and now she was set to go. The quest, the journey, the adventure, her whole life had prepped and prodded her to it—and the time had come. Fame.

If it was to be anyone—it was her. And maybe the pang inside her, it was that. The pain of waiting—waiting for the day when all was set right, and she was made a God. And whenever she found she wasn't a God, the pain worsened—for she, who was so prepared to be a God, was still waiting. And the more she had of this waiting, the more she had of this pain, this malaise, this worry that she couldn't wait forever—because she wasn't a God, and if you weren't a God you were a mortal, and mortals died. And, they died nobody—old and alone. And maybe that was what had always kept her alive—the fear, not of death, but of dying mortal. A death where people didn't say how you would live on in their memories, a death where the world didn't mourn, a death where, every dawn, fans didn't line up to lay flowers on your grave—the death of a no-body. Maybe that was the pain. The fear of that. Dying nobody. Had she been able to convince herself that death would secure her immortality, she would gladly have done herself in long ago. But she couldn't convince herself, not to-tally, so her fear of dying—well, it was the one thing that kept her alive. And, maybe, that was the pain, that she wouldn't mind dying—that she might just prefer it—as long as she could live forever.

Unless, the pain was something else completely—the egg she'd fumbled on the sisal, the word she couldn't remember . . . the pimple she couldn't pop. . . .

Whatever it was . . . fame was the cure-all. Safety, love, it would all be hers. And for this, she was ready. Ready as a hog in a doughnut shop—ready as an ant in a picnic basket—ready as an adder in a lunchbox. The beast in her was re-awakened. *I'm ready. I'm ready. I'm ready.* And it cried out that she was supreme. *I'm great.* The bearer of, well, whatever it was supreme be-ings bore. Glory, mercy, horror, reverence. . . .

Nor would she abuse this power. As a conduit, as a messenger of God, she would be fair, and benevolent—*and like a beagle of light in the dark-ness.* And no, even if she was a beagle of light, she'd be no lightweight, but

john**reed**

rather, would bear the heavy burden of a buoyant heart. Once famous, or refamous, or refamous-plus, she was determined to be the one to provide that thing, whatever it was, that answer, whatever it would be. Her singular intention was to deliver the good news, to bear the blessings of the *it* and the *that*—and to tell everybody the world was a better place.

"Otto," she said, philosophically, as they prepared for her first broadcast from the site of the disaster, the site of the hole, "I just want them to know it's all okay, so they can love me for it."

Since the Peterson disaster, the sad members of the extended family—cousins, siblings, grandparents—had been gathering around the perimeter of the hole. They were visible, off in the distance, watching the search crews (volunteered from nearby Groupersville). They sat in lawn chairs, and sampled food and beverages from their coolers, and comforted each other through sporadic outbursts of hysteria.

For days they had sat in grief, sharing their losses with one another, the intermittent news crew, and anyone else who just happened through. Thing saw in them the television viewer—and the bereaved nation. America was waiting for her help. "I feel your pain," she said, in a preliminary shot that included footage of the family. With that shot shot, the team moved onto the B location, meaning to rid themselves of the relations—but location B was not wholly clear of the kinfolk. And nobody was making any headway in keeping them back, or getting the glum ones to smile.

Thing, however, flipping her hair, got over it, for the camera was there. And a director, an assistant director, and her producer, Matthew (with hair-extension mullet), they were there. And the varying others that she could never keep track of, they were there too. And so were the ever-present duo, Otto, cameraman, and Roth, soundman—though Roth, that bent of nonpersonality with the vim and vigor of a snail on antibiotics, could hardly be thought of as present. Nevertheless, all of them and all of that were there—*them and their paraphernalia of equipment*—and Thing was back on the tube.

"Your hair looks fa-abulous," said Matthew, as he poked his head in front of the camera—

"Search for the middle. Five—four—three—two . . ."

the**WH●LE**

Thing spoke into her microphone—

"This is Thing from the site of the hole. We've returned to the heartland town of Prairie Pooch," Thing looked to Otto for the correction, "uh, the heartland township of Prairie Dog, to report on the middle. But first a farewell homage to Hal and Flipper." For the viewing audience, a montage followed of Hal and the much beloved cameraman, Flipper. Thing talked a little about that, and, reading her cue cards, about what the hole was. An ancient fault line, or a collapsed underground spring or cave or waterway, or a mudslide triggered by rainwater gushing from a broken storm drain—or some combination of multiple causes. (Otto's lens detailed the damage—the hole, enlarging the second time, had taken half of a neighbor's swimming pool, which had in turn flooded the road, and caused a deep crevasse in a nearby driveway.) Regardless, said Thing, geologists had determined that the hole would not be getting any bigger. ("A commission of two hundred top scientists—one with teeth—has been assigned to the task.") The conclusion to this holey disaster, understandably, was an enormous relief to many, as Thing said with a sincere nod. But, equally understandably, it was not a relief to Thing or her people, as, at the site of the hole, nothing was happening. Helpless, the team eventually resorted to interviewing a few rubberneckers and downcast family members—Thing, all the while, worrying about maintaining the ratings, and her complexion.

I've been in the sun too long. I need to wash my face. I'm getting oily. All this dirt from the search and revelry people. The dust is ruining my pores.

For the first several hours, the aftermath of the hole was the primary focus of the broadcast team. But as the wreckage was cleared, the old footage looked better than the new. The torn swimming pool hanging over a shelf of mud. The half barn—timbers ripped, roof in long oblong strips—spilling tools and lawnmowers into the endless depths of the hole. None of that could be topped, and now that it was over, the process of documentation seemed rote and pointless.

After six hours, it was deemed imperative that Thing abandon the erstwhile ruins, as her crew had been reduced to chasing local crickets. ("It's like, it's like—we're bleeding like stuck frogs and we're waiting for the old tickers to stop.") So, that evening and next day, Thing was all over the county—broadcasting news from local hot spots. In one development, simultaneous with the onset of the hole, area chickens had shed their feathers, leaving extensive bald patches. (Word at the neighborhood watering hole was those chickens had seen aliens communing with the cows—and, as that was patently peculiar to the chickens, they had underwent some unfeathering.) The birds raised their heads, as if they were still bold, still proud—irrespective the vast swaths of yellow poultry flesh. (Prickly straws containing new feathers were sprouting.) For the oncoming camera, dogs barked, and cats whisked away. At the gymnasium of the only high school in a fifty-mile radius, cheerleaders tittered, and spoke of how nice the Petersons had been, and specially Bethany, who, the girls admitted, hadn't been a cheerleader. Out in the woods, several teen outcasts were discovered. They claimed to be vampires—dark clothing, excessive makeup— and told Thing and her viewers that they were digging up bodies. It was archeologyish. They elaborated—

Freed slaves had lived on the land the previous century, and the acreage had been passed down in word-of-mouth deeds, until eventually, nobody owned the land at all. Then, the local government of white people sold the land to other white people—stealing the land from the rightful owners. (The white people were yet to build the planned mini-mall and Loews Multiplex Cinema.) In the wooded acreage, there were pit-like sinkholes, and the teens, believing they were graves, had made them the locus of their efforts. Their intention was to find evidence leading them to the rightful owners of the land, who would then be restored ownership. This, said the teens, would appease the restless spirits who had, in an act of wrath, sucked up the Peterson place. Thus would the local outcasts (and vampires) save the locality, and world, from the exacting of any more such vengeance.

Why shore, it was all thoroughly absurd—but the ratings were good, and, back in New York, it was agreed that Thing was once again *onto* something. And whether that something was a voice for disgruntled pubescents, or the thrill of unpredictability, or, indeed, nothing more than crossover from the death of the last guy, Hal, and the rational, or, irrational hope that maybe Thing would get, well, killed too, the kids were showing *an unprece-*

theWH●LE

dented level of sustained attention to news. That notwithstanding, Prairie Dog, ratings-wise, was just too risky (the last broadcast stop was the football game at the stadium the locals had built for their high school team), and Thing and her crew put in a sage bid to wrap and return to the city. Once the retreat was okey-dokeyed, no time was wasted, and as the grunts packed up the van, Thing plumped herself into the passenger seat, called Matthew on her cell phone (the producer had already returned to New York) and resumed an ongoing conversation they had been having about her departure from, and return to, the Viacom-munity—

"Yes, I know leaving was for the best. No, I know the company didn't want to impede my growth—and it didn't, I mean, I really found myself. . . . Yes, I know, for the journalism. . . . Oh yes, wiggle more when I talk. Okay."

Thing nodded and reclined and crossed her legs—and as she listened to her producer, she prepared to light a celebrity cigarette, for she'd been rehired—without the thong. It was her first step towards anchorwoman—and, other than the concession she'd made for spring break, she'd be fully attired.

"Yes, I know. . . . It's all good. . . . I know. . . . Right, I mean, I had to find out what I don't do well, and, uh . . . not do it."

But, as much as Thing's reinclusion in the Viacom-munity was all important, all encompassing and all good, the whole trip to Prairie Dog made her feel slightly sick, as, throughout the heartland expedition, she'd been so ill equipped—though of course there was nothing she could have done about it. But now, as laid out in the *Seven Habits of Highly Successful People*, there certainly was something she could do—she'd get equipped.

Back in New York, she sent a crewman to drop off her bags at her apartment, while she beelined from the crowds of tourists at JFK to the crowds of tourists at Times Square. (Pastel Eddie Bauer shirts, J.Crew khakis, Nikon One Touch cameras, Manhattan Unfolds street maps—and afraid-to-ask directions.) Here, she marched right into the Viacom building, where, without a hiccup of hesitation, she was very shortly sighted rooting around in Hal's desk (which had not been packed up) and Hal's boxes (which had been packed up).

Unhappily, she discovered that there was not too much to find—mostly old sneakers (Nike Dunks and Vans Slip-ons) commingled with a few pairs of stiff socks (Adidas). Also, Binaca breathspray, Chap Stick, Lubriderm moisturizer, Tom's of Maine honeysuckle rose underarm deodorant, Spitfire Skinny Burnouts skateboard wheels, and several handfuls of Bones Super Swiss 6 ball bearings. And, as for paperwork, Ollie's Noodle Shop & Grill, Domino's Pizza and Dallas BBQ—receipts and menus. Still, there was one sketchbook, and to examine it more closely, Thing toted it back to the coveted corner office, which was now her office, as she had taken it upon herself to cancel the lottery.

"That's the luck of the draw," she explained.

She had a few boxes of her own in the hallway—the same ones that had been packed up about a year before—and she felt vindicated, triumphant, in the fact that she had never unpacked them. "Put them in here," she directed an intern, who had fetched them out of storage while she was in Prairie Dog. And, as she plopped into the rolling swivel chair, and scooted around the room, the intern lined the boxes on the nearby side cabinet. Thing, turning away from the youth, thumbed through Hal's pages, which were filled, mostly, with graffiti renditions of HAL.

Most of these signatures were accompanied by ornate cartoon self-portraits of Hal, complete with skateboard and microphone. Many had captions. One image, depicting a smirking, cross-armed Hal astride an Earth apparently about to explode from the inside, was anchored by the legend—

BLOWING UP

Blowing up?

Thing was incredulous. She knew what it meant, in that hip-hop ghetto talk—it meant, getting famous. *Like I wasn't twice the star he was. Like, no way, not even. Like he was ever half the star I was! Like he was ever, ever....*

Furious (and unable to formulate further opinions), Thing wound up and, with full strength, winged that notebook at the boxes. (*Why, Hal was the lowest rung on the totem pole!*) The intern jumped back. And, flapping, the book struck the one new box from Thing's apartment, the one marked "new," and knocked it over. The box spilled onto the floor, and the flapping book—it followed. Among the spillage had been an Aveda eyebrow pencil, a Mars Bar wrapper, sixteen autographed headshots (of Thing herself), earphones for a Sony Walkman, a food container that had once lodged eggplant salad, and an old Prada hand purse (two weeks?) that lay unclasped on the carpet. Likewise, Hal's sketchbook had landed open (facedown), and Thing, feeling refreshed, went over to retrieve it. And when she lifted the volume (onto an unexamined page), there, on the carpet, was a key. Hal's gloating cartoon face looked out over the caption—

Yeah

Thing grabbed the key, dropped the book, and gasped, momentarily unable to take another breath. *Is this the key?* It occurred to Thing that maybe the key had fallen out of her own box. Crestfallen, she inhaled. *The box? The book? The box? The book?* Thing couldn't decide—*I'm vascilining.*

She picked up Hal's book, which remained turned to the same page, and looked to it for the answer—*is this the key?*

And there was Hal, with his answer, "Yeah." A couplet followed—

john**reed**

Yeah Yeah Yeah, Hal's the king
Hal'll tell ya, anything

Thing immediately called a meeting. And, the conference room being empty, there, Thing began—

"I have . . . the key!"

She held up the item, for all to see—and see it, all did, some feeling rather put out, and others feeling relieved to be off the phone, or reprieved from their errands, and still others feeling bemused, or, indeed, awed.

"This is the key," said Thing, her voice quaking.

And, in so saying, Thing turned back to Otto, whom she had acquired for the presentation—

"Roll the tape."

Otto hit a button on the remote control and sat back, and, with the rest of the assemblage, watched the original, uncut montage of Hal and Flipper's poignant, if ill-starred, quarter season on the tube. The rise and fall of Hal, the VJ, and Flipper, his cameraman, soon had every eye in the room puffed up. Lips puckered, chins dropped, throats distended—and the whole assembly, pressed together into that room glassed-in between two hallways, was soon reduced to an aquarium of sick fish.

Thing, herself with eyes as bulging and intense as a halibut on ice, followed up the presentation with some soothing and wise words—

"When I first saw Hal, I had never seen him, or heard of him prior to that, so, at the time, I didn't know him too well. But then, when I saw a few more broadcasts, especially that one where he got bit by the snapping turtle in the Everglades, I got to not know him a whole lot better. And even though there was no way I could have realized it, Flipper had been behind the camera for all those spots, so, the way I didn't know him, was that I was introduced to him through his work. So, to say I didn't know them, is to say I knew them slightly—and I think that was the best way *to* know them!"

Gears ground, sparks flew, Thing's engine was running—

the**WH●LE**

"I mean, I think we all know what I'm talking about when I say that Hal was the most loved man at Viacom, and so was Flipper. And as far as those, those qualities which we all so adored and will miss so dearly, I feel inanimate to say another word. How could I say something that we all know so deep in our gut? I mean, I'd have to groan! I mean, I . . . uh . . . yep, I think that makes it perfectly clear. We all share a terrible thing that's lost. It's too easy to take life for granite, but nothing is etched in stone. . . ."

A gurgling silence ensued, and the attendance reached for greasy handkerchiefs and crunchy Kleenex as Thing garnered strength for what she had to do—

"And now, it's up to us—to finish Hal's work—that ever-so-important work which he was fatally killed pursuing! To see his dream through to the end, even if, well, now, his dream is over. But—criminy sakes!—whatever his dream was, it's probably the same as all of our dreams, whatever they are. And whyever he dreamed, it's probably for the same reason we dream, whyever that is. So, if we want to remember—uh, it's at the tip of my tongue, uh, drat, anyway—if we want to remember what's-his-name, by George, let's see all our dreams through to the end! Why, yes, an end to all our dreams! For we know why we dream, whyever that is, and we know what we dream, whatever that is, so now, there's nothing left to do but it, whatever, whyever it is!"

Suddenly, Thing did remember that dead guy's name, and, pleased, drew herself up to conclude on the high note—

"So, let's do it! Let's do it for Hal!"

A few whooped, and Thing let'er rip—

"And if not for Hal, let's do it for the Flipper!"

The crew, the crowd, the cronies—they went wild. For a moment Thing thought she had overdone it. (Whoops, a table was upset!) But then they quieted, and looked to Thing for guidance. She supplied the details about her most important lead, the key. Hal, a great investigative journalist, on the brink of breaking one of the biggest, most important stories ever, had left behind this one clue, this one key. Thing set everyone in the office to the chore of finding out what that key unlocked. Bus and train station lockers. Safety deposit boxes. Gym lockers. Assignments were given. Nobody intimated that this development

john**reed**

was predictable—straight out of some low-end script, though most of them had seen plenty. It was a lone production assistant who voiced anything but enthusiasm, and even that in a grumble. Shuffling off to her task, she nodded to a fellow peon and cast Thing a sour, she's-so-dumb glance—

"I guess she's seen the movie."

Thing had been expecting as much (verily, had been lying in wait for it) and, upon hearing this affront, she responded, adamant. She knew what she was doing, because, being famous, she knew everything, and, affixing an evil eyeball on the offender, a young woman wearing jeans, bracelets with bells and part of a tank top (outfit by Urban Outfitters), Thing waved her hand up and down her own fashion gear, as if to say—*who's got the pricier ensemble, baby?*

Thing (predominantly Gucci) thumped her hand on the table—not only was she resolute, but motivational. She would be an inspiration to all! *I must spark the flint of excitement to unlock the hidden geysers of adrenaline that drive one to dig deep into the peak of one's abilities.* She sermonized—

"We all create our own realities."

For she, like every other young immensely talented, uh, talent, that she had ever met, was entirely certain that her fame was not merely a windfall, but a debt due her. (And those famous people couldn't all be wrong! Gad, it was hard to believe that even one of them could!) She knew that fame, whether the particular instant required putting up with a manipulative producer or a doting publicist—well, one *always* had to earn it. Spiritually, also, one had to come to a higher place for God to dollop fame and fortune on you. Nothing in life happened by accident. No, no, no! Fame, riches. It was her fate! It was her destiny! God just liked her better! And she'd worked a whole lot harder too! Yes, yes, yes! The autographs, the kissing of feet! Fame! It was her just desert! With a cherry on top!

To drive it home, Thing added—

"Explanation point!"

As far as VJs went, in the brains department, Thing's general placement, by those at Viacom, was somewhat below Honey Crocus, and, on occasion, as low as Stan the Man—which was not high. ("I think she's got drain bammage," said one critic.) Nevertheless, she was *onto* something—the ratings were up there—much as she had been once before. Reality TV was unover—the teens were not turning back on irony or vicarious thrills. And even if, to the churning minds of caffeinated executives, the second time around proved to be as alchemically inscrutable as the first, twice was more than a miracle, and a body had to grant her that grudging respect—that I'll-do-your-bidding which accompanied high ratings—that I'll-slave-away-in-the-hot-city kind of diligence—that deference along the order of, Command me, Madame, while you are stroked and massaged and peeled and sucked as you indulge yourself in a blissful nirvana of long days, buttered meals, and slippery, if plentiful, dollaroos.

Thence, at this juncture (the worker bees were a-working), Thing had to consider herself—first, her appearance, and next, her physical and spiritual health. It was of the utmost importance. For the ratings. Ideally, she would have taken a week (or three) at the Kalani Oceanside Retreat in Hilo, Hawaii. The black sand beaches, the tidepools, the all-natural thermal springs and vents, the botanical gardens. It had been some time since her last visit, and, most of all, she missed the sea cliffs, where she had spent many a peaceful, carefree hour among the sea turtles, dolphins, migrating whales and numerous other celebrities. Either there or the Sivananda Yoga Vedanta Dhanwanthari Ashram in Kerala, India's Western Ghats—and that mystical awareness inspired by the Neyyar Dam Lake, with its coconut palms and flower vistas. Or the Aspen Spa (though she didn't like to ski—such a downer), or the Chopra Center for Well Being in La Jolla, California. But, alas, she couldn't leave town. So, she decided to make the city her spa! Manhattan had plenty to offer! (About seven thou' should do it.) The limo was arranged. Phone calls were made. Otto and his team were alerted. (In a van, they followed Thing everywhere.) The tour was remarkable. Bliss (lower Broadway), Kundalini Yoga East (higher lower Broadway), Soho Sanctuary (Soho), Peninsula Spa (Fifty-fifth Street), and Yoga Zone (conveniently located throughout the city). In her silk bathrobe, Thing submitted herself to a rigorous schedule of phyto-pumpkin enzyme peel, watsu (water shiatsu while floating in a warm spring), stone energy realignment, Phoenix rising acupressure, Native American sweat lodge, Mayan soap washes (antibacterial balsam soap, Mayan clay body scrub & healing sulfur clay), Shirodhara treatments (warm oil scalp massage to soothe the troubled mind), every recipe of cream application (yin balancing cream, yang calming cream, yin/yang muscle comfort cream), four-level facials, meridian conscious manicures & pedicures, Zen meditation and, finally, anal acupuncture (sparingly). People told her that colonics were good too. But after all that healthy stuff, Thing didn't feel like adding anything alcoholic. At home, with her ultrascent aroma diffuser, Thing practiced aromatherapy. Rosemary, for focus. Frankincense, for clarity. Juniper, to reduce water retention. On the town, Thing pursued the perfect salad. Cumin-seared tuna with watercress, tomato and oranges. Cucumber dill. Eggplant arugula. Asparagus, endive and smoked salmon. Also, many smoothies. All the organic city, it goes without saying—establishments, to name but a few, so green as Lucky's Juice Joint, Bachue, Aureole, Ayurvedic Cafe, Hangawi, Souen and Tien Garden.

It was not until a great deal of this had been absorbed, oxygenated, radicalized and expunged that Thing was centered enough to discover her next clue. The day had been undifferent from previous days—she woke, stepped into her spa gear, marshaled the troops, and made off for her first appointment. (A midmorning seaweed body mask—after lunch, she was scheduled for an invigorating Peppermint Sea Twist, "to firm, tone and win the war on bloat.") This morning, it was Ula's, and, as per the usual, Thing, in her robes and slippers, secreted herself out her door and plunged into her limo. Following the Lincoln, the van—and, in it, Otto and Roth had prepared for their typical moil of gathering footage of Thing, who, naked most of the time, would have to be fuzzled out with squares not much to their, or, really, anyone's liking. (The ratings had held—firm as old flan.) On the way out of her apartment building, Thing had taken a moment to give a few words of wisdom to the crazy homeless woman who lived in the pit under the front stoop—

"You don't have to live here," Thing had said, "We are all possessed of free will. You must believe that."

Behind her, as Thing pulled away in her stretch, the crazy woman, who may or may not have understood her, cried out, "Why you take car, honey? Why you take car?" much as she had for the entire week.

As for the day's broadcast, the drill was established—Thing goes into Ula's. Thing gets undressed and lies down naked on funny-shaped lawn chair. (Thing gets fuzzled out.) Thing gets oily massage. (Thing gets fuzzled out.) Thing gets painted in seaweed paste. (Thing, not fuzzled out, is naked under the paste.) But then, there was a revelation. Thing's revelation. On Thing's own silk robe, there was a symbol—a Mercedes-ish flying saucer surrounded by rings. The robe had been in Thing's closet, and as it had no tags (had it been itchy, had she torn it out?), Thing hadn't the faintest whence the item had come. Still, she had grown attached to it during her spa week, and when she saw that her dermatechnician was wearing the same symbol on her robe, Thing nearly hyperventilated. (Otto and Roth captured it all.) Amazed, Thing asked her dermatechnician—

"Where did you get that? It looks just like mine."

"This?" said Sabina the dermatechnician, "I don't know, Ula gets them."

But Thing was convinced there was more to it than that—

"It looks like a hole. Maybe, a growing one, or one surrounded by a fence." (Back in the heartland, a containment fence had in fact been erected at the site of the tragedy.)

"Or, maybe a spaceship," suggested Sabina the dermatechnician, and, with that, opened her robe to reveal her tee-shirt.

And there it was, the same symbol—but big.

"While you dry, I'll go ask Ula."

Thing was satisfied with this, and mugged smugly for Otto's camera lens—*something's bound to happen now*. But then the dermatechnician didn't come back. And it was a top-to-toe different dermatechnician who asked Thing who had started the treatment. One who wasn't wearing the UFO/Hole symbol—not in any capacity. One, indeed, who was named Paulina, and had never even heard of a dermatechnician named Sabina. Ula herself denied any knowledge of the dermatechnician, or the symbol. Thing, Otto, Roth and Thing's producer were, eventually, forced to entertain the possibility that it was an impostor—possibly a crazed fan. Thing knew it should have made her feel ickeroo, but the woman had seemed clean enough—and feel ickeroo, Thing didn't. *Was she really just a crazed fan?*

Or, was it something more?

john**reed**

Meanwhile, all week, dozens of flunkies had scampered about fitting copies of the original key into thousands of keyholes. Mailboxes, elevators, desks and file cabinets. Nowhere did the key pass muster. This, to the viewing public, despite Thing's frequent nudity, was getting to be a drudge—this constant failure. And Thing, who knew that success was all about having the right attitude, decided it was time to go in to the office and give everyone a little nudge in the direction of *victoire*. She wouldn't get angry, she'd just express herself, and rally them to the cause. *My connection with the universe comes from a place deep within. I'm in tune with nature and myself. I believe in taking the world by calm. Be a Goddess*, she said to herself, *be a Goddess.* And, to her subordinates, she planned to say (to ask), "I believe in you—do you believe in you?"

Feeling remade and generally prepared, in that same way she had felt unprepared a week before, Thing scheduled a pep meeting for her people. And the next morning, bright and early (10 AM), the van had arrived, and Thing, having curled and painted and primped for all she was worth (11:30), called Otto and the crew, who had parked downstairs. She was on her way, she told Otto.

"Cool, but hey, Thing, I was in a hurry this m," ventured Otto, who had a penchant for pruning whole words down to single letters, "then I had a cup, y'know, and now I gotta, y'know—u. Ya'think that diner—what is it? the Socrates Diner—will let me use their toilet?"

Several seconds passed before Thing replied.

"Oh, you mean the So-crates place," she finally grasped it. She always assumed the name of the joint had something to do with some species of Greek shipping crate called a "so." "Yeah, they got one, but why don't you use my bathroom?"

After this, Thing hung up. Now, Thing didn't have a telephone voice that many people would call demure—it was more, as one victim had described it, "a cross between an angry owl and a power lawn mower." She seemed to lack faith in the technology, and to rely instead on her own ability to generate amps. Thus, all in the van had heard the uncharacteristic invitation extended to Otto, and, by it, they had been shushed—shushed like jovial budgies by a peckish polar bear.

the**WH●LE**

"Have you . . . um . . . have you ever been up there?" asked Roth, who peppered all his speech with the word *um.*

"No," Otto vociferated—eyes glazed.

There were several gulps, and some wondered aloud what on Earth, what in heaven—what the heck she could want.

Spittle trickling from his wispy beard (he was pooling his strength, but on the upholstery), Otto opened the van door, and stepped into the void.

As it happened, Thing had a second bathroom, and Otto learned not a lot about the VJ's crib—except that the joint was big, had a lot of windows, at least two rooms he hadn't gotten to see, and a couple of unsmiling maids in the grips of an overhaul. Oh, and also, he'd learned the cause of Thing's act of kindness. It had been no more than a practical matter. She wanted him to be ready with his camera when they left her building.

"What do you mean you didn't bring your camera? That was pretty dumb, wasn't it?"

On reflection, Otto agreed that it was, and, after having retrieved the Thing-cam from the van, he was soon accruing footage of Thing locking her door, walking down the hall, standing in the elevator, and arriving in the foyer. Originally, Thing had called in Otto because she hated walking past that crazy homeless woman who lived in the pit under the stoop of her building—but then, something else had occurred to her. Maybe it was time to face up to that old Russian—to finally make a real difference—if not in the world, at least in her public image.

Actually, the previous day, Thing had been captured by Otto screaming at the old bag—

"You stink! You stink! You stink!"

Thing didn't suppose that had been too good for her image—nor too good that she, only a moment later, had also been captured calling the Ninth Precinct to have the "festering bore" removed. By now, however, the witch was back. And Thing would not make the same mistake twice—this time, she had called the precinct before she told Otto he could come up to use the visitor's toilet.

john**reed**

In the foyer, Thing turned to Otto—

"Okay, she's out there, I can smell her."

Otto indicated he was ready (thumbs up), and they advanced down the hallway. Their steps nearly in sync, Thing thought that this bit of showmanship would bolster not only her relationship with the public at large, but with all the other little people, like Otto and the crew, who she had to deal with on a daily basis. Thing noted the formula—*make a good impression on the lowly people, with the lowly people*.

Besides, it was the last time she would have a chance to use the old woman, and sort of a celebration, as Thing was aware of a law enacted by the former Mayor (her hero!) Rudolph Giuliani that allowed the police to arrest, as a vagrant, anyone with less than twenty dollars, at which point said vagrant was given a choice between a city work program and being released back into the street. For those who chose the street, there was the disincentive that they had just registered a felony arrest, and after three of those, they would get put away for life. A remarkably effective system. And, as Thing had already gotten that shrew arrested twice (presumably her shriveled brain kept opting for the street), after this arrest, they'd lock her up for good. (*Rules are rules, she's got it coming.*) And, outside, right on cue, the homeless woman was there, chewing on her lips and sticking out her hand. But this time, Thing, amply armored in a pair of white, elbow-high gloves, met the challenge like a missionary—or, as Thing herself thought, *like a politician, on the champagne trail.*

She cinched the woman's hand soulfully, and then, as if inspired by a deep connection, seized that filthy mitt with her other hand too.

"What can I do for you?"

The old woman was nonplused—

"Shake your hand—no want. Change—want."

"Oh," Thing answered with surprise (didn't everyone want to shake her hand, wasn't that always it?), then compassion, "uh . . . right-ho."

She turned back to Otto, trying to keep an eye on the old bird, who might be dangerous—

"Otto, get me a five out of my purse, will you?"

The camera shook, as Otto, who hadn't known what to make of

the purse comment, eventually understood that he was supposed to supply Thing with a five out of his own wallet. He did. Thing gave it to the woman.

"As always," laughed Thing, shrugging modestly (immodest) for the camera, "she knows I don't keep my change. It takes me too long to count. Besides, there's nothing a person like me could use it for anyway. To a person like me, a cent is nonsense. I mean, I don't even know why all these, uh, homeless people want it. I mean, it's true, I guess, they could spend it. But what could you do with all that gum?"

As Thing turned back, however, she noticed that Otto had lost his composure, and, standing there bug-eyed, had let the camera droop. He was in his own world—having been, no doubt, ticked off by something. But it was unforgivable nonetheless. Thing jerked her head several times, and finally swung out her foot and kicked him—and then he straightened himself out. *What's wrong with him? Is he, like, a fanatical arch conservative? Can't keep up with a little charity segment? Doesn't he know better than that? Or, even if he doesn't, doesn't he know better than not having the appearance of not knowing better than that?* The camera righted, Thing turned back to the woman, who had taken the fiver, but was keeping up her insistence on "change." Thing, embarrassed by the request, tried to hint to the hag that she was mucking up—

"I already told them, you know I don't keep my change."

Then Thing wheeled around to the camera, with a realization, "She must mean like, a change in direction!"

Thing egged the old woman on—

"What change? What change?"

The woman beamed with an idea—

"Honey, why not you ride bichicleta?"

Thing was unexpectedly jarred by this remark, and the old woman nodded knowingly as Thing signaled "cut," and she and Otto walked off.

Ride bichicleta? Bichicleta? Bitch? Ride bitch? Bichicleta? Bichicleta? . . . Bicycle!

Thing had a thought, and shuddered—

"She meant bicycle!" Thing's crew prepared a microphone so she could report the development to her audience—

john**reed**

"You see, I guess a while back I bought this bicycle, and, holy mackerel, you know that key?" Thing fished it out of her pocket and held it up to the lens. "I think it's my bicycle key!" She pointed yonder, with a conquer-the-hill, take-the-bridge, remember-the-Alamo kind of gesture—

"To my—to my bicycle lock!"

Thing gasped with divine inspiration, and then turned back to the source of this new information, the old lady, who, presently, was getting gathered up by the police. ("Yes, she's dangerous," Thing had insisted on the phone, "she sure is!") And Thing looked on that frail, hunched frame with a welling up of emotion—for now she remembered everything! It had been more than a week before that Thing had been walking around downtown buying stuff (Pancho had been out spinning records, and she had managed to decamp), when she happened upon that bike shop on Lafayette Street, where she plopped down her Visa and bought herself a wee gem of a specimen—for a snitch under four thousand dollars. It weighed ten ounces less than the four hundred-dollar models, and this, Thing had thought, was auspicious, because, well, she did want to lose ten pounds. Still, she'd felt a tad silly riding the item home, as, for four thousand dollars, it weighed ten ounces less, and she weighed ten pounds more. It wasn't even lost on her that she could have saved thirty-six hundred dollars on the expenditure just by not eating that slice of pizza from Ben's Pizzeria. That slice she couldn't resist. So, standing there with the bike and the slice, well, she had to hide the bike. So, with her new lock and all, she locked it around a pole, and sat in the park on Spring and Thompson Street and gobbled her extra-cheese, hoping not to be recognized. *Nobody'll see me, I'm too fatt.* (She'd purge when she got home.) Then, after the slice, she was tempted by a lingerie store, for at that time, Pancho, who had once claimed to like corsets, had become self-sufficient in his lovemaking—a circumstance she was hot to rectify. So she went in, and, to make a long story short, that was the end of the bicycle, because after her purchases, riddled as that bike was with guilt, she completely forgot about it. But Thing realized now guilt was irrelevant—the point was, the bicycle was never about a bicycle, it was always about something larger. Was there some form of mind control that had been exercised on her? Something she had overcome with an uncommon act of kindness? (Otto's fiver.) Why yes, she had vanquished the mind controllers (whoever "they" were) with her acuity, strength and empathy. And, through those things, she would overcome this conspiracy. (Whatever it was.) She would find the middle! Thing removed her gloves and tossed them to the ground as she called back to the little old lady, who the police, gingerly, were jabbing into the patrol car—

"Where is the middle, Nina?" Her name, thought Thing, might well be Nina—and, she glanced back at Otto, there *was* the camera. *The audience, like, should think I know her name.*

The crone responded, "What? Eh? The middlement! On your way! On your way!"

Not two minutes later (stopping at the health food store, Prana, for a breakfast smoothie), with Otto and a camera near on her heels, Thing, by way of Motorola, was making demands of her producer—

"No, it has to be the James Bond music! . . . No, it doesn't matter! Get the—get the double O!"

Trying to impart the difficulty of acquiring such a track, Matthew (Brylcreem, à la Ken doll) implored Thing to listen to the voice of reason. But this only inflamed the inflamed Thing, who had been vying, unsuccessfully, for her own producer credit—"Raisin? Who's that? And why would I listen to someone named after an old grape?"

He begged her to be reasonable, but she insisted on being right—and so, to Thing's viewing audience, she did indeed proceed with an accompaniment of James Bond, although in lesser sequences, Thing's frugal financiers did manage to substitute themes from the considerably more affordable *Magnum P.I.*, and the downright bargain-basement *Rockford Files*.

And so it was that only a few hours later, the whole world (or that portion of the world tuned in at 4 PM eastern standard time) would see Thing, accompanied by the James Bond theme music, take a taxi some fifteen blocks down to Thompson and Spring Street, where she discovered her bicycle locked up in front of the Vivienne Westwood shop, where, ten days ago, she had purchased a corset, which she had worn once for Pancho, and then, like the bicycle, completely forgotten about. It had been one of the last of Pancho's auto-erotic sessions (he took it into the bathroom, without her), and the corset, along with the bicycle, the day and the whole kit and caboodle, had been pitched into a dark recess of Thing's mind, which she imagined as a shapeless muddy river, which she called, Denial. And, anyway, that's why she had forgotten the corset and the bicycle, et cetera—because of the tremendous trauma, the mental anguish that she'd endured.

Not too surprisingly, the bicycle she discovered was not that same mountaineering splendor she had left a week and a half before. It was about half a specimen, and what remained was hardly splendorous. Still, the key fit, and she dragged the ruins (no wheels, no handlebars, no gears) over to the van, where she offered it to a crewmember, who seemed to want it. But what had it all meant, she wondered to herself—

"What's the sig . . ."

She turned to Otto, looking for the word, "What's the sig . . . what's the sig . . . What the fig?"

And it was precisely at that point that Thing saw the sign. The symbol. The same one ("leapin' caterpillars!") that she herself had been wearing all week—the same one that, at Ula's salon, had been exposed as a meaningful clue, the meaning of which had not yet been exposed. There it was, when she looked down—sitting right there on her chest, on her robe. And there it was—right there, painted in the window of Vivienne Westwood. An emblem. Why, she realized, the symbol, it was on every piece of clothing in the store. (*That dermatechnician, she was . . . she was . . . a source! Like Sammy the Bowl! Or the White House Mess Secretary!*) Thing animated. She mobilized her crew and got going—right into Vivienne Westwood, for an interview. The salesgirl, unfortunately, was no help.

"I don't know," was all she had to say, "are you gonna buy anything?"

Thing pressed, but the salesgirl wouldn't budge—

"I don't know what it means—probably, buy something."

This wasn't encouraging, and Thing's attention drifted. Through the window, she saw a cute guy drinking coffee at an outdoor table at the cafe across the street. Her roaming eyes fixated, as those of a cat might fixate on a mouse, or, more appropriately, a hamster, as he had long hair.

the**WH**●**LE**

"Longhair" was wearing torn jeans and reading a newspaper, which was okay to Thing, because it looked like the newspaper was a colored one, and those, she thought, weren't so pretentious.

It's funny how long hair makes ugly men monsters, and beautiful men angels, or . . . Gods.

He flipped back his hair—her heart skipped.

Like Axl Rose.

So strong and virulent.

And, it was then that Thing noticed she was viewing Longhair through the Vivienne Westwood symbol. He was framed by it. *Maybe that's what the symbol meant. Find him. It was guiding me. It guided me all this way already, from Ula's to the bicycle to him.* Her destination, the road ahead of her, it was all so clear, so straight—like a one-lane highway in the desert leading to nowhere.

Informed that they would be interviewing the guy with long hair sitting at the outdoor table of the cafe across the street, Otto and the crew got cracking—set up this, set up that, and so on. Thing, meanwhile, sauntered to the other side of the street, lucid in her mind as to what her goal was—to meet the cute guy. She knew it wasn't right for her to introduce herself, but she also knew that more often than not, doing the right thing meant sleeping alone.

In compromise, she sidled up next to him, as if she were going to say something—but then didn't say anything, and waited for him to say something. . . . (Nearby, Otto waited too, as did Roth, soundman.) Longhair, lighting up, thought she wanted a smoke, so he offered her one.

"Cigarette?"

"I know," she said, puzzledly. Friendly enough, but also as if to establish—*I'm aware that's a cigarette.*

Then, he didn't know what exactly was going on. He'd heard about this—skinny blondes with great big breasts walking up and . . .

Hey, he knew who that was!

"Uhh," he said, suddenly agitated, and extremely accommodating, and clearing his throat and a place for her to sit down as if speed were of the essence—

"Cap?"

She nodded, and he called over to the waiter, "Cappuccino, skinny, double mocha."

He turned to her, eyebrows up, "Okay?"

Okay, she nodded, a young girl again—*that was what I wanted. It really, really was!*

"Sit down," he said, "talk to me."

She hesitated coyly—

"I'm not supposed to talk to strangers, but . . . you're only a little strange."

She sat. The busboy served her a glass of water. She sent it back, for bottled water. Her tablemate, caught off guard, was still affixed to that "stranger" remark, so she took the opportunity to ingratiate herself—

"So, now that we're here, I suppose you know my name, and I suppose you know yours."

"Uh, oh yeah, Caesar, or, uh, my friends call me Roy. I know who you are. Everyone knows who you are. A few years ago, I, y'know, wanted to be a VJ, and when I first saw you on TV you were so mind-blowing that I wanted to run to the studio, reach out and break your neck."

Thing bristled, nearly blushed, as that sounded like an excellent basis for a strong and healthy relationship. Shy, she lowered her head, raised her lids, and opened her wide eyes—

"Flatter me, and we'll be friends."

Then remembering the camera, and that this was ostensibly an interview, Thing conducted herself accordingly—reaching across the table, she pulled over the *National Enquirer*, which was lying open.

"So," she asked, "what were you reading?"

Otto zoomed in. The article, "Green Balls in Sky," described three green balls that had been spotted in the sky above the New Mexico desert. They were "a fast-moving big one and two smaller ones," according to the witness quoted. An FAA officer had commented thus, "I've gotten 500 million calls about the green balls. Pilots saw it, police saw it, people saw it. All I can say is it's not an air-traffic control issue because it did not show up on our radar—but it was definitely there." Roswell UFO experts claimed there was no threat, however, as the craft were merely bearing visitors to the annual Roswell UFO Encounter, an Independence Day festival held in the area.

"Oh yeah," said Caesar, or Roy, apologetic, "I wasn't reading it, I was, like, looking at it. It was, like, sitting there. I didn't buy it. Yeah," he added, "I just came from yoga," as if that explained everything.

And, with that, Roy, or Caesar, deemed it time to change the subject. Indicating Thing and her crew, he asked—

"What are, uh, you guys doing?"

"We're searching for the middle," she said, taking a breath and looking at the sky. And, though that cue might prove too enigmatic for most, in a moment, Caesar, or Roy, had nodded—yes, he too was following the story.

"Oh, right, uh," and he shyly snaked his hand towards the ring in her belly button, which was, as always, a trifle infected—

"Here it is."

He smiled, and Thing liked it—

"Well yes, that's my midrift," she confirmed, and she too became shy, and giddy.

From here, Thing didn't really know where to go, so she looked down at her feet, and then her own breasts, and, seeing the lot was still in place, she looked up. And there, across the street, she saw none other than Nancy Hamilton.

Thing ducked under the table.

"What? What are—"

Caesar, or Roy, had started to ask the question, but Thing was quick to hush him—

"That's Nancy Hamilton. Look, look at what she's wearing."

And Roy, or Caesar, he did look. And he saw that she was wearing a pink cardigan and form-fitting white jeans (Ann Taylor).

"Yeah, so? Bookoo suburb, but so what?"

"So," whispered Thing, "I went to grade school with her. And every few years she, like, shows up, and whenever she shows up, that means that scene, like, wherever I am, is about to get like, heavy-duty New Jersey. So, like, whenever I see her, I know I shouldn't be where I am. I mean, like, it means I gotta go."

Thing clambered out from under the table—Nancy had crossed the street, the coast was clear.

"So, you gotta go now?" He didn't hide his disappointment.

"No," she said, thoughtfully, "not that," because she didn't want it to be that, "I think it's more, like, a sign—"

Then Thing interrupted herself, for she'd had an idea—the meaning of the Nancy Hamilton sign had been revealed to her. She was supposed to go away, and probably with Caesar, or Roy. It was such a big coincidence, after all. Ula's, the symbol, the bicycle, Vivienne Westwood, meeting Caesar, or Roy. Most likely, she decided, she and Caesar, or Roy, were meant to elope. So Thing had to make sure there was no misunderstanding—she wasn't going in for that casual kind of relationship. This was too big for something fleeting.

"Y'know, I'm looking for something, like, serious. I'm not playing games. I mean, I'm talking, like, the rest of our lives . . . or, cripes . . ." she reconsidered, "at least, like, the weekend."

He looked at his Swatch. "I've got ten minutes, or five."

"Okay," she agreed.

As it turned out, Caesar, or Roy, was a guitar player and, consequently, a rogue. This, despite his apparent sensitivity (yoga). A pagan with druid tendencies (tree worshiper, he said sincerely), it took little in the way of persuasion to convince him to leave his Catholic, live-in girlfriend (who wanted him to get a job), to go away for a weekend with a movie star (well, a cable-TV, sort-of starlet, who was sort-of washed up) who promised to pay for him, and to keep him around for a weekend, and, well, maybe longer. She'd do her best to introduce him to a few hair bands, in the event that some guitar player overdosed or ran his Ferrari into a cactus, tree or highway divider. So, the weekend settled, the question was—*where to go?*

And, as Thing remembered Otto, who had virtually slipped her mind, this was the question she turned to the camera and asked—

"Where to go?"

Otto, unfaltering in his wisdom, directed the camera to the

the**WH●LE**

National Enquirer, now lying closed on the table. Thing, noting what Otto was up to, saw the tabloid as well.

"Look," Thing shrieked, waving the magazine in front of the camera. Indeed, there was something very akin to the Vivienne Westwood symbol—right there on the cover!

"It's an alien craft," Thing elucidated, reading the headline and returning to the "Green Balls" article—page four. (Otto zoomed in on the alien craft in the magazine, and then in on Thing's emblemed chest, and then in on the window across the street—to make everything clear to everyone.) Thing, meanwhile, proceeded with the article on the facing page, which described a Fourth of July festival in Roswell New Mexico, to which all alien species, and more immediately, all Earthbound alien adherents, relations and enthusiasts (or even mildly curious travelers, or locals) were invited. And, Thing realized, that might be the adventure she was looking for—*because, hey, if you like that kindathing, that's the kindathing you'll like.*

She squirted—

"Ooh, a Fourth of July festival! But when is it?"

And, after it was sorted out that the festival was that weekend, the whole series of ("so-not") accidents was deemed fate, and they were on their way.

"Heavens to Betsey," exclaimed Thing, still dumbstruck by the enormity of the universal order—

"It really was a big coincidence!"

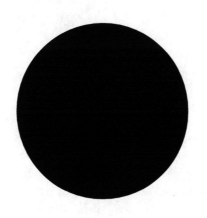

"Oh yeah?" said Matthew (who'd graduated to a stubbly green coif known fondly as the Tennis Ball)—

"Roswell, huh. Kinda beat, but I guess you can always find something dumb in Roswell."

With that, the young man threw his feet off his desk and onto the floor, "But next time, uh . . . Egypt! Or . . . nah, nah, too much work. Too expensive. Vegas. That's right near Roswell."

Thing groaned glumly, for how could she know where this quest would take her?

"We got a deal?" he asked.

"We'll see," she said, shrewdly.

"No," he insisted, "deal?"

"Oh . . . well . . . yes!" she yipped, finally cornered.

Still, she felt that her answer had been clever enough to leave a little wiggle room. But it was a *perceived* concession, and Thing, in turn, was able to negotiate the inclusion of Roy, or Caesar, as a part of the crew. Ticket, et cetera. The truth was, all knew that approval was forthcoming, for, once she got an idea in her head, Thing had, shall we say, a whim of steel. There was no stopping her. To hear her shrill demands was to know, ultimately, surrender. And anyway, it was a desirable compromise—for Thing, by everyone's estimation, was much easier to get along with if she had something like Caesar, or Roy, on the side.

From JFK, Thing and her entourage flew to Dallas. (She in first class, all the others, including Roy, or Caesar, in coach.) From Dallas, they changed to a small plane (Mesa Airways), and after a bumpy flight ("The engine is too loud," Thing kept complaining to the steward) arrived at the equally minor Roswell Industrial Airport, where a rental van was waiting. In it, they drove in a straight line from South Main Street to North Main Street, where they checked into the Sally Port (Best Western) Inn. During the part of the trip that they spent together (for in addition to the first-class/coach discrepancy on TWA, Caesar, or Roy, was not allowed in the Platinum Club lounge), it turned out that Thing and Caesar, or Roy, had a great deal to talk about. He was in a band (the Sickbirds) and so was she (the Headhunters). His band, it seemed, might be breaking up, and hers, which she had formed with Pancho (just the two of them), under current scrutiny, seemed to be similarly close to the reef. (Coincidentally, Otto and Roth, quite independently, were also in bands that were not exactly watertight.) The other delightful revelation (at least to Thing and Roy, or Caesar) was that they couldn't keep their hands off each other. Lips either. This was apparently distressful to the crew, especially to Otto, who reasoned that he was married, and to Roth, who reasoned that he wasn't. Thing, however, did not register this low estimation of her and her guitarist's apelike nibblings, and she proved extremely willing to verbalize her happiness to those who didn't particularly want to hear about it.

"He just has that certain *je ne suis pas*, that certain indefinable something of animal maggotism."

And, indeed, upon learning that Otto was married, Thing and Caesar, or Roy, promptly agreed that they should be wed. (Maybe in Vegas.) And no matter that they had known each other for twelve hours (that is, they would, by the end of the evening), they were unblinking in the conviction that theirs would be a marriage of endless euphoria.

"I've never been so happy!" they repeated to each other and everyone in sight, as they cleaved like chimps. Obviously, they had it all figured out, and Thing rejoiced at their all-knowingness—

"The secret to loving is loving!"

This (the forthcoming domesticity, the homemaking, the cookouts and meaningful family discussions), was all very appealing to Thing. And supplementary to these basics, she and Caesar, or Roy, agreed to adopt several brownish children, and to own a little white dog with curly hair, probably to be named Foo-Foo—although the final decision on the dog's species, and name, would have to be confirmed at a later date, as trends on the matter were apt to change. Oh, the ethnicities of the children too. That would also have to wait.

She exclaimed, "We could live without food!"

"But not without kisses!" he added, joyously.

As the rental van trundled into town, Thing, Caesar (or Roy) and the crew were met by such historical road signs as "The Home of the Famous UFO Event," and "Welcome to Roswell NM! Experience Roswell UFO Encounter: July Fourth Weekend (July 3 & 4)." It being Thursday, July 1, the town was already evidencing preparations for this momentous occasion. There was no store window without loads of UFO junk—and several sported life-size aliens cast in foam (a few busts in plaster). On North Main Street, even at the advanced hour of 9 PM, they were greeted by someone in an alien mask and a shimmering cloak. ("Some dork," noted Caesar, or Roy.) The costumed intergalactic stood in a spacecraft alarmingly reminiscent of *an inflated inner tube.* But Thing, who was doing her best to get into the spirit of the occasion, tried to quit chewing her thumb, and, when waved at by the local dignitary, waved back.

"Promising," said Thing, shakily, as the one disaster that putting-on-a-happy-face could not avert was a ratings disaster. She clutched the arm of Caesar, or Roy. Then, for strength, she looked to Otto, who shrugged his ample eyebrows, as if to say—*aww, don't worry 'bout it.*

Out of the van, she and her retinue oozed into the street, and then, into the hotel, which was right next to the New Mexico Military Institute, which loomed with some importance, though Thing didn't quite know what that importance was. (Otto collected some foreboding footage.) The Best Western, pleasantly enough, was built in the seventies, and thereby fit in completely with Thing's aesthetic. The geometry, the carpets and so forth. . . . There was a pea of a problem with Thing's room, however. A quadrangular building configured around an inner courtyard with a pool and plants, Thing's initial suite was rejected on the grounds that noise from the pool would keep her awake. Her second room was too far from the elevator. (Those halls were long.) The third room, on a corner facing out, was *jes' right*, aside from the carpet, which, to Thing, smelled funny. The fourth room, on a corner with a new carpet, was approved. Otto and Roth and the rest of the crew had all been satisfied with their first rooms, and by the time Thing was settled in, they'd all finished unloading and were, every one of them, sprawled out on polyester bedspreads, staring at floral-print decor and textured wallpaper with Aztec trim—whilst pondering the proximity of the remote control. The one difference in Thing's program of events was that she made Roy, or Caesar, remove the bedspread, because she wasn't sure how often it was laundered, and she suspected an orgy of germs. But, anyway, the bed was soft, nice, so Thing lay on it as she assigned Caesar, or Roy, to the coffeemaker, and the complimentary foil bag of Starbucks Arabian mocha java. Then she and Caesar, or Roy, melted a few items in the microwave, for amusement, and having thus cracked the ice, went at each other. Surrounded by wilting plastic cutlery and one pitifully disfigured rubber tree frog, they were transported—

"On the wings of love," said Thing, "we'll soar to the depths."

Then they were into the wet bar and the few items in the minifridge, and, with silvery laughs, it was mutually decided that it was high time for Caesar, or Roy, to have a trim. Thing couldn't get out of bed because the carpet was likely to be germy (germier, probably, than the bedspread), so Caesar went to go scare up a pair of scissors from Otto ("Sorry, don't have one"), Roth ("Um, try, um, down the hall") and the crew, who, finally, supplied something questionable. Intrepid, the lovers pressed onwards—and Thing, enthusiastic, cut off a hair (or so) more than may have been necessary, or wise. But maybe it didn't look so bad. Maybe it looked okay. *No, it looks good. It looks great!* Then they were off to the hot tub, to rinse off the snippets. With the short hair, she loved him all the more, and they went to sleep in each other's arms.

By morning, however, Thing had donned her sleeping mask, and her Tiffany tasseled earplugs, and Caesar, or Roy, had somehow been relocated to the sleeper sofa. (After all those nights beside cushy Pancho, Caesar, or Roy, with that waif look, as described by its adherents, and that junkie/Somali look, as described by its detractors, was not cozy at all.) When Thing finally woke (nobody on the crew had the temerity to knock on her door), Caesar, or Roy, had already been awake for some time, and she caught up with him in the video arcade. They shared a game of Galaga, and more silvery, if sleepy laughs. Still, by the time the troops had fallen in for breakfast at the Nuthin'

Fancy Cafe, Thing had gotten a chance to take a good long gander at Caesar, or Roy, and he looked kinda old—

"Y'know," she advised him, frowning at his eggs, and, moreover, his sausages, "all those animal products will make you bald, and fatt. Civilized people are turning to vegetables."

He just giggled, but Thing noticed, now that his hair was short, his peaks were a bit on the high side, and his nose was a bit bulbous—

"How old are you, anyway?"

"Thirty-one."

Thing gaped, "You didn't look that old . . . yesterday."

"What's wrong," he asked, optimistic that the mood remained a good one, "can't you love an old man?"

89

She snorted, "Yeah, sure—but thirty-one, that's a corpse."

Charitable nevertheless, Thing tried to make light of it—if he looked twenty-four, and was really thirty-one, well, that would make his true age twenty-six. (Her true age was closer to sixteen. It wasn't so much about age, but making the best of one's good paints.) Besides, she might get used to his age— it always took a few years to get used to one's own.

Maybe it was the hair.

Didn't look as good short. And that was too bad, she thought, 'cause he was poor. But, Thing considered, she would rather have a man without money than money without a man. Money without a man—why, she always had that. Even at home alone! But, well, she would rather be alone than with some wimpy type. And, with the short hair, he did look skinny. . . . But well . . . a little incompatibility was the spice of life . . . if he was as handsome as she was rich . . . well, if she was rich, which she assumed she was, since she was famous.

Curiously enough, though Thing didn't know it, there was actually quite a lot of that with/without calculating going on, as Caesar, or Roy, was repeating to himself—

Put up with it, man. Put up with it. It's as easy to marry a rich girl as a poor one.

Unfortunately for Caesar, or Roy, that hypothesis, when applied

john**reed**

to the rigors of the scientific test, was demonstrating itself to be about as reliable as the formulation that blueberries came from rabbits. A formulation which, regarding the seven blueberries on Thing's plate, Roy, or Caesar, voiced—

"I guess they've only got one rabbit."

"That isn't funny," said Thing, who, having mulled it over, returned to picking despairingly at her fruit plate—the only item on the menu, so she claimed, acceptable to her delicate system. (And even that with comprehensive negotiations.) The Nuthin' Fancy Cafe hadn't seen anything like her since Shirley MacLaine. (The waitress had to tell Thing who that was.)

"I'm totally balanced, in perfect health," Thing informed Otto, Roth, Caesar, or Roy, and her crew, "I mean, if I were, like, to eat what you guys are eating, I'd get totally sick."

That said, she sampled a slice of bacon off Otto's plate, and tucked away at least half of Roth's doughnut.

"Doughnuts are my weakness," she confessed, sucking the powdered sugar and strawberry jelly off her fingers. "They're like, the Achilles' heel of my stomach."

With her fingers in the air, and already on the subject of picking from other people's plates, she surveyed the table—

"Hey, Otto, can I have a few fries?"

Having loaded up on the necessary food groups, the team set out on their day. First, interviews at the golf course behind the hotel—where not too much was disclosed. Nobody even seemed to know what the middle was. "Don't folla that typa thing too closely," said one club swinger, who wore a canary yellow knit shirt (Greg Norman) and purple, weathered twill shorts (Dockers). Another player, when asked of the middle, responded, "Oh yeah," and commenced a discussion on holes 6 through 12, on which Thing was able to report—

"Water hazards are a stumbling block to many."

Back at the hotel, a bellhop had a suggestion. "Looking for answers," he advised, "why don't you go by the museum?" What he was talking about, of course, was the Roswell UFO Museum. And, of course, there, they didn't find any. (Answers, that is.) What they did find, however, were a few mod-

the**WH●LE**

els of aliens, alien spacecrafts and alien everything. (Thing's favorite item was an early Columbian artifact that looked remarkably like the space shuttle, and was made of solid gold—but it wasn't for sale.) One cross-eyed abductee explained that the middle was something a crew from the faraway regions of Galaxy X had found when they rectally examined him.

"The mystery," Thing looked into the camera eye—

"Is getting bigger excrementally!"

Eventually, they did come upon a crossing guard who seemed to have some opinions on the recent happenings in the heartland, and he speculated on the middle, as it was currently represented by the hole in the town of Prairie Dog.

"Could be, there's something in there."

And this struck a chord with Thing—*something is in there*. And, at the next interview site, the Roswell Day Care Center, Thing asked a student, who was himself digging a hole in a sandbox, "What do you think is in the hole?"

The three-year-old answered, "A jar full of mustard."

And while this, perhaps, was not exactly the answer Thing had been looking for, Thing persevered, moving the microphone from his mouth to her mouth and back to his mouth—

"And why is that?"

"Because," the child replied slowly, "I h-a-a-a-te mustard."

After that, they decided the best bet was the famed "impact site." But, their navigational system leaving something to be desired, their discovery of the impact site was not forthcoming, while their discovery of cowherds was not lacking in the least. Cows of every spot, at every corner and turn. It seemed that the quadruped species was in great abundance, while the bipedal, well . . . was not. ("What are all these quadruplets?") Indeed, reasoned Thing's team, the natural inference would be that if an alien wished to visit Earth, cows, and maybe a few people—and yet, throughout, remain undetected—this highway crossing in New Mexico might provide an adequate geography. Thing, however, unlike her fellow cosmic hopefuls, did not see it that way at all. In her estimation, if one were to bother calling upon Earth, the very purpose would be to be *seen*. Why go all that way to go unnoticed? And as for the podunk principality

john**reed**

of Roswell—getting noticed was the only reason *to* visit. Why, the best thing about the place was that when you stood in the desert, you were the tallest thing around. You came to Roswell, it was mostly just you, and those yucky plants, and a few yucky people. Why, you'd have to be mega-yucky not to look *bitchin'* in that company. That's what got her there, said Thing, and if she was as homely as some of those aliens they'd seen at the museum, she sure as shootin' wouldn't be landing in Monaco—it'd be Roswell all the way.

The crash site was yielded after thirty-five minutes on the right road (twice that on the wrong roads) and Thing and her crew endured a tour of a ramshackle ranch house, some rocky foothills, and a toothless man with a placard—

ROSWELL UFO IMPACT SITE

According to reliable military & civilian sources, the Roswell UFO crash of July 4th, 1947, took place within this canyon-ravine. Better known as the "impact site" based on first-hand testimony of those who where here at the time.

Then the Viacom-ites were on their own—left to investigate for themselves the crumbling ledges and vast expanses of sand.

"Wasn't this, like, some kind of *test site*?" asked Thing

"No, that's Area 51, in Nevada," said the rasping Otto. "Near Vegas. It's the size of Belgium."

But Thing didn't believe it. If ever she had seen a location for a test site, this was it. It was so remote, so isolated and desolate, that it was the ideal site for a test. The SATs, probably. The place was so barren, that even the yucky plants were scarce. She, of course, had never considered taking the SATs, but now she could see what everyone was complaining about. Those scholastic amplitude people really were sick. And darn tootin', their test was bi-ased—anyone out here without a sunscreen with an SPF of at least 8, or a con-siderablish base tan . . . well, she didn't know much about sun choke, but if

the**WH●LE**

anything was going to cause someone to choke under pressure, no doubt, this was it. Those underhanded SAT geezers. She had to hand it to them, however, as the gate keepers to that class she was newly a part of, they were doing an excellent job—those dullards would dull the keenest of adversaries. This wasteland would subdue anyone's enthusiasm. . . .

Thing huffed derisively—

"Borr-rring."

Trying to make nice, Thing's guitarist agreed—

"Yeah you're totally right. What this place needs is, like, an atom bomb."

Turning away, Thing grunted at him, disgusted, "Atom bombs cost money. Who's gonna pay for it?"

Caesar, or Roy, he laughed at that, and said—

"Yeah."

Thing wheeled around—

"Don't agree with me! It makes me think I must be wrong!"

And, back in the van, Thing began to think that maybe she was wrong, maybe it wasn't the desert that was boring, maybe it was him. He was always talking when she just wanted him to shut up and listen. And listening to him—he was so boring that she was afraid he was gonna make *her* boring.

"Don't talk to me," she advised him, "maybe then we'll be okay."

She didn't want to jeopardize her career—

"Don't feel bad about it, but you're like, a carrier. Y'know, of, like, blandness. You might be contagious. Don't worry about it, though. I think I'm a carrier too—herpes, warts and, I think, ulcers."

For lunch . . . they returned to town, and after a quick stop at the hotel for a few equipment exchanges and adjustments, ended up at the Grinder Coffee Shoppe. The decor was Barbie and Marilyn Monroe, and Thing, charmed and hungry, quietly abandoned her diet. (The bathroom was clean, and fairly well soundproofed—so there was nothing to hold her back, or her meal down.) Espresso milkshake and a sandwich—smoked turkey and cream cheese with green chili. Her guitarist wanted a wrap—cream cheese, olive and pecan. But Thing was further annoyed by him—he had no money and she was sick of paying for him. And, sensing this, he just salivated, and didn't order anything.

"I'm not hungry."

But, as he sat there and fiddled with the fifties knickknacks, Thing was even more annoyed. He kept taking her chips. He had already eaten her pickle.

"Go get some more," Thing told him.

"But I haven't had anything," he asked, "how could I get more?"

Thing didn't understand him at all—

"Getting more than nothing? That's easy. I don't think you could get less!"

It was as they left the Grinder, falling out onto the sidewalk, heading for the van, and a few more locations, that they encountered some sort of cult member hooded in a red sweatsuit. He had a metal pot, in which he collected pocket change, and swung a hand bell as he sang to the tune of "Santa Claus Is Coming to Town."

You better not talk, you better shut up, and if you don't
we'll make you out to be a crackpot.
The UFOs are landing, on E-a-a-a-rth.
The aliens are coming, to enslave the human race,
But if we elevate our consciousness, they'll blast back into space.
So . . .

Thing asked if he could answer a few questions about the middle.

"All questions will be answered," he said.

And, resuming his ditty, he presented a handout to Thing and her crew. Directed to "interested parties," it mapped the route to an "important meeting," which, however rife of potential, did not surpass the prospect of driving around to collect random footage. There were some nature preserves and a zoo. So, they drove around, saw a few ailing animals and a lot more sand.

"Haven't we been on this road?" Thing kept asking. "Is this private property? How do we know that trespassers won't be violated?"

the**WH●LE**

Then, the air conditioner in the van quit working. It took a while for anyone to notice the humming gadget was diligently filling the cab with hot air, but when it was noticed, everyone noticed, and in an ill, overheated, rip-snorting humor.

"AHHHHHHH!" yelled Thing, in no mood for it all—

"How could anyone pass the SATs if they drove around out here without an air conditioner?!"

Roy, or Caesar, was in no mood for any of it either—

"What? What are you talking about?"

It was all Thing could do to cast him a sidelong glance. He was so stupid that she didn't have the patience to explain—it was like his mind couldn't make the simplest of leaps. And, there he was, even after that disobedient remark, waiting with dopey eyes for her to say something pleasant. But it was too hot, and she was fed up with this puppy dog following her around. And it really was like he always had his tongue hanging out—waiting for her, loving her, looking at her. And it was just too hot. Way too hot. But maybe . . . maybe if he could—

"Fix the weather," she said.

He regretted to inform her that he couldn't, even when it was cleared up that what she had meant (because she knew only God could fix the weather) was—could he fix the air conditioner? This, sadly, was as remote to our guitarist as had been the possibility that he could wag his finger and produce rain.

"You're getting to be a letdown," she said.

Even handy Otto offered little hope. Nobody seemed to know much about air conditioners, aside from the fact that when they broke it wasn't worth repairing them, and that they polluted the environment as they moldered away in dumpsites.

It was decided then that the team should advance to the meeting recommended by the Christmas cultist. All the way, Caesar, or Roy, trying to defend his personality, reminisced about the days when he was "wild." He had a theory that the finer men were formed from their mistakes, and that, in this regard, a man became good by being kinda bad. It seemed to be the contention of Caesar, or Roy, that the more guilt one had, in general, the more generally honorable one was. That was his principle, anyway, and our heroine could hardly forgive him for having such a thing. And, after much postulating, Roy, or Caesar, ungrinned upon by the stars, was meeting with success in convincing Thing that he was down-to-earth and morally fibrous. She summarized—

"Yeah, you're a drip."

Thing was irritated not only by him, but by herself for having picked him out—*how could I know he'd wanna, like, set a good example?*

The cultist's lodge was a single-story eighties-style ranch structure. At the door, Thing and her entourage were asked to remove their shoes. They had no trouble with the camera, however. The cultists were a subtle mix of hyperaware and absolutely oblivious. They wore green tunics tied at the waist, and pointy, cone-shaped hats.

The meeting, already in session, was held in an inner gymnasium equipped with basketball backboards without hoops. The leader of the session was a thin, bald man wearing a red suit with white trim.

"Welcome to our question and answer session," he said, waving the crew forward. Though they chose to sit in the back, Thing already had a question—

"What's with the Santa suit? And the elves?"

The esteemed leader of Heavenly Light, Rector Sandoby, answered, smiling and undithering—

"We're a Christian Alien group."

Thing didn't get it—

"So?"

"So, Nicholas, the children's saint, was a visitor from another world. That wasn't a sleigh he was riding."

The others present at the meeting (green tunics, pointy hats) gave a knowing chuckle, which was followed by a "ho, ho, ho," from their great leader. Thing whispered to Roth that the scene was giving her Claustrophobia.

Launching into his preliminary discussion, Rector Sandoby explained that the lost city of Atlantis was the home of a semi-aquatic alien race. During their time on Earth, this semi-aquatic race, through genetic manipula-

the**WH●LE**

tion, developed three types of servants to attend their needs—whales, dolphins and humans. Between these three, the aliens had physical labor covered, in and out of the water. The alien methodology for said genetic rendering of servants was a process of combining their own DNA with that of a donor species. Subjects were selected from among the mammalian population, as mammals were most compatible with the Star Race, as the aliens called themselves. The use of apes and monkeys produced an early attempt at man—Neanderthals. But the aliens were disappointed with Neanderthal, and therefore created Homo erectus, a more versatile and intelligent servant, and, from there, went on to evolve Homo sapiens, our own species. Hippos were used as the base DNA for whales, and later, whales as base DNA for dolphins, which was borne out by the evolutionary evidence. (There was a significant similarity between whales and an ancestral artiodactyl, an early hippolike aquatic mammal.) By charting parallels between dolphins, humans and whales, it was becoming growingly possible to approach a rough model of the original alien DNA. (Through public access to the genome program, Sandoby and his followers had undertaken the gargantuan task, and were well under way.) Some human beings possessed more alien DNA than did others, and there were quantifiable traits likely to be found among these Star People. Physically—extra vertebrae, unusual blood types, low body temperature and chronic sinusitis. The leader directed himself to his audience—

"As a child, did you feel that your mother and father weren't really your parents? Did you have friends invisible to adults, such as playmates, elves or angels? Do you have hypnotic eyes? Have you ever received the message, *Now is the time*?"

A third of the people on Earth, the leader claimed, were such Star People (Thing thought she was probably one of them, as did each member of her crew, as well as Caesar, or Roy), and of those who weren't helping the Santa's Light sect to prepare for the alien landing, most Star People were, in some fashion, preparing themselves to aid their Earthborn cousins to survive an impending cataclysm (which might come in the form of volcanic activity, global temperature and geological changes, full-scale social collapse, a planetary electromagnetic field reversal resulting in the shift of the Earth's magnetic poles, or, possibly, one or two of the above, or even all of them, or, anyway, something). According to Sandoby, Star People tended to be the socially responsible members of our culture—doctors, teachers, police officers and psychic counselors. And while Sandoby explained that only those Star People of Santa's Light were alert to the alien transmissions imparting higher awareness, anyone, including an ordinary person, could see it—

"Look around you, it's there. The government doesn't want you to think about it. But how else could it all fit together? There's no other explanation."

The leader continued in the same vein on the subjects of Mayans and Egyptians and the great pyramids, and the dozens of other pyramids on Earth and, of course, on Mars, and then, suddenly, Thing interrupted the proceedings. Roth, Otto, Caesar, or Roy, and the other New Yorkers were, every one, sick with horror—abashed, in a society of maniacs, at not being one. But Thing had raised her hand, and, without waiting to be called upon, was asking—

"And how, uh, did they send you those transmissions, again?"

Fortunately, the inestimable Rector fielded the question with ease—

"The Star Race communicates with light. We, at Santa's Light, interpret the planetary signs, or, what appear to be planetary signs, and what are in fact transmissions sent to us in the form of planetary signs. Other peoples, other cultures, throughout history, have utilized this same interplanetary interpretive method. We are by no means the first, or the only stargazers to make the discovery."

And, having imparted that vital bit of information, Sandoby moved on to part two of the evening—mingle with the new initiates.

"Why don't you have a cookie? Sometimes you must give up your will to share in a greater power."

No less than a dozen men and women in green tunics and pointy hats came at Thing and her crew with pamphlets, cookies and fruit punch. And, thus it was that the Viacom entourage began with polite apologies and started for the door. Santa's little helpers, pushing their refreshments and literature, were left closing in on themselves in the gymnasium, while Thing and her people waited in the front hall, where another elf (his hat was tasseled) promised to fetch them their shoes.

Having escaped unscathed, the team took the opportunity to congratulate themselves on their return from the brink of the abyss with all that awesome footage.

"Golly," noted Thing, "everything really is always for the best. I mean, if the air conditioner hadn't quit working, we never would have known to come here. Or, maybe we were meant to come here, and then we weren't going to, so the air conditioner quit working, so we did." She turned to Otto—

"Did you get it all?"

Otto nodded—he had.

"I mean, yowza, I've never seen so many harelips in one room!"

"Yeah, I got'em all," said Otto, and then, there was sniggering all around, and Thing tried not to remember something (about harelips) that, well, she refused to think about. Something that she distinctly remembered having had an excellent reason to forget—

"Hey, where's our shoes?"

And then, all at once, the elves were in the front hall, renewing their efforts to provide refreshments and literature. And, it was quickly realized by Thing and her ensemble, these weren't small elves. ("We're outnumbered," squealed Thing, "because there are more of them!") The offerings were mighty suffocating. A menace of pamphlets, cookies and punch. The slavering, yuletide zealots really wanted them to try some.

"Have some cookies!"

"Have some punch!"

"Read about our philosophy!"

Otto was the first to wise up, "Hey, if we wait for our shoes, we'll never get out of here!"

Indeed, Thing had already reached for a cookie and a Dixie cup of punch (the cup had pirates telling jokes printed on it), when Otto took charge—

"Run! Run! Run for the van! Run for your lives!"

He knocked the Dixie cup from the hands of Thing and the rest of the crew.

john**reed**

"Don't eat those cookies," he screamed, as they all, glassy-eyed, had the oatmeal raisins at their lips.

"Quit that!" he yelled, as they lifted up their pamphlets, to peruse them while they snacked—

"It's—it's—suicide!"

Roth was the next to snap out of it—

"Um, hey! I don't even like oatmeal raisin!"

Thing too blinked her eyes with lucidity—

"You think these cookies are made with refined sugar? What about the punch?"

"Yes! You bet they are!" shrieked Otto. And then they ran—scattered out doors and floor-to-ceiling ranch-house windows and scrambled for the van.

Behind them, the cultists yelled—

"Cookies!"

"Literature!"

"Punch!"

"Shoes!"

"Here's your shoes!"

"We have your shoes!"

Once Roth had been dragged into the van with an overhand grab of the belt, Otto slid the door shut with a slam and a hoot and a pat of the Thing-cam, "Got it all! Got it all!" Having thus effected their escape ("That was, like wow, out of this world!" exclaimed Thing), they all picked up Olympic flip flops at a 7-Eleven. Nobody seemed to care much about the loss of their sneakers, except for Thing—

"They were DKNY," she pouted, but with a smile on her face, as there was always a newer pair of sneakers out there.

"Hey," said Otto, as they re-crossed the 7-Eleven parking lot, "I could go for Indian, y'know, to cleanse the system."

And, in a coincidence that Thing, as their trusted captain, could not ignore, it was precisely at that moment that Otto discovered a menu under the windshield wiper of the rent-a-van. So they went to eat Middle Eastern at a

theWH●LE

restaurant called the Dark Pyramid, which was significant, not just because pyramids had already figured substantially in the Santa conspiracy, but because Thing had a hunch that Egypt had something major to contribute. It was an oily joint, but happily, the food was too, and it satisfied something deep within them all.

"Spicy food's good for the heat 'cause, like, it makes you hotter inside than out," explained Caesar, or Roy.

As they walked carefully to the van through the gravel parking lot (flip flops), they were approached by one of the cultist elves. This little helper had his cap pulled low, and looked like he probably worked in the machine shop. The temptation was to flee, to speed away without a glub of hesitation. But once Thing saw that this elf was not only alone, but something of a midget, she held up her hand—

"Let's hear what he has to say."

Nervously, the aberrant elf twisted to and fro, as if to double-check for lurking enemies before divulging the reason for his appearance—

"All dat," he looked over his shoulder and whispered, "all dat ya jus' saw, a'da compound—dat was jus' misinfermation. I can bring ya tada real t'ing."

"What—what's that odor?" asked Thing, her nose twitching, "smells like raw onions. Maybe they're delivering them to the resta—"

"No," admitted the nervous, impy man, "dat's me, Mitch." And Thing smiled, nodded and stepped back, as Otto got the camera rolling and Mitch continued—

"Ya wer lucky ta ged ouda dat Christian compound alive, dough. If yuda gotten yer shoes back, da'insoles wulda been oudfidded wid tiny liddle needles designed ta prick ya, so ya don't feel 'em, ta inject dis undedectable poison dat causes cardiac arrest, or drug overdose, or suffucation, which could later be disguised as suicide by hangin'—or, even worse an' da most probably, wuld make ya suscept'ble ta da power of suggestion, an' all dem deviously persuasive arguments."

"Uh, Mitch," said Thing, fumbling at her microphone, "did you follow us from the Santa's Light compound?"

"Yeah," said Mitch, pulling on his helmet and stepping onto his gas-powered scooter—

"Now, yu folla me."

So, Thing and her crew, without anything else planned, waved their hands—*why not?*—and took to the highway, collecting footage of the mysterious scooter rider in the green frock.

"Not too inconspicuous," noted Caesar, or Roy, of the leprechaunlike figure and his Go-Ped Geo Sport. Nevertheless, Mitch was continually scanning the horizon for unseen opposition.

"It's like he's afraid someone might notice him," said Caesar, or Roy, a bit too enthusiastic with his sarcasm.

"You think," Thing asked Otto, "he was the one who put the menu under our window shield? You think it took him all that time to catch up to us, I mean, like, riding his scooter, like, twenty miles an hour."

Otto, tired of talking, raised his eyebrow—

"Could be."

Off the highway onto a twisting dirt road, the Go-Ped and van eventually arrived at a near-empty trailer park. In the door of a rickety rig, a black man stood ushering forward Mitch and his guests. Thing wasted no time getting to it—the interview, and, as Mitch had phrased it, "da real t'ing." Inside the camper, the black man had finished preparing a slide lecture—he clicked the slide carriage back to the start.

"I'm ready," he said.

"How'd you know we were coming?" asked Thing.

He didn't answer.

She asked again—

"How'd you know we were coming?"

And though he didn't answer, again, the question brought a beaming smile to the lips of the black man in Lee jeans and a White Album Beatles tee-shirt. Then, Ponte, the King of Aztecs, as he introduced himself, was unwilling to sign the required sign-away-your-rights form. Otto, still behind the camera, finally convinced him. Thing immediately had a question.

the**WH●LE**

"Uh, Mr. Ponte, are you and, uh, Mitch . . . uh . . . are you two lovers?"

Once again, Ponte ignored Thing's question. And as the King of the Aztecs began his lecture, Mitch, that pot-bellied, greasy little dude who smelled like onions, shushed everyone into silence.

What followed was a series of images—cowboy hats, cowboy boots, a McDonald's restaurant, a man on a bus, et cetera. Slides of a seemingly innocuous nature—but not so, according to the Aztec King, who explained how these slides constituted a mere picayune of the extensive evidence he had assembled. Aliens, he said, had invented cowboy boots in the 1800s to disguise their one big toe—triangular—that might more aptly be called a claw. This he demonstrated, with photos of cowboy boots. (But no pictures of toes—triangular—that might more aptly be called claws.) The Aztec King alleged that nothing other than a large alien population could account for the prevalence of "cowboy boots" in the region of the Southwest.

Thing tried to encourage the delusion.

"Why, like, obviously—cowboy boots are so stupid looking, why else?"

"Yeah," Ponte turned to Roth, who was shuffling into a corner— "How would you explain it?"

"And the middle?" Thing furthered.

"I'm getting to it."

And, he was. The McDonald's he had photographed turned out to be not at all an ordinary McDonald's. It was, said Ponte, the entrance to an underground complex—five miles in diameter—the center of which had been located beneath the suburban home of the Peterson family (the same Petersons who had, lately, been sucked into a hole). Much of the town had followed. And Ponte knew the reason why. He proceeded to the next slide, a man on a bus—

"This is the inventor of a type of, in layman's terms, beamer machine, which is either a time portal, of limited usage, or an intergalactic portal, of limited usage."

Originally, the device had been meant to be no more than a transporter, a *Star Trek* beam-me-up-Scotty technology. First farm animals, and then volunteer convicts had been employed to fine-tune the mechanism, and eventually, kidneys and eyeballs, as truculent as they had been about the undertaking, ended up arriving (after transport) safely inside their owner's abdomens and, respectively, eye sockets. (The initial design of the machine had been cadged from the darkness of Egyptian burial chambers—hieroglyphs and diagrams.) Still, there was a problem—one in every 250 convicts would disappear. Never to be retrieved. (Where did they go? Nobody knew.) Then something else started to happen—things arriving in the machine, quite on their own. They were parts to a new machine—an improved machine. Improved how—that was unclear. But built it was. And disaster ensued. The hole had appeared. More and more of the stuff of the military compound, and the Earth in general, was being drawn into the technological vortex. Was it an alien mining operation? An invasion from space? From the future? The past? Was it a gigantic mistake? Or, was it the Chinese, with another clever method for stealing secrets?

"Whadeva id'is," said Mitch, who could scarcely follow it all himself, "id'ain't doo good!"

Thing, however, as much as she wanted to believe, was skeptical—

"This is all swell, but don't you have something else besides, like," and Thing hated to say it, "pictures of guys sitting at bus stops?"

Ponte was thrown into a rage. The compound. The government. None of this was for popular consumption! There might even be enemies among us—aliens, time travelers or the Chinese! Or all three! And, the McDonald's. And the bus stop outside the McDonald's. That compound. Well . . . Ponte tossed the slide projector angrily, and started raving about security at a place like that—

"Don't you think it's well guarded?! They're not—"

Thing interrupted—

"Who are 'they'?"

He answered—

"The Olympic committee!"

And, as Thing and her crew looked to their flip flops (*it was a big coincidence*), Ponte broke into song. ("Mitch and I, we love your show," he informed her.) As manic, as crazed as he was, the King of the Aztecs had seen the Olympic committee score a point—and he knew the time was right. So he reached for his saxophone, blared forth a few notes, and started to croon—

> *They hide your shoes. They short your sheets.*
> *They bend your keys while you're asleep.*
> *They sour your milk. They warm your beer.*
> *They drool on your pillow in the middle of the night*
> *   and whisper insecurities in your ear.*
> *They run down your batteries in a sinister plot.*
> *They switch the caff and decaff coffee pots.*

Mitch, beatific, bobbing his head and fluttering his arms, provided the chorus—

> *You'll stub your toes and knock over your stuff,*
> *'Cause they've moved your furniture just enough.*

Then . . . sirens pierced the night, the trailer and the song. Ponte asked, rhetorically, "You see." Mitch looked to Ponte—

"Sounds like pigs."

"Yeah, comin' for us," confirmed Ponte.

Then, all was a-whirl. Ponte was in and out of the trailer, here and there, pulling up stakes and locking cabinets. Mitch did what he was told, and in hardly a minute (the sirens growing nearer), Thing and her crew were vacated from the motor home. Then, Ponte's 1989 Winnebago Warrior was screeching out towards the highway—posts cracking and breaking away, lines and hoses snapping and dragging, the patio awning tearing off, sailing up, and skidding into the dirt. . . .

At the brink of the clay road, Ponte threw his head out the window and brought the RV to a clamorous halt. He yelled back to Thing, who, with her crew, stood amidst the wreckage of the campsite, the crickets chirping.

"Find the dark pyramid!"

john**reed**

Thing listened, awed—

What? What? What dark pyramid? Oh—

"The restaurant?" she cried out.

"No," cried Ponte, emphatically, "not the restaurant."

"But, at the restaurant, do they know?"

"Well, yes," he answered, "but no more than you or I."

Then, he was off, like Pancho, never to be seen again.

Thing and her crew watched the trailer barrel away. Shortly, three cop cars followed (or, to be exact, one car, two trucks), with the trailer ahead of them. And then, out at the highway crossing, for all to see in the wide, empty desert, the trailer drove straight, and the police vehicles turned left—lights still flashing, engines still blaring.

Thing was agog—

"Hehhh?"

"Those idiots," throaty Otto shook his head, "the cops aren't after them at all. They want some other psychos."

"Oh," said Thing, who then, having made an association, perked up, "you think they're, I mean, the cops, you think they're on their way to a doughnut shop? You think there're Krispy Kremes out here?"

The Krispy Kreme idea—it hit home. Among the crew, she triggered a powerful craving for a between-meal doughnut. But there was no Krispy Kreme on the map, so it was decided the best course of action was to resume the investigation—to return to the Dark Pyramid restaurant for more information, and maybe dinner. (The fried banana fritters, those were pretty good too. They could all use a few more of those.) Sadly, their route was not direct, but lopsided, meandering—and during a we're-not-lost-I-know-exactly-where-we-are excursion, there was little in the way of stimulation save the four-legged kind that moos.

"Dag," said Thing, "even with the festival and all, I think we've seen more cows than people. I mean, like, if an alien wanted to visit, why would it want to visit all these cows? I mean, and why do they kidnap and dissect cows and stuff? I mean, if aliens are like Gods, what's with the cows?"

After this, Thing retired her critique of alienology, although Roy, or

Caesar (who had been retired himself, after an unsuccessful stint as navigator), had an explanation—

"Could be like maybe, to those, uh, aliens, cows are Gods. Could be those cows, they're, duh-ha, Bovinity."

Thing was incredulous—

"Huh?" she screaked, "You don't know what you're talking about—if anyone's Bovinity, it's me!"

This outburst was not met with laughter, but a sickening silence, through which Thing's slighted heart could be heard beating. She was near tears, but sucked it in as best she could.

"I know, I know," said Roy, or Caesar, trying to calm her, "you are, like, a deity."

In his dealings with Thing, Caesar, or Roy, had taken to practicing sincerity, which was not effective. Thing didn't mind a little sincerity, but too much was, to her taste, a bit like too much salt. So, when Caesar, or Roy, explained himself (that to him, she was like a God, because he worshiped the ground she walked upon), she warned him that he was laying it on kinda sick. "I mean, thick," she corrected herself.

"But I love you," he insisted. "It's the truth."

She looked away—"If truth's so great, then why don't you keep it to yourself?"

After that, Thing had no more to say to him. They had shared a perfectly good illusion, but he had overstated it. And now that the illusion was ruined, by his oafish handling, she couldn't trust him. And with the trust gone, the lying was over.

The Dark Pyramid restaurant was closed by the time they got to it. Everything was closed. No Krispy Kreme was located. No Dunkin Donuts even, though they all had a vague memory of having seen one. They returned to the hotel, under the erroneous impression that room service was all night, which left them in the lounge eating popcorn, beer nuts and Doritos. Also, stuff from the vending machines in the hotel lobby. The bar was open, so some nutritional value was to be had there. Roth had an atomic nectar (rum, vermouth and gin), Otto had an alien's blood (vodka, crème de menthe, blackberry brandy and lime juice), and Caesar, or Roy, had a kryofluid (spiced rum, lemon vodka, orange curaçao and grapefruit juice). Seated at another table, the rest of the crew drank CIA specials (whiskey, rum and vodka). Glass and plastic wrappers (vending machine) flew hither and thither in an orgy of sugar and alcohol. The conversation grew heated—frenzied. Eventually, Thing was so annoyed by her guitarist, who was talking about *anarchy*, that she had to seek a change of venue.

Spotting the Black Rabbit, who happened to be in town, she took a Mounds bar off the table and sauntered over to join him at the bar. There, the Black Rabbit already had a fresh pink cocktail waiting for her, which he promptly deposited under Thing's inquisitive nose—upturned and wriggling.

But Thing . . . having already knocked back a couple (the pink cocktails were always there when she wanted them) thought better of it, and tended to decline—

"Although," she admitted, for the set-up was scintillating, the ice a-shimmer, the liquid a-sparkle, "it *is* a temptation."

"Ah yes," said the Black Rabbit, with a buck-up expansion of the chest, "well, there are several fortifications against temptation, I suppose if cowardice serves you, then—"

But that accusation, Thing wouldn't hear of it—

"I'm no coward, and you know it. I'll do any crazy, stupid thing—bone-cold, stone-dry sober. I know you're trying to fumi—uh, lubri—uh, masti—uh—"

"Manipulate?"

"Yes, manipulate me. What you want is that I say I'm no coward and drink it. But *that*," said Thing triumphantly, "would be the cowardly thing to do."

"But you want it?" asked the oily Rabbit, "no?"

Thing jerked back her head, confused. Her eyes crossed, and, after several short breaths, faltering, she stuttered, "But it's not cowardice, it's my . . . it's my . . ."

"Conscience?" Furry head tilted, ears flopped—

"Same thing."

And to that, Thing had no answer.

the**WH●LE**

"Well," said the Black Rabbit, now kind, now debonair, "the only way to rid oneself of temptation is to yield to it."

"Okay then," said Thing, unable to find fault in this faultless logic, "I guess the one thing I can't resist is temptation."

The Black Rabbit was then obliged to take a call from his stockbroker—so Thing, with cocktail, returned to her table. Unfortunately, Roy, or Caesar, was still talking about anarchy, and newly reseated, Thing was not inclined to again uproot herself. This time, it was the guitarist who had to go.

"Roy," she commanded, "or Caesar, go get me a glass of water."

To this imperious issue of orders, Roy, or Caesar, smirking timidly, retorted—

"If you want a glass of water, get it yourself."

Thing could not contain her disappointment. She yelled—

"Don't you get it? You're major minor-league! I'm so much better than you, you should do whatever I say! And you would too, if you weren't here with me! It's just your head's all . . ." She exhaled impatiently, not sure how to let'im have it. Then, she ran off, ostensibly, to get her own glass of water, but, in fact, down the hall, up to her floor and into her room. There, she soaked a towel in the toilet (which, need I inform the reader, had not recently been flushed), and returned with the dripping object to the lounge, where she hurled the article, wadded into a ball (about the size of a canon ball) right (SPLATO!) into Roy, or Caesar's, unsuspecting head. The guitarist had made an easy target, whether it was, as Thing suggested, because his head was so big no one could miss it, or, alternately, because Thing had fired from point-blank range. Regardless, for a split second, the towel stuck to the young man's head, and a portion of his face. Then, the towel began to unravel, and, in so doing, slid downward, slopped over his drink, and came to rest, finally, in his lap. The drink, toppling, followed shortly.

When Roy, or Caesar, looked up, shocked (along with Otto and Roth, whose chairs, miraculously, had shot back several feet from the table, and that quiet little world which had so jiffily gone eco-disaster), Thing had only this to say—

"Wrap it around your head! Maybe it'll reduce the swelling!"

john**reed**

As might be expected, this turn of events did not go unnoticed by Roy, or Caesar. And, as a result of Thing's misbehavior, or, to wit, his mistreatment, he summarily removed his scant supplies from Thing's room, and vamoosed. (Otto and Roth were asked to bunk together—they and the crew went for a sauna.) And soon, he and Thing were installed in their beds, talking to each other on the phone. The feeling was sad, and sulky, and maybe an itsy-witsy bit sexy, and they spoke for a long time. . . .

Then, Roy, or Caesar, finally made the observation, "This is ridiculous."

So he returned to Thing's room to "just watch TV." And, lickety-split, they were watching porn (pay-per-view). Not long after, mammalian behavior kicked in, and they were at it. Nonetheless, it wasn't all that it had been, and though the fundamentals were diverting enough, Thing didn't like the kissing. Finally, she broached the subject—

"The kissing makes me, uh, uncomfortable."

"Oh," he said, "I don't want to make you uncomfortable. I mean, I uh, like it, I mean, the kissing, but, yeah, anything to, yeah . . ."

This, of course, was no discouragement, or, rather, no encouragement not to kiss. And it made Thing feel deeply guilty, which made her kiss him more, which made her feel more uncomfortable, which made her more guilty, which made her kiss him more and more, which made her more and more uncomfortable—and, well, she soon grew to hate the whole situation, though she saw no way out. . . .

It was just an oops fuq, she thought, afterwards, popping another piece of gum into her mouth, as the one she had in there, with all the activity, had gotten a little hard. Then she began coughing, which reminded her, they had cigarettes. Chewing wetly, she lit one. But then, he exhibited some negativity, pinching his face, as if to ask—*gum and cigarettes?* She sucked and puffed, smacked and popped. And finally, he asked—

"Are you gonna chew that gum all night?"

"No," Thing shot back, "I'm not gonna chew it all night. I'm just keeping it in my mouth!"

"Yeah," he said, "uh . . . don't choke on it."

the**WH●LE**

Indeed, thought Thing, it really was just an oops fuq—but for him or for her?

And, after a moment or two of silence, Thing observed—

"It's such a weird mistake, to think that good-looking people are smart. A pretty face says a dumb thing and we listen—and we don't think it's stupid, but totally like, uh, pro, pro—"

"Profound," he said.

"Yeah," said Thing, turning to him, with sudden dread. She was no psychic, but she had a kind of uncanny inkling that he wouldn't like getting called dumb. She did call him a pretty face, though, and was already preparing a defense. Interestingly enough, however, he didn't take it personally, but regarded her with a queer contortion of the features, as if, for his part, he agreed, and wondered how she was reading his mind—*why is she saying this about herself?*

"Yeah," said Caesar, or Roy, "I guess so," and then, as if to make that final, inevitable leap—

"And uh, all celebrities are beautiful."

There was a bit of a pause as Thing digested that. It seemed, oddly enough, absolutely correct. Why, all celebrities *were* beautiful!

"Yes," she said, compassionately, "I know."

Then she patted Roy, or Caesar, on the cheek, as if to say— *that's so very sweet of you my poor, poor mortal, to call me beautiful when I've called you stupid, to concede the truth, to take it so well, that I'm breaking your insignificant heart—*

"I'm so, so sorry, honey."

And then they went to sleep in each other's arms, completely at one, and not understanding each other at all.

The next morning, Thing left Caesar, or Roy, sleeping on the couch, and marshaled her troops for departure. (Eternal happiness. What had she been thinking? It would be a living hell.) There was a celebration brunch at a Mexicanish restaurant called Mario's. It was uncertain as to whether the celebration was for success, or failure, or simply Thing's new freedom (she felt so liberated without her guitarist), but Viacom was paying, and nobody on the crew was turning it down. Eggs. ("I'd like them poached . . . no, fried . . . no, the whites

john**reed**

fried, the yolks poached.") Grilled Cajun catfish. Shrimp. Salad bar. Fajitas. Pineapples. And beer and wine too. New Mexico wine. And Mario's own beer— Alien Amber Ale. An earnest green alien peered out from the label of the beer. Roth kept several bottles as souvenirs. They all ordered desserts. Thing rose, and rose her glass—

"For your loyal service, I'd like to offer all of you a toaster."

They sat befuddled—she indicated that they should rise. They did. She continued—

"I think we all know what we're celebrating, and if . . . then . . . and . . . well . . . you can bet on it! Roger dodger . . . uh-huh . . . I think we all understand each other. . . . We've taken the bull by the teeth, and . . . yes sirreebob . . . it was as easy as falling off a piece of cake . . . I mean, flexibility is the bedrock cornerstone of this house of cards. . . . And . . . so . . . to us! And . . . to reaching even greater platitudes of achievement by rising to that higher standard above our potential! And . . . of that . . . I'm confident we're all capable!"

Before they drove to the airport, they stopped by the Dark Pyramid restaurant, as it was open by then. (1 PM.) And, as they had been told, at the restaurant, nobody seemed to know anything about anything, except that if there was a dark pyramid, it was, maybe, in Egypt.

"Aha," the VJ's suspicions had been confirmed—

"Egypt!"

So, Thing called in to the offices to have the flights booked from JFK. Then, all piled into the van, and Otto, Roth and the crew took their phones out of their pockets and fanny packs and called their families and loved ones to inform them that the trail led straight to Egypt. . . .

At the airport, Caesar, or Roy, caught up with them. Thing and her people were nearing the metal detectors when they heard the voice—

"Hey! Hey! Wait for me! I'm here! I'm here!"

He greeted Thing with a kiss. She recoiled.

"Thanks for letting me sleep," he cooed.

Roth, Otto and the crew were off, through the metal detectors, for they, unlike Caesar, or Roy, knew what was about to go down. . . .

Roy, or Caesar, started for the metal detector himself.

theWH●LE

"We better go," he said, looking ahead to the gate, "I, like, wow, barely made it, huh?"

"Yeah, well," Thing said dryly, resuming her place in the metal-detection line, "it was very sweet of you to see me off."

"What?" he said, eyes like lemur. "What about me? I mean, I need my ticket to go through security."

"Sorry," said Thing, moving breezily through the station, "your ticket was one-way."

She really was surprised by him—*can anyone be so naive?* She looked back at him—glum on the other side of the barrier. And it was then that Thing realized how blown to bits his heart was—*aww, I've popped his pumper.* She marveled at the strength of human weakness—as he stood there, with his hands in his pockets, his look altogether downcast, and his body quivering. *Why, why—he's shaking like a Jell-O fish!*

Bands of tourists came and went. Some wearing "My grandparents went to Earth and all I got was this lousy tee-shirt" tee-shirts, others dragging polyethylene aliens. Still others bore luggage with "I $upport UFO Research" pins. All with their cranberry-eyed optimism, and their surety of . . . *the revelation.* This was the one hope that could not be dashed. The one confidence. If it wasn't in their lifetime, it would be in their children's, et cetera. And, maybe they were right. But the bitterness of their own lives, here was the battery that powered this lightbulb—and the light suffused everywhere.

An announcement was made for Thing's plane.

Thing turned away. She could feel him watching her walk—leaving forever. She could feel he was crying. She saw the mugs, the toys, the sweatshirts and flying saucer posters. "We're here! We're here!" The insistence was plaintive, unconvincing. *We're here? Watching football games and drinking frozen orange juice? We're here? Buying postcards and eating donuts? What is it? What is the answer?*

With an ephemeral compassion, she turned back—

"Good luck Roy, or Caesar! May you . . . uh . . . uh . . . live all the days of your life!"

john**reed**

Then she was on her way. *You're closer—closer to it. To it. It. Only you. For you. The it.*

The breakup . . . yaahz, was a woeful thing to remember, a reminiscence, like so many others, that throbbed and tugged like another time in her own body. But, well . . . promises and pretzels were made to be broken. And there was such a lingering sense of remorse over a broken pretzel—never to be looped again, forever unhitched and incomplete. No, it could not have worked out between them—*rich girls don't marry poor boys.* That was the natural order. And she couldn't feel guilty either—if God hadn't meant for there to be people poorer than herself, He, or She, or It, wouldn't have given her all their money. She remembered once that the Black Rabbit had told her that it was impossible, the way things were, not to, at least once in a bit, look down your snoot at someone. . . .

Too bad, thought Thing, *he was so good-looking.* But she was too. "Jeepers," she exclaimed to Otto, "beauty skins deep."

At JFK, the logistics of Egypt began to weigh on Thing. The interpreters. The permits. The guides. The drivers. The hotels. The equipment. The customs officers. All too much. And then it occurred to her that even if the answer *had been* in Egypt, there was no saying *it was still* in Egypt. The truth, as she was learning from that whole Caesar/Roy episode, was a slippery customer. There was nothing, as she had always assumed, permanent about it. Rather, the truth was a mercurial element. One that was in constant flux. It was like, in some nook of her brain or tummy, she had always known that the big bang theory was flawed. And then, like, it was—she had seen a show on the Discovery Channel! And though she'd never bothered to learn the math to prove it, it was clear to her that everything proven by science was eventually unproven—and that this pointed to the essence of all answers. There were no limits. Not the edge of the Earth. Not the sound barrier. Not the speed of light. None of that really mattered. And as far as the universe, who was to say that the laws of its governance weren't also in constant motion? Evolution, just like living things. Even plain ol' elements had three stages—solid, liquid and glass. Maybe more, that we didn't know about. By gosh, the sun itself was changing—living.

the**WH●LE**

We had seen so very little, who was to say there weren't big chunks of the story we knew nothing about? Who was to say that we didn't understand, or didn't only half-understand, or didn't only hardly understand, what amounted to less than a nano-micro-nothing in the largeness of all? Who was to say the answer hadn't advanced from, well, going all the way to Egypt, to, well . . .

Thing knew what to do. *Be a Bovinity. Be a Bovinity.* And, as they walked through the airport terminal, Thing tried to become fully conscious of her every thought. *I don't feel like going to Egypt.* It kept running through her mind, and, as Thing considered, she decided it wasn't so much a fear, as an authentic inclination. *It's too far. And I don't want to ride a camelot.* She concentrated on being in her body. She slowed down, to feel herself breathe and walk. She sensed her body's subtle energy, and let that guide her. She asked her intuition—*where do I go?* As Thing and her crew neared the outlet to the baggage claim area, one of many waiting livery drivers stood holding up a sign for his party. He had long hair. *Is it Caesar/Roy?* Thing looked again. *No, it was just a fragment of my imagination.* She read his sign. "Miss Cones." Then, a section of the airport under construction, there was a line of cones. Thing stopped. She saw the liveryman staring at her, as if to ask—*Miss Cones?*

Miss Cones? Miss Cones? Miss cones? thought Thing. *No, I'm not. No, I didn't.* Otto called after Thing as she took to the bizarre task of following a line of cones through the airport. But there was no opposing her, so he assigned Roth and the crew to their duties, and pursued. The cones ceased abruptly at the foot of a travel billboard, and Thing too, here, abruptly ceased.

Otto, bringing up the rear, glanced worriedly from Thing to the poster of the leaning tower.

"Looks like a birthday cake, doesn't it?" asked Otto.

"Yes," said Thing, seriously, "it does."

"Or maybe," proposed the word pruner, "a wedding c."

"Yeah."

"You know," Otto pondered anxiously, "I think it's really far away, like France, or Spain or something."

"No, it's not," snapped Thing, "it's in Italy. That's the leaning Tower of Pizza."

john**reed**

"You wanna go to I?"

Thing deliberated as she drew out the words—

"No-o no-ot ree-aally."

She consulted her cameraman, "Doesn't it sort of seem to be pointing, sort of, to this other poster?"

"Hmmm," said Otto, "could be," and together, they turned to the next poster.

"But uh," Thing pointed, "what's that?"

"That's Las Vegas," said Otto, as the advertisement displayed an evening skyline of the gambling/family-entertainment town.

"No," said Thing, "I know. Not that. That. That huge triangular cube." And with a mounting excitement, she shook her finger at a black triangle in the panorama—a mysterious black hole in the city.

"Oh, that? That's the Luxor pyramid. It's a hotel. Everything else in V's got lights. But it's like this humongous glass pyramid that's all black. So late at n, it stands out by being dark."

Otto noticed that Thing's jaw had come unhinged. He'd seen her awestruck before, but it always dismayed him.

"What," he asked, "am I fired?"

To silence him, Thing held up her hand. As for words, there were only three, and she gasped them—

"The Dark Pyramid!"

In daylight, *mais oui*, the Luxor pyramid was impressive—but so was everything else. At the intersection of Tropicana and Las Vegas Boulevard alone, there were four tremendous hotels. The Tropicana, the MGM Grand and the Excalibur, which was next to the Luxor. Everything was wild and inviting. Limousines, red carpets and any fantasy that concrete could shape.

Of course, the Luxor was a little outside the budget of Thing's producer, Matthew. And, anyway, when Thing asked around, nobody at the Luxor knew anything about Egypt. Then somebody said they thought there was something with Egyptologists at the convention center. . . .

But first, Thing and the crew had to check into the Lady Luck, which Thing thought was appropriate enough, and where a two-fer deal had been worked out. Thing was satisfied with her eighth room and it was arranged that she would link up with her crew in about fifteen minutes, in the lobby, after everyone had freshened up.

Two hours later, when she made it down to the lobby, Thing couldn't find the team, but eventually located them in the casino, which was bright and airy with huge picture windows, and rows of slot machines that were danged appealing. There was a huge slot machine called Big Bertha, and yet, yet . . .

"What's wrong with all of you?" Thing motivated her crew, who, side by side, were taking up an entire row of machines—

"We were supposed to leave two hours ago, and I've been ready for five minutes!"

The team then mobilized, and it was into the rental van and off to the steel-and-glass behemoth—that was so typical of the American experience—to kick off the daily broadcast.

"Here we are," said Thing, "the Las Vegas Conventional Center."

john**reed**

With the team's outstanding press credentials, they were led directly to the main lecture hall, where the *entomologist* conference was already underway.

"Um, that's not the same as a, um, Egyptologist," warned Roth.

"Oh," said Thing, "don't be a party, uh, sport, uh, sporter, uh, I mean, don't be a spoil, uh, spoil, uh, don't be a spoil pooper!"

A small man with bifocals was commanding his audience with a spellbinding address on genetic manipulation. The underappreciated species *Drosophilae melanogaster* had been bestowed antennas with eyes on the ends of them.

This was exactly the kind of breaking news story Thing was hoping for, until she realized that the slide show had misled her, and that the *melanogaster* was not seven feet tall, but more like three millimeters long, and that it was not an alien species either, but, rather, a fruit fly.

The talk broke up then, and Thing was soon engaged in conversation by another short, bespectacled man who kept rubbing his foot against the side of her leg. He was a scholarly-looking fellow, however, and seemed to have something incomprehensible to say, which meant that it was probably important.

He kept going on and on about her "erroneous zones," and how he'd like to attend to them in various fashions, but she wasn't at all sure what he meant. That is, he went on and she wasn't at all sure until she asked what fruit flies had to do with pyramids and Egypt. Then the situation was reversed, and a blank gaze was stretching the circumference of *his* eye sockets—

"There's been some confusion. I know of no relation between fruit flies and the ancient pyramids in Egypt. But the humanists are down at the other end of the convention center, and, stringent as they are about the scientific method, they may have come up with a correlation. Several people had this entomology talk confused with the etymology talk in room 1511."

Thing then understood—*it was they who were in the erroneous zone*, as they were wanting that other talk in room 1511. As a matter of fact, a "humanish" convention sounded extremely promising, for if one were "humanish" it stood to reason that, even if one were very nearly human, one was not human at all!

the**WH●LE**

"Oh," said Thing, "why thank you," and she extracted her leg from the rapid-fire motions of the man's foot. (Although his expression had gone doleful and craven upon learning that Thing was in no way involved in the entomology circles, he had not in the least abandoned his foot on the foreleg approach.)

Thing and her crew then hurried up to room 1511, where the lecture, "Etymology and Mythology of the Omphalos," was, likewise, already underway. A fellow with a paunch animatedly delivered his nasal discourse—

"The wisdom of the Omphalos, i.e., the wisdom of the World Navel, represents the threshold—the entry into the sacred zone, which is the universal source."

Thing gasped at the coincidence—*erroneous zone, sacred zone*—it just seemed that everyone was talking about her zone!

"Ehem," the lecturer resumed, "the World Navel is the all-that-is-everywhere. It is the 'maybe.' It is victory and defeat. A place of infinite risk, and the ultimate sanctum sanctorum. It is ubiquitous, and the origin, as well as the conclusion, of all existence. Ugliness and beauty, sin and virtue, pleasure and pain, are, to the Omphalos, not only of the utmost importance, but of the utmost irrelevance. A human object of worship, or, for that matter, disdain, might represent magnificence or goodness, or repulsiveness or evil—or, they might transcend any scale of human value. Likewise, a place may simultaneously encompass and preserve opposites. A good example of a man-made location that bears such a burden of the horror and the sublime is a Mayan sacrificial temple. A naturally occurring example might be an earthquake, or, simply, the ocean. Neither are these inherent self-contradictions and similitudes strange to the arts. To quote Heraclitus, 'The unlike is joined together, and from differences results the most beautiful harmony, and all things take place by strife.' And to quote Blake, 'The roaring of lions, the howling of wolves, the raging of the stormy sea and the destructive sword are portions of eternity too great for the eye of man.' "

Thing, who assumed the presentation was, as impossible as it was to follow word to word, addressing the subject of herself and the hole, got the general gist of it. Yes, the hole was scary, but thrilling too. And yes, she was lovely, and loving, and all the world should love her—but surely, everyone also knew that she could be terrible, and terrifying, and all the world should be in terror.

Then the man droned on some more and Thing began to think there had been another goof-up. She perused a program, and, after several minutes, discovered that the conference was for "humanists," not "the Human-ish." This, Thing immediately deduced, was not so exciting.

"Humans?" she blurted out. "Is that all you're studying?"

The professor, mistaking Thing for a student with a questioning mind, deployed his speech on why the humanist education was important—i.e., the classics and stuff.

"Yeah, yeah," said Thing, annoyed that she had been challenged on camera, "I know what a classic is. It's a great book. But if I already know it's great, why do I have to read it?"

The professor, interpreting this as a critique on reading as an outmoded method of communication, tried to impress on his audience, and on Thing in particular, the importance of the age-old practice.

"My winsome girl," he was saying, giving her the once- and twice-over through his glasses—

"Ehem, yes," he cleared his throat, "You see, what I was—"

"Yeah, yeah," said Thing, "I know. I know all the arguments. You couldn't read, you couldn't make sense of the TV guide. Blah, blah, blah."

The professor then suggested a few plays and novels to Thing, so that she might judge for herself their value.

"Listen," said Thing, "I don't have to read *Hamlets* or *Moby Duck* or *Great Expectorations* to tell you whether or not it's great. Just gimme a name. I heard of them—they're famous. They're famous—they're a genius. They're a genius—they write great books. So, like I said, you know, like, it's a classic, or, like, whoever wrote it's famous, you know it's great, and that's all you've got to say, because nobody else read it either."

Thing, glancing over to her producer (Matthew, now onsite, as Vegas required him) realized that she had gone too far, that she was revealing, maybe, a national secret—but thanks to thick quinking she was able to discharge an incontrovertible recant.

the**WH●LE**

"Oh, but, thank you, Professor, I'll make it my very first priority to lose no time reading those books."

The team withdrew. Thing believed it was likely they'd find something relevant out on the Strip. At the Circus Circus, or the Mirage, or Caesars Palace, or the show at the Riviera, or one of those feasts at the Excalibur—*at a feast, there had to be plenty of vegetarian food. And maybe some crispy roasted pork too.*

The rest of the crew, on the other hand, was exhausted by their travels—and all they wanted to do was go to Wimpy's to pick up a chili dog and a milkshake and possibly a banana split, and to advance from there to the hotel pool, and from the pool to the hot tub, and certainly, in the end, to initiate a direct link-up with the cable television that was so prominently featured in every one of their rooms.

Thing was encouraged to continue her investigation without them, however, and she did. She lost almost a thousand dollars in almost seven minutes at the Wheel of Fortune in Vegas World—and then happened into the Black Rabbit, who had a few pink cocktails waiting on the bar. Thing, still focused on the lost dough, was desponding.

"The problem with you," said a sympathetic Rabbit, edging a martini glass in her direction, "is that when you're not drunk, you're sober."

"Yeah," said Thing, "gimme that. Reality is for people who can't handle a drink."

Three pink cocktails later, Thing was, not drunk, but, as she said, overserved. The Rabbit had left Thing alone at the bar, as he had, he was sorry to inform her, several investments that needed looking into. She went out onto the floor and gambled until some guy wouldn't let her anymore. Then there were pink cocktails, from somewhere, and not sure exactly how many she'd had, or how much she'd lost, she slumped over her stool at the roulette table and wondered if she could stand up straight enough to get laid.

Thus did Tim and Tina approach, for Thing, they recognized, was depressed, desperate and, well, overserved—which was everything they were looking for in a companion.

Tina, a hairspray Q-tip of a girl, was often unliked by others of her own sex. But Thing, who didn't mind that Tina and Tim were a package deal, immediately took a shine to her, and managed to lift her overserved hand to stroke the gal's cheek.

"Oh," said Tina, "you're like an angel with a halo." And after it was explained what a halo was, Thing agreed—

"Oh yeah, like, held up over my head with my horns."

Then they told Thing how gorgeous and brilliant she was and how they had been watching her on television for years—not that she looked any older—and that, talking turkey, Thing was the foremost wonder of the world.

Of course, Thing knew all that. But it was nice of them to say, anyway. And she accepted graciously—

"I have nothing to say except I'm famous."

As it turned out, Tim and Tina weren't famous. But Tim was a Getty, and his pockets were bulging with the sweat of the honest working man, and Thing was delighted to make his aqueasance.

"You see," said Thing, anxious to communicate that she and Tim were on an equal footing, "half the world is standing on the other half's head, which—"

Tina interrupted—

"Is okay if you're on the top half, like us."

They all toasted to that, as it was true, evidently, that they were all on the top half, as Tina had married her way in, by being wed to Tim—which didn't bother Thing in the least. Nor did it bother Tim, or Tina, that it didn't bother Thing. Nonetheless, there followed a moment of reflection, for there were a few details about being on the top half that warranted footnotes, if not complaints, and Tim voiced the sentiment—

"Difficult to go for a walk, though."

"Yes," Thing readily agreed, "they're always squirming down there."

"Yes," said Tina, and they toasted. (Miraculously, Thing realized, they were all drinking pink cocktails!)

Then Tina fired up into how unbelievably rich Tim was—which culminated in Thing coming down with a case of the shakes.

"Be careful," warned Tim, "you'll give her a heart attack."

the**WH●LE**

"Ye-ye-yeah," stuttered a still-trembling Thing, "Cadillac arrest."

Meeting a man of Tim's credit rating was a great stroke of luck—for Thing had no idea how much money she had lost, and wanted no part of finding out. All she needed to know was that there was plenty. And here, clearly, with Tim and Tina, there was plenty. Indeed, Thing thought it was quite lucky that she had lost the money, because she was so naturally inclined to being lucky, and, moreover, rich, that by disturbing the order of the universe, that is, by unluckily losing some money, the heavens had looked down and felt obliged to drop her a gold goose.

Or, geese.

For there were two of them.

Tina was stroking Thing's thigh, and there seemed to be not only plenty of money, but plenty of love to go around.

Tim and Tina were staying at the Mirage, where even Thing had to admit she was impressed by all the modern inconveniences. They walked through the indoor tropical rainforest, and watched the volcano erupt. They examined the shark in the fish tank at the front desk. Then they made the voyage to Tim and Tina's room, which was packed, every inch of it, with items that Tim had recently bought Tina. Mink coats, Versace dresses, et cetera. Tina remarked that Thing could have whatever she wanted, and, as Tina was Thing's size, Thing immediately stripped down to her transparent Calvin Kleins and began trying things on. The availability of the treasures fit slap-bang into Thing's way of thinking (as she did into the clothing) for, to Thing, genuine riches meant other people's money.

"Take what you like." Tina flipped her fingers grandiloquently, banishing recompense—

"Knickknacks from the gift shop."

"Not," Tim said, almost apologetically, "that we're saying you need it, or that," he took a deep breath, "you're poor."

"Oh," said Thing, dropping the stole and answering defensively, "I'm not. I'm not," and, here, she took a deep breath too, "poor."

"We're all equal, us three," said Tim, waiting for Thing's confirmation.

"Oh yes," she concurred, "way."

johnreed

And yet, Thing knew all that silk made a difference, and she was hungering to prove to them how worthy she was. Hopefully, she thought to herself, even without the money, the fame would keep her afloat.

"Do you," she asked primly, "have a hot tub?"

They did. They showed it to her. At the sight of the jacuzzi shell with jets and a mother-of-pearl finish, Thing found herself pants-antsy—and feeling, for some reason, dirty all over.

"Oh it's a fine tub, all right," she cocked her hips defiantly, "but does it hold water?"

They claimed it would.

As much time as she'd spent in a thong, and as often as she'd swapped duds on location (usually, right out in the open), Thing was unshy about the undies, which was all she was wearing. And, in short order, she was unshy about shedding them too. She flicked a switch, the water gushed, and she waded in. Tim and Tina, stripping down, followed.

"You're right, Thing," said Tina—

"We better test it out."

Tim turned on the red overhead light, and turned off the other lights—and, bubbling in their jet streams, they looked at each other. Tim said something about ambience, and Thing agreed.

"Yeah, I feel nice and sexy, in this ambulance."

Tim and Tina were feeling it too. And after a few rounds of Truth or Dare, Thing's growing knowledge of French was drawn upon, and a *fromage à trois* was proposed, ratified, and enacted.

They woke at half past noon, and ordered room service. Thing, still in a Parisian temper, had French toast, medium rare, and a bowl of raisin cereal with the raisins on the side. They had the bellhop bring up the newspaper too, for the horoscopes.

Tim and Tina read theirs, and Thing nodded like she was paying attention, and then came hers—

Wedding bells and negotiable bonds—
good tidings are in your near future. Don't miss the opportunity.

the**WH●LE**

The horoscope was thrilling to Thing, and equally so to Tim and Tina.

"I'm rich and good-looking," said Thing, "I'm half-married already."

"Yeah," said Tim and Tina, "us too."

"Yeah," said Thing, "and three halves make a whole."

Hence, the three, all together, decided the horoscope meant they should get married. There was another sentence in Thing's horoscope ("You'll discover, in an unexpected place, the path to answers you've been looking for") but since they couldn't figure out what it meant, they decided, well, so what they couldn't make sense of it? and advanced with the wedding planning.

"Uh, wait a minute," said Tina, not wanting to burst anyone's bubble, but addressing a question that nevertheless needed addressing, "do you think it's a problem that Tim and I are already married?"

"Uh," asked Thing, "is it?"

"Hmmm," said Tim, considering, "I don't think so. Polygamy's legal in Utah. We'll go to Utah."

"Ah yes," said Thing and Tina, "Utah!"

So they hopped a plane that hopped to Utah.

Then they took a taxi from the airport to the Inn at Temple Square, which was the best hotel downtown (on the authority of an airport poster), and near the Mormon Temple too, which was where they assumed they were going to get married. They checked in, then walked over to the temple, which looked a whole lot more like a medieval castle than had the Excalibur, back in Vegas. The granite walls were soaring, and there was a gold-plated statue atop the middle spire that Tina, putting a hand up Thing's dress, said wasn't nearly as adorable as another angel she knew.

And no, thought Thing, she was not marrying Tim and Tina for the wrong reasons. No, not for money. She was marrying for love—and loving for money.

And Utah was *so* the place to be. And the temple towering over them, that was *so* the place to get married. Unfortunately, they ran into an obstacle—in the form of a guard (Mormon) at the pearly gates.

"Why are you here?" he asked.

john**reed**

Tim answered, "We're here to do God's work."

"Uh, yeah," Thing lent her support, "whatever that is."

The guard directed some test questions at the wedding hopefuls, which they failed. Whod've thunk it—but monotheism was not a gift from the Gods, and when good people died they did not go to Paris, and when bad people died they did not go to Mexico.

At any rate, Thing was relieved to be disabused of the Paris and Mexico mix-up, as she'd been terribly afraid that her French wasn't up to the challenge, and that she wouldn't be able to drink the water in hell.

Thing, thinking of hell, had an idea, "Hey, the guard's guarding the temple, but who's guarding him? I bet we could take him."

So, there they were, standing on the corner, discussing the possibility of rushing the temple guard, when a guy in a black suit came up to them. And as hot as it was, the man, in his suit, didn't look hot. He looked too tired to be hot. Actually, he looked like he thought he should be nervous, but was too weary for even that.

"Hey," he said to Tim and Tina, "didn't I see you guys at the Bunny Ranch? What're you doing around here?"

Tim answered, "I didn't know priests went to brothels."

"I was on a holy mission."

Tina lifted her eyebrow, "Didn't we see you in Vegas too, at Fun City, at the craps table?"

"I'm trying to save a few orphans—is it my fault they're not lucky?"

Thing told the minister they wanted to get married, and that they couldn't even get into the temple.

"Oh yeah? I'll marry you," he said. "A hundred bucks each."

"You'll get us in there?" Thing angled her head.

"Yeah, but I'll have to marry you in the basement."

A cash machine was located. Accounts were overdrawn. The guard at the temple gates was placated. (Another hundred.) And the trio was in the holy temple. Then, past the interactive videos, the murals, and one exhibit after another, they were into a breathtaking worship hall, which they walked through on their way to the basement.

the**WH●LE**

The minister recited the service, which he seemed to know more or less by heart. And then he told them they were married, and that he'd send the license to their hotel.

"But," Thing objected, "isn't it, uh, custum, uh, cust, uh, kisstomary to curse the bride?"

"Oh yeah," the minister said to Tim, "if you want to, go ahead and kiss her."

Tim went at it—with Thing.

"Oh," said the minister, "okay, I guess you can kiss her too."

Then Tina.

"Yeah? You two too? Oh, okay."

Tina and Thing. Tim watched.

"Yeah, okay, that's enough."

Thus betrothed, the trio was excused and led out of the temple by a choirboy whose curiosity in Thing and Tina was unholy. Then the newlyweds wandered out into Temple Square, and, walking through the gardens, they were inspired by the sound of voices and an organ issuing forth from the tabernacle, which was shaped like a huge, round bread loaf. Very comforting. And, so comforted, so inspired, Thing and Tim and Tina skipped down the paths with, on their lips, a singsong—

"I'm rich and famous, now. I'm rich and famous, now."

At La Caille at Quail Run, the waiter ran through the elaborate French menu twice, explaining every nuanced flavor and delight. Thing thanked him for his knowledgeable presentation, and ordered macaroni and cheese. Tim wanted a burger. Tina put in for chicken soup.

When the check came, there was some question as to who was responsible for paying it, as Thing was Tim's bride, and therefore responsible for the cost of the wedding, while, looking at it from another angle, Tina was probably Thing's bride, and already Tim's, so Thing was responsible—unless it was just dinner, and Tim was responsible, because he was the man. They decided to split it three ways. They each presented a credit card. They joked how rich they were, but how they were also having trouble with their credit cards, and they hoped the charge would go through. Then they kept joking when all three charges did go through. But somehow it didn't seem funny.

Back at the hotel, they were still a tad hungry, and ordered oysters up to the room. Tucking into the second dozen, the three discussed tapeworms, which, as much as they admired the easy lifestyle, they were afraid they might get. Then Tim started to make a confession.

"Hey, Thing, you know what a termite is?"

"Yeah," said Thing, taken off guard, and afraid someone might ask her to prove it, "do you?"

"The kind of termite I'm talking about is one that lives off rich people, like, in their houses, or, uh, hotels. They just sit around and eat."

"Is that what you're calling me, a termite?" Thing was ready to whip a Blue Point in Tim's direction, but then his answer baffled her.

"No, it's not you," he said, "Tina and I, we're the termites."

"Huh?" said Thing, stupefied.

"Yeah, we are," said Tina, "but we really do love you, and we want to stay, uh, your husband and wife."

"You fools," said Thing, dropping her oyster.

"Yes, we're the fools," said Tina, "not fools for money, but fools for love."

Thing started laughing, sorta, and crying, sorta. Tim thought he knew the joke—

"Yeah, I heard that before too. You look at any marriage—there's always a fool."

"Yeah," said Thing, now hiccuping (the laughing and crying had been too much), "but there aren't always three."

"Huh?" said Tim.

"I don't have any money either," said Thing, "I don't think."

That didn't sound good to Tim, or Tina, and suddenly, by the look on their faces, one might surmise that the oysters had been, perhaps, elderly.

"Okay," said Tina, picking up the phone and ordering three bottles of Veuve Clicquot, "let's drink like sponges."

the**WH●LE**

"Why not?" asked Tim, shrugging—

"We are."

Thing shrugged too.

Then they drank from their bottles, only to realize that they weren't sure that, between them, they could cover the hotel and room service.

Thing picked up the menu—

"To add insulation to injury," she said, "these prices are exuberant."

"Maybe we're not even married," offered Tina, "maybe that guy at the temple was just a janitor, God help us."

With that, room service delivered a package that had been received and forwarded to their suite by the front desk.

Tim opened it reluctantly.

"It's the license," he confirmed, "we're married."

Thing looked over his shoulder—

"Your name is Gettry?"

"Oh yeah" said Tim, "Gettry."

"Not Getty?"

"No, Gettry, with an 'r.' "

Thing had been holding out the hope that Tim was a poor relation—in line for something when someone keeled over. The fact, however, that he was a Gettry, left little chance that any of that Getty money was ever going to grease his pockets.

"I suppose the Gettrys aren't in oil too?"

"Uh, no."

"They are kind of slimy, though," Tina added, sullenly.

But then three pink cocktails presented themselves, and stuff didn't look so bad anymore. *You've buttered your bread*, thought Thing, *now sleep in it.*

After that, true love was just around the bend again. They called room service one more time. Thing, ascertaining that garnish was free, ordered a plateful of it.

"The most important thing is love," said Tim.

"Yeah," said Tina.

john**reed**

The marriage was then consummated again. This way, and that. And that, and that, and this. Then Thing crept out of bed for one of those Diet Kiwi Strawberry Snapples that was available in the minirefrigerator, for a small inflated fee. Then to the bathroom for a postcoital unwinding, and unloading. (She reflected on how she had gotten to take a close look at the inside of every toilet bowl in every hotel suite she stayed in—and how limber her finger was. Maybe she did have some ancestors in Bulimia, wherever that was.) Back into the bedroom, she laid claim to the second of the queen-size beds—not because she didn't want to sleep with her husband and wife, but because there was more room. Then she couldn't sleep, and plugged some Walkman headphones into the television, and part watched, part dozed. There was, at some point, an intriguing infomercial—and she wrote down a website. But in the morning she couldn't remember what it was for, and, well, that scrawl—she wasn't sure she could make it out. Those wigs and wags and scratches and dots were most indicative of hieroglyphs (or, as Thing would have phrased it, whatchyamacallits). But, while perhaps onerous, the task of decoding was also one of self-appreciation—for however unintelligible those marks were, Thing perceived that they pointed to a highly evolved intelligence, or something.

She proceeded unhurriedly, for it was 9 AM, and she knew that Tim and Tina wouldn't be getting up anytime soon, as Tim had detailed a theory that a person who woke up before noon was squandering his or her life on daylight, and, far worse, being awake. After forty minutes of scrutinizing the scribbling, Thing arbitrarily ruled a successful conclusion to the deciphering process ("700thwxyl2"), and, having come up with a credit card that still had a few more ducats on it, attempted to log on to the hotel-room desktop. Eventually, she got going, and after wading through the two hundred e-mails she'd received since she last checked (all were outdated, irrelevant, or advertising some internet product or benefit that she didn't understand), she tried the website address that she had deciphered—and it didn't work. Error number something or other. Then she tried again, and it didn't work again. Then she tried it over and over and over. Always, error number something or other.

It was extremely discouraging (ding-dang it!), because she felt there was a good possibility that this website related to her ongoing investigation—namely, the hole, and her search for the middle. As annoyed as she already was by the e-mails, this roadblock on the information superhighway was especially irritating. Finally, through another nettlesome failure, she apprehended that the number, the error number, was ten digits—700, et cetera—and that this might constitute a phone number!

Ahh! The soup thickened!

Error. Error. Error. Yes, *she had been in the erroneous zone*. And now, well, yes, without question—she was meant to call that number!

She dialed. There was ringing. Someone answered. He said, "Hello?"

She answered, "Yes, who is this?"

She'd been demanding, and the man on the other end of the phone was equally demanding—

"What do you mean? You called me. Who's this?"

"You know who this is. If you didn't, how'd I get your number?"

"Uh, maybe you've got the *wrong* number."

"If I called the wrong number, why did you answer the phone?"

"Look, I'm Leon. Does that help?"

"No, I don't know any Leon. That can't be right. You must be someone else."

"Naw, Leon."

"No, someone else."

"Naw," he said, having had enough, "Leon!" And, thus asserting himself for the last time, he hung up.

That, of course, didn't resolve much, and Thing thought she might be in the erroneous zone again, that is, until she noticed a penny on the carpet. She knew that if it was heads up she was on the right track, and when, upon examination, it was, she puzzled over her latest clue.

Naw, Leon, she repeated to herself—*naw, Leon.*

N'Awlins!

New Orleans! That was the answer! New Orleans! Then she recalled the last line of the astrological outlook—the one she hadn't understood. Well, she understood it now.

john**reed**

You'll discover, in an unexpected place, the path to answers you've been looking for.

That's it. Yes, she was on her way. Yes, to something.

She retrieved the column. As she expected, she didn't see anything new. Just the horoscope. But then an advertisement, in the margin beside the horoscope, caught her eye.

Discover the wisdom of the Creole Mystic!
Find your guide to the winding roads of life!

Discover the Creole, thought Thing, and realized that was prezactly what the astrological column and the "Naw Leon" man had been talking about. A New Orleans Creole! Obviously an ancient and venerab, uh, vener, uh, venereal tradition. There was a phone number, and, when Thing began to compare that number to the number she'd copied off the internet, well, she began to think that maybe they could be the same number. Was that 700? No, it was 900, then something else, which might be, well, the number in the ad. She had written the number down just a few minutes ago, but, well, it was awfully hard to read her own writing. But, luckily, she had the number right there in the magazine!

Thing snuck into the bathroom with her cell phone and the magazine. She dialed. The line was answered by a woman with a Creole accent. But also, there was some New Jersey in there.

"Is New Jersey near Louisiana?"

"Uhm . . ."

"Are you from New Jersey?"

"Uhm, yase child, but the swampy side."

"And that's right next to New Orleans, right?"

"Uhm, yase, child."

"Was it a trailer park? You sound trailer park."

"Uhm, yase, you and me mus' have a cosmic connection, child."

"A trailer park in the swamp."

"Yase, honeychild. I'm having a vision. I see, I see that school was never the right place for you. That you were always under—"

the**WH●LE**

"Yeah, exactly."

"Underestimated, child?"

"Uh . . ."

"Underachieving, child?"

"Uh . . ."

"Understimulated, child?"

"Yeah, understimulated by the teacher after school."

"Uhm, yase, child."

"Under the desk, and the chairs and, gee, I liked it all right, but I didn't learn much, I guess, because even when I thought I was doing really super-duper with my reeling and writhing, I never understood what they were talking about on the tests."

"Uhm, yase, child."

"So anyway, I got into this pickle of a dilemma. I got married, and now I'm in the bathroom talking to you—and my husband is in the other room with this woman, who's our wife, and I'm feeling, well, like all I want is for someone to hold my hand, and . . ."

Thing couldn't help it, she began to cry.

"And you're wondering about love, child."

"Yubetchavich," gurgled Thing, "love. Is there, is there any—"

"Yase, child, I see, that out there, there is, the one."

"Yeah," said Thing, her snuffling mollified, "I think, I think that too."

"Yase, there is the one."

"Yes," said Thing, "I can feel it too, right behind me—like a hand that's reaching out for me just around the corner!"

"Yase," agreed the Creole psychic, somewhat uncertainly, "the one is, uhm, very close to you."

"Uh," Thing paused, also uncertain, and glanced at the door behind which Tim and Tina lay sleeping, "is the one just one?"

"Uhm," the psychic hesitated, "maybe not, child."

"Uh, how many?"

"Uhm, two?"

"Oh yeah, that's amazing."

john**reed**

Then, a moment later, Thing realized she was disappointed.

"So, uh," she asked, "my husband and the other woman that's our wife, are they the one?"

"I didn't say that," said the psychic, who seemed to have just received some of that divine inspiration she'd been waiting for. "I can see that you're not done yet, child."

"Done yet?"

"Done yet, child."

"But there is the one? Even if, well, it's a they."

"Yase."

"You mean," Thing said brightly, "the one's still out there?"

"Yase."

"But I know who the one is?"

"No."

"But I thought you said—"

"Yase, that the one was very close to you, child."

"But I'm all alone."

"Yase, close to you, but far from you now."

"Huh?"

"Close to your heart, but far from your body."

"Oh yeah, like, I'm supposed to be with them somewhere, but I'm not. I'm here," Thing sadly agreed. "Yeah, I mean, I'm lost. I mean, I must be. I mean, I know right where I am. But it's Utah."

"Yase, you feel so disoriented."

"Yeah, how'd you know that? I have been having trouble with my stomach."

"Yase."

"And I'm confused about where I am too."

"Yase."

"And who I am."

"Yase—but you'll find you're the one who's where you are."

"Huh?"

"You'll find yourself."

the**WH●LE**

"Oh yeah? And what about that charm bracelet I lost when I was eleven, will I find that too?"

"You'll find everything, child."

"Like, like a room of lost things?"

"Yase, a room of lost thing, child."

"Where is it?"

"Wait, I'm having a vision, child. Yase, that it's, that it's—"

"On the river?"

"Yase, on the river."

"Wow! Jigger me timbers—that's mondo incredible."

"Yase . . . on the river, child."

Thing took a deep breath. She knew it was a river. But why? Was it . . . was it . . . Yes, she knew that river! It was the river where forgotten things went. Ideas, mittens, earrings and even that charm bracelet she lost when she was eleven. Why yes, her whole life she had known about that river, or, sort of maybe somehow knew about that river—

The River of Denial.

"Yes," Thing gasped, "square dinkum, I'll find it on the river."

"Yase, child, I see it."

"Uh, since you're a psychic, let me ask you, I lost my cigarettes somewhere. Can you see where I put them? Did I smoke them all? I think I have to—"

"I'm having a vision of you going to the store, child."

"Wil'ya fawncy that! I was just thinking about a trip to the store."

"But also, child, I'm having a vision that you'll call me back."

"Absotively-posilutely."

"Extension 444, or, ask for Myrtle."

"Myrtle? Is that Creole?"

"Yase, child, we're all Creole here."

Thing stole out of the room, just for some cigarettes, and, could be, a short walk. But she also took her stuff. For safekeeping. She'd dreamt of being happily married forever-after since she was a baby girl. She had always known she'd have a house and a lawn and a pie in the oven. But now, it was

john**reed**

like, maybe that wasn't so realistic, after all. Maybe those days were gone, and those dreams were no more than nos, uh, nos, uh, nos, nostalgia, she remembered victoriously—and, well, the nostalgia just wasn't what it used to be.

She found some cigarettes at a convenience store, and once she started smoking, she understood what had happened to her. Yes, she had gotten married. But her particular vows should be discounted—analed, as they said—because she had been under the influence of some monstropolously powerful emotions that had made a mess of her better judgment. The emotions had been so passionate—violent, insane, misleading—that they had left her completely unable to make good on her promise to, well, keep up that state of passionate, violent, insane and misleading emotion, well, forever. Really, she thought, love was so debilitating, that if you were in it, you shouldn't be allowed to make any major decisions—and, most of all, if you were in love, you shouldn't be allowed to get married.

Gadzooks, there were so many laws, and when it came to something so common sense as that—something that would undeniably protect a lot of people from some dreadful things happening—well, there was no law at all. No, not even a public service announcement.

Humpf, decided Thing, resolving not to go back to the hotel after all—

Include me out.

Then she fled. She ran. She ran harder than she ever remembered having run before. . . .

She ran so hard that she could barely catch her breasts.

Meanwhile, up at the Inn, Tim and Tina had woken—realizing that Thing had gone out for cigarettes, and realizing also that here was a good chance to stick her with the hotel bill, as the deposit was on her credit card, and their financial situation was, uh, cash-poor. The marriage too would have to be sacrificed, but that was a minor concern, they agreed, when faced with a hotel bill. Besides, they were students of life, and they knew well enough that, for them, to be content without wealth was too hard a lesson. So they packed up their stuff, and they fled, and ran too. They were, at that, more accustomed to running, and ran faster than Thing, and, after about four blocks, they caught up

the**WH●LE**

to her, as she, winded after two hundred yards, had decelerated her velocity from gallop, to canter, to slog. When she turned, and saw it was them, they saw too that it was her. And then she and they began running again. But this time, away from each other. Finally, Thing found the bus station—and slept in her double seats all the way to Vegas.

Back at the Lady Luck, her hotel room was cleaner than she'd left it. And it probably wasn't the maids—but a miracle. A miraculous sign that showed she'd done the right thing. None of the crew had noticed she was gone. Even Otto, Roth and Matthew (who appreciated the chance to get his hair cut at a local joint) had assumed she was hungover and that they had the day off. She didn't tell them otherwise. "Yeah," she admitted, "it was the cocktails. All I could face was, uh, down. It was a pillow fight just to get up."

Besides, in the last thirty-six hours, nothing had happened, and even when the team did get to work, the spot they churned out was so lackluster that it was only aired because Thing, who'd apparently had some inflammation of unhappiness or insecurity that nobody could understand, insisted that Anita the stylist and makeup woman smear her in so much beautification butter that, had she been squeezed, the VJ would have shot skyward like a prune pit. Thing, backdropped by one hundred ten-thousand-dollar bills at the Horseshoe, provided lead-ins to a few clips from the Roswell July Fourth festival. It was all very interesting, but Thing assured her viewers that while her team had missed the Roswell celebration, they had not missed any crucial clues. "Don't worry," she said of the mysterious hole, "we'll get to the bottom of it, by hook or ladder!" There was also some news on the Petersons. "Their deaths leave a void in the community that will be hard to replace." As for the hole, there was nothing to report but that it wasn't doing anything. Not getting bigger. Not getting smaller. Nothing. Thing did her best to stay upbeat, in any case, and tried to put an exciting spin on the lack of razzmatazz—

"The slowdown's accelerating!"

Later that night, Thing was in her hotel room watching a rerun of some ancient cartoon show called *South Park*. But the plot was a mite complicated, so she flipped through the channels and settled on *Sesame Street*—even though she knew most of that stuff.

john**reed**

The regular programming was then interrupted, however, with an important nude flash. The hole had enlarged again. "Aha!" exclaimed Thing, ready to jump up and get gone—until she realized she was too tired and depressed to crawl out of bed. The marriage thing—it made her feel like she'd been poisoned, like she'd drunk poison wedlock (which, someone had recently told her, was what'd killed So-crates). But that was the thing about television, something important could happen, they'd interrupt what you were watching, and then you'd turn the channel to watch that other show you wanted to watch—which is exactly what she did. And, well, it turned out that cartoon show wasn't nearly so complicated as she'd thought!

The next morning, the crew was ready to go, and Thing was ready to go, and they went. Flights were booked, vans were rented.

On the drive to the new perimeter, Thing called her psychic, Myrtle.

"So, the hole is growing, and I have to go there, but do you think I should really be going to look for them, I mean, the one? Or do you think maybe they're at the hole? That it's like, the same thing? I mean, is that where I'll find the one, at the hole?"

"You think so?" asked Myrtle.

"Maybe."

"I think, maybe."

"You think so?"

"Yase, maybe."

"Yes, I think so."

"Yase," Myrtle was firm, "I think so too."

Packed into the rental van, the crew drove through hills of dry grass, and roadside produce stands, towards the country storm that hovered ominously over the horizon. Closing on the phenomenon, the team saw that the hole was the anchor of the storm—which intermittently erupted into thunder, lightning and rain showers. Beyond the fence erected by the military, soldiers stood in the bright sun.

Thing made her broadcast. ("Troops of the Fifth Infancy have accordioned off the area.") All of Prairie Dog had been engulfed, right up to the border of Groupersville. Interviews—coincidentally, at the same McDonald's and bus station featured in Ponte-from-New-Mexico's alien exposé—revealed that every last person Thing had interviewed in Prairie Dog was now missing, and probably dead. Them, and everything, gone. The high school. The football stadium. Even the archeological site of the Prairie Dog goths. The Groupersville high schoolers, among them, the Groupersville football players and goths, commented on the deaths of their sister-town equivalents, and rivals. The Groupersville goths, indeed, had managed to complete the work of the Prairie Dog goths, and had located the descendants of the former freed slaves who, a century before, had been dispossessed of their land so that a suburban community of white people might be established. (The restless souls of the dispossessed former slaves had consumed the Peterson lot, which had once been the site of a black schoolhouse.) Although the land was gone now (into the hole), litigation had nonetheless begun, and at the section of fence nearest the disputed missing land, a black power group from Georgia had taken up the cause. In turn, a white rights group had taken up against the taking up of the cause. And while the Holy Church of Prairie Dog had been, alas, holed, the two sides disputed the significance of the church's roadside cross, which remained, teetering on the chasm. The Georgian African cult, which, it turned out, lived in a compound that consisted of a series of black pyramids, interpreted the cross as, primarily, a symbol of Malcolm X. "A bit of Malcolm is always walcum." The white supremacists thought the symbol was, contrarily, an evocation of their heroic Klan brothers. Jesus was white, they reminded the opposition, who replied that no, Jesus was black.

The hole was the white man's punishment by God—the black messiah was coming!

No, the white messiah was coming!

Thing had been standing far enough away from the fence (and the cross on the other side of it) that when the hole reenlarged she wasn't sucked in. The Georgia black power group, however, was, as were the white supremacists, who had hailed from Pennsylvania.

It was an extremely popular segment. "Wha—aahhh!" screamed the black extremists. "Wha—aahhh!" screamed the white extremists.

A press conference was called. At the Groupersville Sheriff's Of-

john**reed**

fice, it was explained that, besides the extremists, the Groupersville High School and (sigh) football stadium had been engulfed. A few football players (sigh), a few cheerleaders (sigh) and a few students were dead. Oh, and (sigh), the sheriff reiterated, the football stadium was gone. Some federales and geologists then took the floor. No, they assured the questioners, the hole would not grow again. It had only been an aftershock, which they had expected. The politicians agreed. As did the lawyers, who were regarded as experts, for some reason.

Finally, the floor was opened to reporters.

"Gentlemen," shouted Thing, "for your information, I'd like to ask a question. Why has the hole sucked up all the places I've been?"

"Yes," answered some someone who evidently knew something, "we've noticed that." He chuckled. "All the places you've been, and all the people you've interviewed—to be precise." He chuckled again, as did everyone else—and then he addressed the room.

"But we must resist the temptation to attribute relationships that don't exist. Science is not superstition, and there is no relation between Miss Thing and this rare geological phenomenon. It's a total coincidence. Thing's story is not the story of the hole."

With that, Thing noticed the Black Rabbit was signaling her from across the room. As he pointed a long rabbit padtip dramatically upwards, Thing immediately understood what he was trying to impart. *Get out! Out! Now!* Thing assembled the troops. They pulled back—as the press meeting continued. Van to airport to plane, all live, Thing moved her people off the front line. Matthew was so angered by the retreat he unthinkingly grabbed his head and flattened the ridge of his stiff hair. "And," he'd snarl fitfully, with a dull look in his eye—

"Explain to me once more why we're missing the press meeting."

From the twin-engine charter, Otto captured Groupersville getting swallowed by the hole. The Sheriff's office (and press conference) went first. Altogether, eight thousand people were killed, or rather, "went missing." In Prairie Dog, it had been six thousand. The nation mourned, and got on with business. Thing, the survivor, was celebrated (as was Matthew, *the producer who had taken action*). A national memorial was planned (a former dump outside Washington D.C. was earmarked). Geologists and politicians and lawyers agreed, the hole would not grow any larger—the Groupersville incident was an aftershock, which had been expected, and it was not, as had been falsely reported, eight thousand in Groupersville and six thousand in Prairie Dog. It had been eight hundred in Groupersville and six hundred in Prairie Dog. It was the summer, and a lot of people had been on vacation. And, besides, the evacuation process had been well under way.

Thing and her crew, meantime, were off to Cleveland, where, on a local daytime talk show, the Pharaoh of the Georgia black power cult, and the Grand Pooh Bah of the Pennsylvania white supremacist cult—neither of whom had been present in Groupersville to get sucked into the ground—were going to go face-to-face before a live audience. The two leaders had both faced allegations from former cult members of physical, psychological and sexual abuse. Throughout the show, a continuous stream of callers chronicled horrifying, albeit unsubstantiated stories, relating to the misbehavior of the two self-proclaimed prophets. Coincidentally, both men, for their races, claimed ancient roots—reaching all the way back to the first civilization, which was probably Atlantis.

Small-featured and pale-skinned, the Pooh Bah contended that his people were descended from a small-featured, pale-skinned, blue-eyed and gold-haired super race.

The Pharaoh had something similar to say—similar in structure, but not in substance. Having researched Thing's broadcasting history, he'd composed an explanatory ditty—

> *Why is whitey so cold-hearted?*
> *'Cause whitey got no soul.*
> *And musically retarded?*
> *'Cause he bred with Neanderthal.*

Fists flew. Slurs were slung. Security was slow.
Commercial break.
For the next segment, Thing introduced a bunch of white kids

from Indiana who thought they were black kids from Los Angeles. Then came the "proud to be an oreo" group, who maintained that most black people, on the inside, weren't black at all—they were just trying to be cool. Any unbiased eye could see, they argued, that the overwhelming majority of black people couldn't dance either. Battle ensued. Of course, it was hopeless, and pointless, and made for a great broadcast. Congratulations all around.

The ratings, as of late (especially since the annihilation of Groupersville), had been picking up—up and down, really, but mostly up. Thing was, according to the publicity department, "Connecting with her audience, fueling their passions, challenging their thinking—creating fresh, relevant, risk-taking entertainment found nowhere else." Questioned by Charlie Rose on the inspiration for her search to locate the middle, Thing explained—

"I hatched the idea a year ago, but it didn't catch fire until I jumped in with two feet headfirst. Since then it's been, like, snowballing."

This was her time, she told the popular television interviewer, to take the bull by the tail and look it in the eye. And yes, Charlie agreed, Thing was a diva of such immense talent that after her broadcasts there was seldom a dry seat in the country.

As if to echo the sentiment, there was even a crowd of fans outside the usually serene Charlie Rose studio. Charlie caught them on tape. They waved their arms. Many of them wore bikinis, and one, noticed Thing on the monitor—there was one who looked like her, but ten years older. Thing shuddered—and told Charlie it was because she felt such a deep sense of responsibility to her fans, because, just imagine, without her they'd be nothing.

Thing was then invited to the White House Correspondents Association dinner. She had been nominated for some award. All the other important reporters were also going to be there—David Letterman, Jay Leno and Brooke Burke. Thing hoped she might be seated near Ozzy, who was always there, even if he'd kicked the bat heads years ago.

It was only a bounce from New York to Washington, and on the US Airways shuttle, Thing sat with the Black Rabbit, drinking pink cocktails and discussing this and that. But the bunny was not his usual hoppy self, and Thing inquired if he was, perhaps, a bit down in the, well, hole.

the**WH●LE**

The Rabbit, flipping back his limp ears forlornly, acknowledged that yes, he had been preoccupied—

"My apologies, dear girl. You see, I have had a petite setback with an investment of mine."

"Oh," said Thing, commiserating, "you're broke?"

"No, but . . . bent."

"Might I ask—"

"No Worries Munitions," said the Rabbit. Then he and Thing proceeded to evaluate the unexpected downturn in the company's profitability. It seemed that NWM (No Worries Munitions) made these really smart bombs, while the military made these really dumb maps.

"They can't tell a munitions yard from a schoolyard," grumped the Rabbit.

"But," objected Thing, trying to console her perkless amigo, "that can't be all bad, I mean, if they hit a munitions yard, there are usually a few children romping about a munitions yard."

"Ye-e-es," said the Rabbit slowly, and then he was twitching his whiskers, helpless to Thing's charm—

"That's true," he said, lifting his glass to tink against hers, "they can't hit a schoolyard every time."

Limousining to the White House dinner, Thing promised her audience she was onto some top-secret information—information she was planning to broadcast, even if it killed her! But, she reassured them, there was no cause for alarm, as she'd remain fair and omnipotent, and would only broadcast that secret information if it wasn't dangerous, or classified—

"Anyway, don't sweat it, I'm hot stuff, and totally cool-headed, and nobody's ducking this investigator, 'cause I always pull my punches."

She was, as she informed her viewers, going to interview, like, senators and junk, and get herself her own scandal even if she had to go undercovers to do it! The hole, the middle and all that—this was gonna blow up like Nixon and Waterloo!

Or, she asked Otto, was it Napoleon and Watergate?

At the dinner, a bunch of guys to her right said that the hole was the result of morality gone awry—that traditional American values had to be restored. The guys to her left countered that there was nothing to fear, traditional American values were alive and well—genocide, aggression, conformity, emotional and cultural repression, and the worship of consumer goods.

Thing, natchatively, was in full accord, with everyone—

"Yeah," she exclaimed, "the world must be safe for hypocrisy!"

Thing couldn't get any top-secret information, however, nor could she find any representatives of the Olympic Committee—two facts that she found alarmingly suspicious.

Discussing the difficulty of securing those top-secret answers, some senator asked Thing, in confidence, about her retired bikini, and if he'd soon be seeing her in it again. Perhaps a private showing.

"Like, you and," Thing pondered, "maybe, me?"

"Yes, you, me, and the bikini—that would be just the tops."

The senator said he had a firm appreciation of the female form, and Thing promptly agreed, knowing exactly what he was talking about. She was, she told him, something of a lymphomaniac herself. Anyway, the conversation went on, and finally, Thing, by her estimation, managed to negotiate a "secret exchange," in the parking lot, in an hour. And once it got around that Thing was looking for candy dates, and that if you gave it to her in the parking lot she'd keep the secret, she had twenty-seven appointments.

And, in the basement parking lot, she did find out some things. First, that the alien stuff was only a tiny part of what was going on. Did she really think that the government spent two thousand dollars on a toilet seat? There were, she reported from the blackened corners of the garage, tiny bees that were in fact mechanized spy cameras and microphones, and computer tracking chips that were regularly implanted in people by, for example, the CIA, FBI and NFL, and that the government was experimenting with improved lungs for soldiers fighting in conditions of diminished ozone, and that all the cownappings that had been going on had to do with testing cows for irradiated milk, which wasn't as healthful as it sounded (nobody knew what division of government was conducting the study).

As for the hole, it was the site of underground experiments involving "digger bombs," which were sort of like those Russian dolls—one bomb in another, in another, in another. The detonations were oriented downwards—the application being that of blowing a bomb shelter, or anything like a bomb shelter, and whoever was in it, into dirt.

Also, at the site of the hole, a machine was being developed that could move objects or organic matter well beyond the speed of light, and, hence, into alternate states of existence. The machine, it was reported, had had some problems, and a conflict of alternate states of existence had developed within the hole. ("Ponte and the beamer machine!" Thing reminded her viewers.) In turn, this process had been deemed worthy of investigation as a weapon that might raze mountains and hills, or, even, create valleys or lakes. Entire enemy military bases, reported Thing, might be gulped into the ground—blamelessly.

Additionally, it must be noted that, besides recording the top-secret information, Thing's crew recorded twenty-seven drunken propositions (mostly, Thing and her informants sat in her limo behind a tinted window). And, twenty-three times, Thing said, "No." Twice, she said, "Later." Once, she asked, "Again?" And, on the single least decorous occasion, Thing just sighed loudly, while the unidentified senator scrambled for his side of the Towncar, apologizing, "Oops, sorry."

In the days that followed, Thing's broadcast triggered a Washington debate on the hole. Some argued that this was the first time that something like this had happened in America, and something should be done. Others argued that nothing should be done for the first time. Old footage of underground testing made its way into the media circuit, and seemingly confirmed that something similar might be going on at the site of the hole. The footage dated back to 1954, and the fashions left Thing convinced that there was indeed a real danger of, rad, uh, rad, uh, retroactive contamination.

"I mean, why did people in the old days dress so funny? I mean, we know better now."

Eventually, steps were taken. Twelve Navy SEALS got sucked in. Then, a team of twenty-six crack-climber Green Berets. Then, two helicopters. Then, a team of four paratroopers wearing jet packs. Then, a guy, for want of the covert-ops terminology, shot from a cannon. In one instance, half a guy—two arms, a leg and a head—got expelled from the hole, like a gob of cheese by the Heimlich maneuver. Otherwise, no one came back.

Via the footage of these failures, Thing's ratings, resultingly, swoled. So did her crowd of fans. Occasionally, she and Otto and Roth went into the street. Hands fought to touch her. The throngs, having joined into the enthusiasm of the search, screamed, passed out and expressed their own interests in Thing's finding the "plump-smack, slab-dab middle."

Though flattering, yes, the adulation did have its drawbacks. And not just that there was always some photographer in the building across the street trying to get a shot of you on the toilet. Or, over it. (There were no rights for Bulimians!) Way creepier to Thing, there was that woman who was ten years older that looked like her. She was always there. With the fans. Behind the next streetcorner. But never close enough to confront, or even get a good look at. She *always* wore sunglasses. (Mostly Ray Bans. A few pairs of Black Flies.) It went so far that Matthew, Thing's producer, realized he had his own fan, who looked just like him who was ten years older, who was following him. It was all laughable—those fans were so old! But then Matthew, panic-stricken and hysterical, called Thing in the middle of the night to tell her that the older fans who looked just like them were actually themselves from ten years in the future, traveled back in time to take over their younger selves. Matthew, who was twenty-eight, and not really, thought Thing, that young, was under the impression that his youth would be stolen from him by this temporal invader. And then Matthew disappeared for three days, and when he reappeared, he had no such fears, and looked tan and fit and great, and maybe like he'd had a laser peel and a few shots of Botox, and he had this certain air of wisdom that was so terrific, and an incredible prescience of stuff that hadn't happened yet, and, anyway, there was obviously nothing to worry about. Matthew (cornrows) said it himself.

More and more favored in the public eye, Thing was looking forward to getting invited to better and better events. But, lamentably, it was July, and the Nantucket Film Festival, Sundance, the Academy Awards, the MTV Awards . . . well, ugh, it wasn't now. As wanton as she was to travel the world and have her name called out as she strolled onto the red carpet, the season, though perhaps good for apricots, was not ripening any good parties. The fashion shows in Paris were okay. But the clothes on the runways were for winter, so you couldn't see too much flesh, so the turnout on the leading man front was not what Thing had hoped it would be. Then the season really dropped off, and all Thing could find to do was go back to Manhattan for the opening of Shakespeare in the Park, which Thing learned, was to take place, oddly enough, in a park, Central Park. But it wasn't even a Shakespeare play. It was Chekhov, and, to be frank, Thing hadn't had the faintest idea that the *Star Trek* officer was a writer. A few days in the Hamptons was equally unexposing (though Thing did get a little tabloid action by going topless), and the VJ was ultimately forced to resort to Los Angeles for the gay and lesbian agenda—the Annual Gay and Lesbian Film Festival, Outfest, et cetera. Thing was outed after Tina (Thing's ex-wife) turned up on a talk show, which was briefly exciting, and then she was un-outed by Tim (Thing's ex-husband), who managed to get himself on a different talk show. Then, it was the wrong season in Los Angeles until she couldn't stand it anymore—the Hollywood Movie Awards gala, the Paramount Pictures anniversary bash, and the Teen Choice Awards, where Thing won the Female Choice Hottie Award, which, to her dismay, was not a statue but a surfboard. She loved L.A., but even Thing had an inkling that getting a surfboard for your mantel wasn't going to get you any closer to world domination. As for getting the surfboard on her mantel—well, that would take some doing.

It was a good thing that the video journalist (as she was increasingly known, as opposed to "video jockey") was soon requiring some rest and relaxation, as everything was fodder for the ratings, and fodder was just what the recipe called for, and Thing undressing for a massage on a beach in Hawaii—that was pretty respectable fodder.

From Hawaii, there was a bump to Maui and a weekend on the beach and a past-life regression. Thing, it was revealed, had lived a former life on a planet far, far away. And, more recently, she had been a Native American Indian—probably a chief's daughter, that is to say, a princess. Then it was back to the waking world, and the United Kingdom—first to the Millennium Dome in Greenwich, which was a bore, and then to London, which was better. Thing picked up the accent, which remained well into her trip to India, where she was enlightened, and she lost the old sniff-sniff, what-ho, cucumber-sandwiches twang that had so overwhelmed her.

As for the financials, in view of the fact that Thing had decided there was no way she still had money in the bank, she resolved not to trouble herself, and to just use her Visa, because, well, she knew that something would happen. It always did. And the remarkable thing was that, as always, something did happen. Shortly after Thing started using her credit card, she started getting more and more offers for other credit cards (she was already approved!), and, soon enough, the tally was fifteen and counting. And the greatest thing about it was, you could pay off the old credit cards right at the same 1-800 number you called to get your new credit card!

And not only was Thing living large, but loving large!

Yes, all the while, the dating. The success! Then, the failure.

Otis promised to pay her rent, to buy her dresses. Over dinner at Indochine (New York City), he laid out a foolproof smuggling operation, involving Amsterdam and a pet bird. And she was convinced that it really did sound like he knew what he was doing. But, predictably, once he won her, the promised dresses and rent checks, they were not spoken of again. Then he went to Amsterdam, and didn't come back. When she finally did hear from him he needed a lawyer for getting nabbed for smuggling drugs from Amsterdam. She got the message on her voicemail, erased it, and never heard from him again. Well, what did he think? He may have managed to hide that he was a dope from her, but he never should have tried it with the dope-sniffing dogs.

Next were the ducks. The ducks of Danziger, who was, as he liked to say, an impecunious Duke—although Thing rapidly deduced that he was lying, as he was entirely penniless. Nonetheless, on Danziger's Moroccan side, he was the rightful heir to some dukedom. (Thus, the moniker "Merganser.") And here was the one thing that Thing genuinely liked about Danziger—that if they were married, she'd become a duckess. So, the ducks. Stuffed. Ceramic. Glass. Plastic. Wood. And elevator magnets. Duke Danziger . . . or so the story went, for if he really were a duke, why wouldn't he sell out some sir-doms for a bit of cash? Well, Danziger wouldn't even talk about it, and, as Danziger's friends said, he refused to sell knighthoods—either because he hated the idea of royalty, or because he wouldn't sully his duckdom. Thing questioned him about it regularly. He smirked and kept silent, and Thing gradually began to suspect that the whole rumor was his own fabrication.

"You know," said Thing, "I don't believe you're a duke anymore."

Danziger shrugged enigmatically.

"You're no duke—and I'm no dupe."

And Danziger shrugged again. And Thing told him that next time he passed by, she'd appreciate it.

Then, a trip to L.A. and a boy whose endowment was, well, equinomical, as he was lacking in all the other critical assets. Money. Smarts. Family. Power. Not even chicness. Regardless, Thing was planning to hold on to him—to clamp down like the feds on a death-row inmate. The circumcissal evidence was in, she said—and he was hung. But when, one night, he started pushing her head down into his lap, she started getting screamish.

"Eek!" she screeched. "Two words—impossible!"

After that, she suggested their relationship be plutonic.

"Yeah," she clarified, "me on Earth, you on Pluto."

Then there was Humphrey, an Englishman who Thing quite approved of, aside from his propensity for meatloaf and oxtails. ("You're probably one of those people who wants to turn Puerto Rico into a steak.") Finally, she was forced to explain to him that his dietary proclivities were going to land him in an artificial inseminator.

"Eh, respirator?" he asked.

"Yes," said Thing, but she had made her point, and now commanding his undivided attention, she informed him that it was time to get in the saddle and ride the tiger by the skin of its teeth.

"Eh," he began to ask, "you mean—"

"Yes," said Thing, "it's time for you to vegetate. I don't want to cast asparagus, but the food you eat is abdominal! You need to learn about stuff like unnecessary roughage, and green allergy."

"Eh, you mean algae?"

"Yes," said Thing, not liking being corrected, "that too."

He, wan, miserable, took to the challenge, perhaps forlornly reminiscing on beef pies and flank steaks, but, nevertheless, with surprising grits. Indeed, he didn't complain all that much about the alfalfa—but rather, the wheat grass and seaweed, though one would have thought the alfalfa would be featured.

In mere days, however, Thing noticed that he was getting skinny, and, worse than that, sick. She couldn't abide his runny nose. The enter, uh, entel, uh, lentelprise had been a failure. Thing tried to break it gently—

"You should never lead a gift horse to stop in the middle of a stream of water, just to look in his mouth and make him drink."

"Eh?"

"Oh, you get it."

"But I'm changing."

"Don't change, I want to forget you just the way you are."

Next came William, a fellow New Jerseyite on a pilgrimage to India. ("What kind of name is that? Every Tom, Dick and Harry is named William!") Then, back in New York, came a hothead named Kirk, who didn't like finding out that monogamy, to Thing, meant that she was only dating men. ("Don't leave mad, but just, just, leave.")

Then there were others, such as Mark "Frasier" James, who, up on a bear-viewing stand in Alaska, kept sneezing. He blamed Thing's sweater, but Thing knew there was nothing wrong with that sweater, as, generally, when she wore it, men would drop to their knees salivating, which meant they were perfectly healthy. What he had, she realized, was a serious psychological problem. She happened to have seen several documentaries on the subject, and it was the last thing she needed—a boyfriend with a crippling phobia. Angoraphobia.

Thing's dating achieved record density upon her subsequent return to New York, over the course of an evening that stretched well into morning, and, even, a little afternoon.

For dinner, she went out with number 1. They had a nice time and he went home at about 11:00, as it was their first date and he had to get up for work in the morning. Then Thing went to a club to link up with number 2 and number 3. Number 2 was her date, and they danced until 1:00, when he went home. Then she danced and drank pink cocktails until about 4:00, when she decided to go home with number 3. She did, and only when he was entirely drained of all life force did she leave his apartment. She arrived at her own apartment at about 7:30 (AM). The phone was ringing. It was number 1, who wanted to meet her, at 10:30, for a round of golf. He had decided to take the day off. She agreed. Then, number 2 called. He wasn't taking the day off, but he wanted to meet her in a hotel room on the way to his office. She met him. Then, he went to his office. Then, she went to the links, where she and number 1 shook some bushes from the inside.

So, anyway, as one might expect, Thing sometimes found the dating rousing, and sometimes way too much of the same old thing. And, as far as the boys themselves, sometimes they were the apples of her eye, and sometimes, grains of sand that were scratching up her cornea.

And, throughout, Thing was getting more famous. Always in the tabloids with a new man on her arm. "Half those lies aren't true!" she retorted, at a press conference during which she announced that she was considering suing several of the gossip rags for deformation of character. Viacom, sorry that it had only captured a small sampling of Thing's social itinerary, had a dating show in the works for the next season, in which she would be host, date and shopping/decorating guru.

And, with the fame, came the fans—more fans following her, it seemed, everywhere. There was even that old one who appeared to have had some sort of cosmetic surgery to resemble her—although, queerly, after whatever it was she'd had done, while the woman still looked a shade older than the celebrated VJ, she looked, maybe, not as old as she had looked. . . .

It was at the Redneck Pride Festival in Jigtown, Mississippi (Thing way needed some better parties), while preparing for her shoot—getting her haircut by Anita the stylist—that the VJ began to suspect there was more to all the fans and parapottis than she had thought. Always with the cameras—everywhere. And even if, for the life of her, she couldn't have summoned up the word "surveillance," she knew that she was under it. Anita the stylist and her datebook, the videostore and its record of rentals, the parapottis, the overhead security cameras—well, it was all a matter of record. Why, they knew everything!

john**reed**

Leaving Anita's hotel room, Thing rode in the van to the fair-grounds—the whole time being followed by the parapottis and security cameras, and, even more annoying, a colossal green fly.

Oh, as far as Redneck Pride, the festival was entertaining, and run of the mill. Your average "mudpit belly flop" competition, and flat-bed truck "limousine service," and "bobbing for pig's feet" contest, and "toilet seat toss." A lot of stuff like that. Not too many shoes, or shirts, though. Thing interviewed a few winners and got into the groove by spitting some watermelon seeds (fuzzy cubes when she came out of her shirt), but, overall, the day was hot, and dull, and despite what Matthew had told her, this wasn't anything like the X Games.

To make things worse, the green fly never left her. All day it buzzed infur, infur, infragrantly around her head. For the whole nation to see! Finally, she nailed the bugger with a bag of chips, and it was partially disabled. The crew was already packing up, and Thing, realizing that the fly, in fits and starts, was trying to *get back to somewhere*, resolved upon a course of tracking her erstwhile tormentor.

After twenty minutes of shadowing the ordinary green fly, Thing began to suspect that the injured creature wasn't ordinary at all. Why, for her to be following it, it had to be extra-ordinary. Probably, it was one of those miniprobes that she had heard about in Washington. (She really must have possessed some superhuman speed to swat a supersecret spy fly.) Eventually, the damaged robotic insect (a highly sophisticated and expensive bit of equipment) led her across the road to the high school, and a large janitor's closet. Inside, Thing, much to her surprise, discovered her long lost charm bracelet. Placing it on her wrist and jingling the amazing find, she was certain that even if the chain was a little different and it didn't have any of the same charms, it was definitely her charm bracelet! And she was pretty sure those were her mittens too! And that notebook, maybe! And that StarTAC and Wiffle bat and hula hoop! Why, this was the room of lost things!

Then Thing saw the fly was still struggling, and, following the device into a dim corner, there, Thing saw the possessed fan, the one that looked like her but was older, but not as old as she had been. But now, she didn't look older, anymore. Too shiny to be old.

theWH●LE

But the woman did sound old, or, older—

"Happy Birthday."

Then Thing understood, this wasn't just the room of lost "things," it was, as Myrtle the psychic had said, the room of lost "Thing." She herself was the lost one. She had entirely forgotten her own birthday.

It was tomorrow. July 29th.

"I'm sorry," said the woman, "I'm not ready to give you your present yet. I haven't had my dermabrasion." And with that, the woman crept behind a pile of coats, and when Thing went to it, she saw the woman was gone.

At that moment, some math teacher dipped his head past the open door—

"Oh, so this is the lost and found."

And then Thing saw that, yes, she had found that she was lost. And not just because she was in Utah, or Mississippi, but just because she was. Because she hadn't even remembered she was turning twenty-four. And because she wasn't too sure that she wasn't turning twenty-five, or twenty-six, or—only God knew how many birthdays she had forgotten.

And all she had wanted was the charm bracelet she had lost when she was eleven.

But it would have been better to forget it—you remembered something like that, next thing you knew you remembered you were thirty-four years old.

Just like her producer had told her—ten years older.

Otto and Roth, ever-lurking, had caught most of this on tape (all except the face of the strange woman, which was obscured in darkness), and so too did they catch Thing's expression when she realized that she wasn't too pleased to discover whatever it was she had discovered.

Just like her producer had told her—she was ten years older. A thirty-four-year-old hag who wished she was young again. A hag who wished she was young and famous. More famous than she'd been, even, when she was young. More famous than anyone. A hag.

Then, Thing ran, determined to forget all this—whatever it was.

john**reed**

She ran—and Roth and Otto followed. All she wanted was to forget, and to have the whole world remember her for it.

"Please, don't forget me! But let me forget!"

She sobbed as she ran—

"Please, I don't want to remember anything! But remember me!"

Eventually, Thing stopped running, as did her crew, who had come up, in mass, behind her. (The troops were far quicker than the general.) They had arrived at the bank of the Mississippi River, and there was no more running, no more going anywhere—not unless they hopped a ride on the Mississippi Boat, the *Delta Queen*, which, moored on the Jigtown dock, was boarding for someplace.

Thing instructed her people to go back to the hotel in Jigtown to pack up her bags, and their own too, while they were at it, for, as she said, she wasn't going to miss that boat for a million years.

They left (to soon return), and Thing, sanguine, waited—for here, she knew, she had found the River of Denial, and she would go wherever it took her.

New Orleans, as it turned out. No, it was no coincidence—and Thing put in a call to Myrtle the psychic to consult on the significance of the development. Myrtle said it meant that Thing was to come in for a person-to-person reading (three hundred dollars), and that there was no avoiding it, as she had already had a vision about one, and there was no changing the future, so they might as well schedule for tomorrow. Thing readily consented. She was surprised, however, to find that Myrtle was not located in the French Quarter, but in what sounded like a lower-class suburb called Jervis.

By any standard, Jervis was worse than it sounded. Thing's crew documented the fact that only half of the cars in the community had tires. Also, Myrtle's complex was not what one would call regal, but more like, rectal.

"What's with the camera and all these people?" asked Myrtle, dismayed, "they can't come in for your private reading!"

Then, having had a psychic insight, Myrtle softened—

"But I guess they can each come in for their own readings, since they're here."

theWH●LE

Thing was led to a back room, complete with crystal ball and shining satin curtains, and a small black dog that wouldn't leave her alone. Kept grabbing at her purse, that animal.

"I mean, I love you, Myrtle, but can't you cu, cu, uh, club your dog? Doesn't it have a noose, or something?"

But Myrtle, dog-wise, wasn't taking suggestions.

"Love me, love my dog," she snapped, and directed Thing to sit down.

"Uh, okay," said Thing, releasing the Prada strap, and relinquishing her purse to the mutt. For all Thing cared, that dog could go to hell in her handbag, but she had business with Myrtle the Creole psychic—

"On that true love person, or, uh, persons, how about a name, or, uh, names?"

"Uhm, John?"

Thing let out a cry, "Ahhhh!"

"Uhm, Mark?"

"Ahhhh!"

"Uhm, how about . . . Roy?"

"Ahhhh!"

"Timothy?"

"Ahhhh!"

"Alex?"

"Ahhhh!"

"Uh . . . Wally?"

"Ahhhh!"

"Dimitri?"

"Ahhhh!"

"Eric?"

"Ahhhh!"

"Kirk?"

"Ahhhh!"

"Raul?"

"Ahhhh!"

john**reed**

"Miles?"

"Ahhhh!"

Yes, Thing realized, screwing up her face, if Myrtle was planning on dredging up every old name from the past, this was going to take a long, long, time.

"How about," asked Myrtle, fairly confident by now, "Bobby, Peter, and Sam?"

"Hmm," considered Thing, relieved, "Bobby, Peter, Sam. Sounds familiar, but, no, no, no."

"They may be in your future."

"Okay, enough with the names."

"Uhhm," the psychic stroked her dog, which had climbed up onto her lap with a bone or something, "I see, uhm, a child?"

"Yeah, in my past?"

Myrtle looked up from the dog toy, or whatever it was that she and her dog were fiddling around with—

"Uhm, yase?"

"Uh, no. I never had a kid, only an abortion."

Thing's cellular phone rang. It was Matthew, who wanted her back in New York, and pronto, which was a good thing, as Thing was getting bored anyway.

"Well," said Thing to Myrtle, wrapping up, "I may have had an abortion, but I have a career too." And, after wrestling her purse back from Myrtle's dog, Thing, her crew trailing behind her, was en route to the airport.

In the Platinum Lounge, Thing had trouble with her credit card. Or, well, not so much trouble, as it went through on the second try, but something else, as it was only one solitary credit card, and unaccompanied by the fourteen or fifteen or twenty others that she thought were in her purse, via her wallet, which was slick with dog slobber. Anyway, she didn't dwell on the mystery, as those credit thingies were easy to misplace, and they were bound to turn up.

In the back of her taxi, as she was pulling away from JFK Airport (the team had disbanded for the evening), she noticed something that did rattle

the**WH●LE**

her, however. There was that woman, who looked like her but ten years older. But now she looked younger. Maybe even younger than Thing. (*Dermabrasion?*) Her cab followed Thing's cab. Down the block from Thing's apartment, her cab pulled in when Thing's cab pulled in. Thing paid her fare and went upstairs. Then she went back down, for some cigarettes, and to see if that woman was still around. She wasn't. But then, Thing caught a glimpse of her, and she was. Thing had donned her jogging suit—and, in the seventies Puma collectible, which had yet to be sweated in, she took chase.

After a block, Thing dropped her cigarette, and after two blocks, her pace fell off considerably. Luckily, the woman she was chasing had also slowed considerably (she too had retained her cigarette for the first block). And thus, even if the bad news was *Thing wasn't getting any closer*, the good news was *she wasn't getting any farther away*. And for some time, that's how it went—nobody gaining ground, and nobody losing it.

But at the central crossing of Tompkins Square Park, Thing found that her fox had flown the coop, and she was all alone. Dejected and wheezing, and finally able to enjoy a cigarette, she staggered homeward.

Oh, that's kind of a big limousine for Tompkins Square, she was thinking, straightening herself out—when the hand came around her face and pushed the chloroform-soaked rag under her nose.

Then she was in the limousine, which was driving. Those fans had really gone too far. Or, maybe, this was her shrewd awakening, and those fans weren't fans at all, but something else entirely, something, well, that had been sent in, to well . . . well . . .

Swoop in and pluck me dry!

Thing was terrified. She cried out—

"I've been, uh, uh, catnapped!"

"No," said the familiar voice beside her, "you haven't been kidnapped, it's more like custodial interference."

"Is that you?" asked Thing.

And the Black Rabbit took Thing's trembling hand in his long, fuzzy paw.

"Yes, I think so."

john**reed**

"It's so scary. Not just this, but everything! And I'm so, so, mor, uh, mor, uh, I'm so worried!"

The Black Rabbit patted her hand, "Now, now," he said reassuringly, "don't let worry kill you."

"Okay," said Thing, snuffling, "I'll let you help."

And then she thought that if the Black Rabbit was there, things couldn't be all bad. And after one, two, three pink cocktails, the swaying limousine rocked her to sleep in his fuzzy arms. And then, she dreamt.

She dreamt of ten years in her life. Ten years when she wasn't famous. Ten years when she was never rehired by Viacom. Ten years that began with dating Pancho for four years, and were filled out by five years of punch-flavored barbiturates distributed in paper cups—and were culminated in an elaborate plot involving video-rental clerks, Anita the stylist, spies posing as fans and/or dermatechnicians, green fly insect probes and time-travel abductions. Yes, the plot, it was all clear to her—it was just like with the producer, Matthew, who, she realized, had only been replaced first to test the plan and technology, and, moreover, to help clear the way for the next replacement. . . . The replacement of Thing herself.

Now ten years older (dreamt Thing in the limousine), she was prepped and refreshed on her past. Through a time-travel beamer machine, she was transported ten years back in time, where she followed her former self until she was sure she could resume her former life. Then, briefly returned to the future, she was given a face-lift, and liposuction, and an eye job, and a neck job, and a forehead job, and jis' a nip of a nose job. Then, finally, after one more visit to the past, she underwent a series of aggressive dermabrasion sessions—and she was ready to replace her old self. They—the Olympic Committee—had chosen the older version because she would be wiser than her younger self, and the task set to her required an older, wiser self. And thus (dreamt Thing), having lured the young Thing to Tompkins Square Park, and, there, having captured her in a limousine, she had replaced the young Thing. Then (dreamt Thing) the young Thing was brought to the future, to live out the life of the self who had replaced her, or, in other words, to remain a drugged-out zombie, forever unable to reintegrate into society.

the**WH●LE**

And then (Thing dreamt) came another ten years—this time, the ten years of her old self in the life of her young self. And it all went splendidly. And yet, it wasn't over (she dreamt), for at the end of those ten years, much in the same way as the previous ten years, Thing was initiated into a plot to take over her self ten years in the past, or, well, ten years in the past minus a few minutes, as, this time, the young Thing had to be taken over just before she was taken over ten years before. But for this upcoming cycle of ten years, the technology was improved, and Thing's old brain was transplanted into the young body. And (in the dream, though it was more like a *hallucidation*), these ten years were even better than the previous ten years—she was more famous, more rich!—because, remembering the previous ten years, she could improve upon them. And then came another kidnapping and replacing, and another ten years where, as a result of remembering the first ten, and, more importantly, the second ten, she was even more famous and rich and worshiped. Then, the whole thing again—with yet even more of the good stuff, as she could now improve not only on the first and second ten years, but on the third ten years . . . and so on, and so on, forever. . . .

Or, well, not forever—but until she knew everything and was a Goddess. And then, as she dozed in the fuzzy arms of the Black Rabbit, she forgot all about the dream—although, in her, that inexplicable conviction that she was destined to be a Goddess who lived not just forever, but forever young, was inexplicably strengthened.

Then the Rabbit woke her. She wore a blindfold. He helped her out of the limousine, and led her across an avenue. Then, into what sounded like a restaurant. Then, up two short flights of stairs into a bar. Then, they took off her blindfold. It was Le Parc! There were noisemakers, paper horns and cupcakes with candles!

It was a surprise party! For her twenty-fourth birthday! But, surprise, there were only seven people there. "We planned it a few days ago," said Matthew, "when the ratings were up."

Hopeful that, later, the party would sardinify, Thing opened her presents. She did her very best to forget that horrible lesson she had learned in Mississippi, in the lost and found room—that one never really gets anything, except older—but the impression lingered. Oh, she put on a brave face, pulling ribbons, tearing tissue, but there was nothing she wanted, except maybe for the eighth present, which she didn't think was from the Black Rabbit, though it might have been. Anyway, it was a rabbit-ear vibrator—and the nose and buckteeth looked like they would, well . . . and the ears looked like they would, well . . . It looked like the item would work. And, well, like any good rabbit, it looked like it had some kick. Probably, it was a jackrabbit.

Unfortunately, the party did not pick up. Indeed, the DJ never arrived, and it was so quiet that Thing heard her cell phone ring every time it rang in the next thirty minutes. ("Yoiks, it's hard to believe it's been half an hour when it's only been thirty minutes!") There were a dozen calls—all from her various credit card companies—to inform her that her cards were running up suspicious charges and would she like them canceled.

"Perish the thought!" she told the first few of them, but then she began to think that maybe something was wrong. Maybe it wasn't just a coincidence that she didn't know where her credit cards were and now there were all these suspicious charges. Maybe . . . they'd been swiped! Finally, her bank called to tell her that she had been writing so many checks that she was in excess of the twenty-thousand-dollar allotment of her checking plus. That's when Thing knew something was wrong, as she'd always been more of a cash and card girl, and she didn't really have enough confidence in the whole check-writing thing to write, or even deposit a check without help—and she would definitely have remembered at least a little of all that help.

Unable to withstand the barrage of disquieting calls, she decided to make a few calls herself. Actually, there was someone she had to call. Someone who, probably, maybe, could save her. Luckily, her phone book was still in her purse, and she managed to locate the Black Rabbit's phone number, which, for some reason, she had.

The Rabbit answered—

"Ah, yes, Thing, allow me to extend my regrets for my early departure. My investments required attending."

"Oh yeah," asked Thing, unready to let fly her own problems, "how's that going?"

theWH●LE

Well, the Rabbit explained, there had been some trouble with protestors, and it was driving stock valuation way down.

"A few skirmishes, a few bloated CEOs, a few toxic corpses, a few noxious smokestacks, a few cadmium-rich wells and nine-legged frogs, and everyone's crying."

"It sounds to me like they should be buying."

"Unquestionably—those are excellent fundamentals."

From the Rabbit, Thing got the inside scoop, and once she'd determined that the company was Swedish and that the presidents and vice presidents all had blue eyes, she could not understand what the problem was. It just didn't seem fair that a taint like that could so sully them. Now, if they were Muslims or crack dealers or something, then she could see it. But their guns, and she and the Rabbit quite agreed on this, were only sold to those who knew what was best—those who were pure, honest, and of noble intent. Senators and stuff. There were law books and congressional debates and these war things didn't just happen. These were catastrophes of enormous political and economic consequence, over border disputes and channels of trade and issues of national identity. It wasn't like No Worries Munitions was selling their guns to gangsters in Los Angeles, who wanted to shoot someone to sell more crack on their particular corner, or to avoid getting a low-paying job, or get some payback. Shucks no, that wasn't NWM's market at all. (Except for some mail order, internet and gun-show business.) Why, that was much too low end! Yes, even to the Rabbit, there was the shadow of a suspicion of a twinge of something akin to regret over that ninety-caliber rifle (which happened to be NWM's top mail order, internet and gun-show seller, at twelve thousand dollars per). It could tear through tanks or bulletproof, or even ballistic-proof glass, in one shot. Nevertheless, Thing and the Rabbit were certain that there had to be some private citizens who had a lawful purpose for such a weapon. No, not terrorists. Not drug lords. Hippo hunters, maybe. Why, NWM had only sold six thousand of the guns the previous year. And there had to be twice that many hippos!

The Rabbit, with that, seemed to be feeling a little better. But there were other concerns, he said, such as the fact that the far lefties and far righties and even a few of the far centrists were proposing, as an alternative to warfare, outright buyouts of troubled countries. Some had so strayed as to suggest that littering a nation in diamonds would be more cost effective than littering it in bombs.

This, Thing conceded, did sound rational, and therefore represented a threat.

"Perhaps," the Rabbit proposed, torturedly, "there's something we can learn from those peaceniks. . . ."

After a pause, Thing admitted that there was a reason she called. She knew the value of money, she said, and therefore was trying to borrow some. And, likewise, he said, she therefore wasn't getting any. This, consequently, made her reassess the value of money. *It was worth more than she thought!* So she tried to borrow it again, but this time more, and, likewise, again, made less progress.

"It's like, it's like, they're erasing me—or taking me over."

"You know," said the Rabbit, "you look lovely."

"What? What's that supposed to mean?" asked Thing.

"Well," the Rabbit said ruefully, "it means that, owing to my investments, and, uh, fiscal troubles, all I can afford to pay is a compliment."

With that, Thing suddenly realized, whatever the conspiracy was, they had gotten to the Black Rabbit too. Or, maybe, that the Rabbit had been working for them all along.

"What," posed Thing, "do you have to say about the Olympic Committee?"

"Uh, nothing whatsoever," said the Rabbit.

"See?" cried Thing, "I knew it! You're a part of it! But I don't need you. I'll climb this mountain all by myself—right to the bottom of it! I'll change the world—and I'll do . . . whatever . . . well . . . whatever's next!"

So saying, Thing clapped closed her cell phone. And, appreciating that she was facing poverty, she felt, first ridiculous, but then ennobled. Yes, now she knew the struggle of the disadvantaged. Yes, now she'd felt hardship firsthand. Now she was at one with the struggle of the lower classes. Yes, ennobled. She too was a noble savage.

Then she thought that maybe her psychic, who was her new best friend, would maybe lend her some money.

the**WH●LE**

First, Thing thought to ask Myrtle about the credit cards. Myrtle agreed with Thing, that the cards had surely not been stolen. No, no, Myrtle soothed the anxious VJ, there was no reason to cancel those cards, as she had a very clear vision of the credit cards, and that they weren't stolen—and, to prove it, she identified the one credit card that Thing still had in her wallet.

"Triple A Visa."

"Oh yeah!" said Thing, checking the card. "How'd you know that?! You're like a psychic psychic! I mean, I had about fifteen or twenty cards, and you picked out that one as the one I still had! And you were right, I still had it! I think that one had the lowest credit limit, though. Did you know that too?"

"Uhm, yase."

Seeing as how Myrtle knew all about Thing's temporary cash flow problem, and Myrtle was Thing's best friend, besides, Thing felt fairly comfortable asking Myrtle for a loan.

And of course, their friendship, as true and real as any friendship in heaven, it would endure forever, or rather, it would have, had the subject of lending not been broached.

"I gotta go," said Myrtle.

And that was the end of that.

Thing looked around Le Parc.

Pretty much everyone had drifted off. It was almost 8 PM, and, uh, as people said, it was getting latish, and, uh . . . It was only Thing, Otto and Roth, slumped in their chairs, staring at the projection screen (put up for the party), wondering about, well, sort of everything, and, well, sort of nothing.

Then, the live update.

As rendered by digitized satellite images of the Earth, the hole was growing. Brian Williams of MSNBC reported—

"As was warned by geologists, the hole is again increasing its circumference. This, scientists have verified, will be the final episode in this natural phenomenon. Homes and businesses to the northwest, to the north, to the east and to the southeast have been evacuated and secured by the Army and the National Guard. The desert land to the southwest is owned, as a result of a

164

165

johnreed

1911 treaty with the United States, by the Lawimi Indian tribe, whose population, over the last century, has plummeted from 30,000 to 712. Lawimi elders have agreed to cooperate fully with the United States."

By now, the satellite image had zoomed in—and one began to grasp the scale, the enormity of the earthly phenomenon. What looked at first to be a troop of ants scuttling slowly away from the breaking perimeter, had transformed into a herd of wild horses running from the sand that was roiling up and crashing behind them like a wave into the surf. And as the cloudy wave submersed them, the horses, one and then the next, plummeted into the egress—legs akimbo. And then, an odd thing happened—all the horses stopped, turned, and trotted into the storm of sand. And they fell, and sank into the churning ground. And the satellite image cut to a close-up of an Indian elder.

"Must be Lawimi," said Otto.

Matthew, who had reappeared for the broadcast, was desponding, despite the taut skin of his forehead—

"You think you've done it all before—blammo, an Indian tribe you've never heard of. They're not gonna let us in, are they?"

"Shhhh!" sibilated Thing, listening, and, what's more, maybe onto something.

"The Lawimi," said the Lawimi chief, "as a sovereign nation, have agreed to fully cooperate with the nation of the United States. Only members of the Lawimi tribe will be permitted to visit the holy site of the hole, which we believe fulfills ancient Lawimi prophesies."

"Only Lawimi tribe members," groaned Matthew, but Thing had something to say to that.

"Get that geezer on the horn. I'm a Lawimi princess!"

This was a surprise. But Thing was full of surprises, and not four minutes had passed before, yes, the geezer was with horn.

Thing explained to him that she had been past-life regressed, and that she remembered, if not a whole lot of detail, at least enough to know she had been a Lawimi princess.

The elder, quite reasonable about the assertion, unhesitatingly accepted it.

"You see," he said, "we believe in reincarnation, and since now there are so few Lawimi, we believe that peoples not Lawimi carry Lawimi souls."

"Okay, so I'm Lawimi. Can I come down?"

"Yes, but you must pay your tribe dues."

"Tribe dues?" Thing prepared herself for the worst. Matthew nodded, and prepared as well—

"Find out how much they are."

Thing asked, "How much?"

"We are a very poor nation. These dues are our primary source of revenue."

Thing was getting impatient. This was obviously going to be expensive.

"How much already?"

"Twelve fifty."

"Oh, twelve grand?" Thing was nodding yes. Matthew was nodding yes.

"No," said the elder, "twelve dollars and fifty cents."

"Oh yeah," said Thing, "that's what I said, twelve dollars and fifty cents." Matthew was really nodding now—so hard that his ears were shaking in sync with his crooked Mohawk.

"And," Thing furthered, "what about the crew?"

"Twelve fifty."

"Each?"

"Yes."

"And, uh, not to beat a dead sore point with a horse, but, uh, they aren't Lawimi."

"We believe all people come from the Lawimi. Even if they don't remember it."

Thing was giving the thumbs-up.

"Teriff!"

Matthew was giving the thumbs-up. Otto and Roth were thinking about packing their equipment.

"But first, we must make a trade."

Thing held up her hand. The chief wanted to make a trade.

"Uh, what kind of trade?"

"In one hour, we are going to have a ceremony. If you are to bring your culture to ours, you must also allow us to bring our culture to yours."

"Airtime? How long?"

"Two minutes. The priest's prayer."

"Two minutes," said Thing to Matthew, "priest's prayer."

The producer bobbled his head from side to side, tormented—

"Okay, done."

"Done," said Thing.

"Good trade," said the elder.

"Just out of curiosity," asked Thing, "what's the ceremony for?"

"To bring more Lawimi."

Right on schedule, one hour later, the chief made his brief introduction, explaining that the feathered, painted dancers were Lawimi tribe members, and that the tribe was calling on lost members, and that they had already sworn in Thing and her crew, who'd all come across with their twelve-dollar-and-fifty-cent membership fee. Then the Lawimi cameraman was directed to the priest, who commenced his prayer.

Tracing a circle in the dirt with his toe, the priest, who was especially brightly painted and feathered, flapped his hands in the air and offered these words—

"The circle is a nest. It is drawn by the toe because the eagle builds with its claw. Much as the eagle makes a nest to hold its young, so did the Sky God make a cradle of the world to hold people. If you climb a mountain and look around, you will see the heavens touch the Earth on every side, and the circle in which we dwell. This circle I make with my toe is not only like the nest of birds, but like the cradle of people. Also, the circle is the kinship group, the clan, and the tribe."

theWH●LE

The priest clapped his hands and, with a shuffling dance, wiped out the circle in the dirt. Then, he said to the camera—

"Now, we invite all people to know the circle, that they, like the young eagle with its feathers, may spring from the nest—that they may see their wings are strong, and they may leave the circle far behind, and fly in a sky without limit, and see into a horizon that is infinite."

Thing knew she wouldn't be talking to the Rabbit for some time. (That spat over the money.) Maybe, she thought, this was her chance to quit with the pink cocktails, or, well, not quit, exactly, but take the focus off. For a long while she'd sort of been quitting, or, at least, taking the focus off. Fortunately, the Rabbit, even if he wasn't availing himself to her, had left four thermoses of cocktails in the plane that Viacom had chartered to take her and her crew back to the hole.

Everything's still the same, she told herself, *it's just a little different now.*

The hour was late, and Matthew, Roth, Otto and the rest of the crew drifted off in their seats. Thing, after what she guessed was the equivalent of two cocktails (straight from the thermos), began to feel sleepy herself. But first, she unpacked her brand-new rabbit-ear vibrator, and discovered that the batteries were in it. It did buzz, and she did make a few noises, but she didn't think anyone woke up while she checked the engine.

Then, she too nodded off, and only groggily awoke to transfer to the rental van—and the obligation of a live broadcast. She swigged from her thermos and smoked a few Virginia Slims, though actually, she wasn't smoking either, or, rather, she wasn't focusing on smoking either—but she was coughing continuously. It took five takes to get it right—

"It's live."

"It's live."

"It's live."

"It's live."

"It's live."

Then, they chose the livest-looking option.

"It's live."

john**reed**

And from there, they proceeded with the update.

"As you can see, we're in the desert, live at the site of the hole, which recently got bigger. The fence is over there, and we're the only ones around, and, uh, well, the crutch of the matter is that's the whole kettle of fish in a nutshell."

Really, there wasn't anybody around. It was just Thing and her crew, and a thousand miles of desert. Her tent was the sole interruption on the horizon, that is, aside from the van, where the crew would be sleeping.

"Oh," said Thing to the crewmembers who had, after some false starts, managed to erect her personal nylon pavilion, "thanks for your help. It's deeply depreciated." Then she had them bring in her bags and inflate the blow-up mattress. Somebody had forgotten the pump, and Otto and Roth, volunteered by Thing to do the inflating, almost lost consciousness. As soon as they were able enough to stand, Thing got them up and out, and settled in to go back to sleep. She dug out her rabbit-ear vibrator and tested it again, this time on the loudest setting. She was a measure louder herself too, so, afterwards, she felt she had undergone a recuperative release and went back to sleep. Rest was peaceful, knowing that, aside from her crew, it was just her, the hole, almost three thermoses of pink cocktails, and an ocean of desert.

When she woke up, it was to a band. Initially, she thought her crew had put in an alarm clock—those cuckoos! But then she realized the band was live. She opened her tent flap and peeked out. It was Straw Dogs, said the announcer, and they were opening for Nick Cave, who was opening for Bob Dylan.

And tonight, neither lie, nor the colors on the sky,
Will replace any ache, though you try.

Off in the distance, she could see that two other stages had been constructed. Matthew had attached a note to her tent—

the**WH●LE**

9:00	Cyndi Lauper, Paula Abdul and Pat Benatar
9:20	Bono
9:40	The Olson twins (Mary-Kate and Ashley)
10:00	Courtney Love
10:20	Aaron Neville & Linda Ronstadt
10:40	Gwar
11:00	Madonna on Courtney Love
11:20	Ross Perot
11:40	Shania Twain
12:00	P. Diddy
12:20	Flock of Seagulls
12:40	Dalai Lama
1:00	Lunch, and the afternoon schedule

Thing couldn't believe it. There, on the third stage, Diana Ross, Janet Jackson and Jennifer Lopez were singing the Sister Sledge hit "We Are Family."

As it turned out, being their own nation, the Lawimi tribe had opened their section of hole to a multifaceted deal that encompassed cable, internet, television and the print media. Initiation fees were paid for whole swaths of the country. (In a survey of MTV's young adult viewers, 64 percent said, "I like to meet new people.") It seemed the entire nation was becoming Lawimi. (Fifty-seven percent said, "I'm always looking for excitement.") Thing, as a reincarnated tribe member, called her lawyer to have him investigate as to whether she was entitled to a cut. Since she had been a princess, she reminded him, she should probably get most of it. That little money problem, she suspected, was over. She never should have fretted over it. (Seventy-seven percent agreed, "I am satisfied with my life.")

Aside from the Lawimi initiation fee, there was no admission price, but, as it was late July, and 101 degrees by 10:30 AM, it was assumed that, aside from all the advertising money, the four-dollar soft drinks and three-dollar bottles of water would reap their reward. Also, popcorn, hot dogs, pretzels, ice cream, candy and veggie burgers were available. There were two

john**reed**

hundred Porta Pottis, and by two in the afternoon, twenty thousand concert-goers. (Sixty-nine percent said, "I like visiting new and strange places.") Charter flights were landed directly on the nearby clay flats. Buses caravanned the spectators the ten minutes down the road. There was plenty of beer available too—as well as other refreshers and mind-altering substances, if you knew where to look. Vendors were not far behind, with tie-dye tee-shirts and foam visors. Also, everything else, from the alien antennas of the alien groups, to the Santa's Helper baseball hats sold by the Santa's Helper cult.

When the construction crews had finished putting up the giant tent that topped the third stage and audience area, Dido and Radiohead started up a duet. Then, at the first stage, Dylan wound down his last song, and the construction crews went to work on a tent there—which, upon completion, was populated by metalheads Marilyn Manson and Ozzy and Kelly Osbourne. The tent at the second stage was opened by the Chili Peppers and Bjork.

All had been made Lawimi tribe members. Not to forget the security guards, and the police, and three or four platoons of soldiers—now, Lawimi braves. (A few had even gotten so far into the spirit of things as to have their faces painted.) Their presence was a veritable prophylactic against danger or mishap. Any eventuality would be promptly handled. Indeed, if their competence was at all akin to their prowess as mud wrestlers, the world had nothing to fear.

A few of the Indian elders echoed this sentiment. Nothing to fear. The hole won't get bigger. Geologists (who'd also been made Lawimi tribe members) had analyzed the site, and were certain the hole would grow no more. The clouds and rainstorms that intermittently formed over the hole had no significance at all.

Surrounding the hole, it was sunny. There were Absolut vodka Jell-O shots circulating, and the Coppertone was going on liberally. There were so many bikinis that Thing, directing the camera over the panorama, described the moment as "peak season." She herself had donned a bikini for the temperate hour. A black-and-white ensemble with cow spots. Finally, she realized, she was the Bovinity she deserved to be.

The interview opportunities were many. First, there was Mitch,

Thing's Roswell source, who smelled like an acre of onions. He led Thing and her crew to Ponte, who explained that all the signs were there—Atlantis was rising to the surface.

The Santa's Helpers group had also made the journey from Roswell. Now with holes drilled in the middle of their foreheads, the cult members wore green Nike sweatsuits with the shirt hoods drawn tight. In addition to their "third eye," the cultists, in a coordinated movement, dehooded to undrape shaved heads with curving scars that looped, zipperlike, up, over and back down their skulls. Like softballs. Then the cultists popped beady glass eyes into the hole in their foreheads, and fixed their tri-eyed gapes upon their leader, Rector Sandoby, who wore a red Nike sweatsuit.

Sandoby discussed recent articles in *The New York Times* that had detailed the homicidal proclivities of dolphins and whales—and assessed that this bore out his theory that aliens had manipulated man, whale and dolphin with alien DNA. Having proffered this appetizer, Sandoby then moved onto the main course. A representative of the aquatic alien species of Atlantis, who had created man, dolphin and whale, had recently made a visit to the cult leader, and guided him on an informative morning tour to a distant galaxy. The alien, said Sandoby, resembled a human lobster, soft-shell, and had traveled in what those of the old world might call a flying sleigh, but what we of a more modern inclination would call a shuttle. At great length, the alien had spoken to Sandoby of the lobster-esque race, the Santans. (Misinterpretations of "Santan" counted such monikers as "Santa," "Satan" and "Santana." Two members of the seventies band were incognito Santans—the aliens loved rock'n'roll.) Though an ancient and highly advanced race, the Santans had but recently attained a perfect harmony among themselves. Up until about four hundred years ago, there had still been evil intergalactic travelers of their race, who would occasionally turn up and cause trouble on Earth. "Beelzebub" was the name of one such troublemaker. "Niclaus," known on Earth as Saint Nicholas or Santa Claus, was an alien philanthropist, who had a fondness for human offspring. It was no myth, Sandoby said the alien had said, that Beelzebub, or, for that matter, Niclaus, knew everything about everyone. And to prove the point, the alien took Sandoby to "the planet Astra, in the Doria Galaxy." Here, in an immense hall that defied description, the basic personality of every human being who had ever lived was sorted by birth date, that is, by the stars, which was the only true constant. DNA makeups were kept current, as were basic sociologic histories—and thus, every human being might be judged and measured as having either exceeded or fallen short of his or her potentiality. (Such judgment would be taken into account when the aliens, who were soon returning to Earth, assisted the human race to a more evolved incarnation.)

Along with the dolphins and whales, men had been created to serve the alien Atlanteans as laborers. In the case of each species, subspecies were created to suit more specific tasks. Thus, the differentiation in the races of men. Originally, the Santans had a negative impulse in their population that they had not yet overcome, and they had utilized these racial differences to foster, in humanity, an intolerance that helped to guarantee that humans would never be able to cooperate with one another and achieve independence. And, despite some crossbreeding (including some comingling with the low-caste servant, Neanderthal), the racial prejudices had remained intact after thousands of years. Also, disparate languages had been introduced. (The Tower of Babel.) But since the aliens themselves had reached a higher level of consciousness, they were planning to return to Earth, to rectify their previous wrongs. Not only would they do their best to undo their destructive DNA manipulations, but they would rid the world of the racist tendencies that the negative lobster aliens (who had since been rehabilitated in Chinese reeducation camps) had made such a prevalent part of the human psyche.

Despite the fact that the alien/lobster city of Atlantis had long fallen due to its own internal conflict of good versus evil, the aliens had continued to exercise a significant influence on humanity. The Santan race was sort of the intergalactic older sibling of the Earthling, and that relationship, for better or worse, was evidenced repeatedly throughout human history—especially as represented by religion and mythology, as science, among humans, was only eighty-odd years old. In this role of big brother/big sister, the Santans were presently setting about the task of raising the ancient city of Atlantis, which Sandoby's escort alternately referred to as a "dome," and a "dark pyramid." Over the millenia, the former aquatic city had been protected, underground, by the same

the**WH**●**LE**

superstructure that had previously protected it from the ocean. A restoration of the city had been initiated, and the metropolis was now ready to be drawn from the depths. That's what the hole was—a preparatory procedure. (Atlantis, much older than anyone realized, had been located in North America when North America was still underwater.)

Then, after a commercial break, Thing and her team brought, to their viewing public, other cultists—religious extremists and extraterrestrialists. One group believed that soon the heavens would be sending the messiah to convert everyone to Christianity, including the Christians. Next, the Satanists, along with the Goths, voiced the theory that the hole was the mouth, or the rectum of the devil—which was evidently a good thing. One of several cow worshiper sects interpreted the recent rise of cownappings by UFOs to be a result of visitations by aliens who themselves worshiped cows, as the cow greatly resembled a now-extinct alien creature that the aliens had once tended and farmed for organ transplants. And, indeed, said the Earthling cow worshipers, the aliens had been selecting suitable animals from Earth's cow population to utilize for this very purpose.

Another theory was that the cows were only involved insofar as, from them, the aliens had adapted a form of smallpox to infect the planet. Still others said that it was an accident, that Mother Nature, or God, or the aliens, or whoever they were, gave us viruses to keep us in check—to keep our cities from getting too big, our consumption from getting too destructive. But the upshot of our own arrogance, selfish meddling and gratuitous weakening of the immune system of the natural world, was that one of those viruses (for instance, smallpox) had jumped to another animal, and that animal was the Earth. (The hole was the blister. Global warming was the fever.)

Of course, there was also the possibility that the hole indicated an immunization (a pockmark scar much like those that once resulted from, interestingly, cow-derived vaccines) which was designed to *protect* the Earth from planetary smallpox. Maybe the aliens were looking out for us—maybe, even, the hole was just a tiny part of their efforts to assure a healthy Earth that was habitable for humans. Unless they were trying to destroy us, or trying to make the Earth habitable for something else.

john**reed**

As the viral/pox theories encouraged Thing to rub the pimple in the middle of her forehead and wonder why everyone else was getting a pimple in the middle of their foreheads, she was relieved to move onto a series of theories involving environmental catastrophe. The hole, said the environmental radicals, was a planetary herpes sore. (Damn, that didn't distract her at all—*rub that pimple, rub that pimple.*) We hadn't been taking care of ourselves, and, as the idea went, the stress was showing!

Others, maintaining that the hole was caused by bacteria—possibly a biological weapon gone haywire—claimed that the only solution was to give up our immoral ways of technological sin and return to a simpler way of life. Several submitted the opinion that it was up to us to bring about Earthly paradise. The hole, for example, represented a world out of control. Society and culture itself was now surviving on us, like a ringworm, and had manifested, fittingly, as a ringworm infection. There were the anarchists, the hippies, the punks and the People for the Ethical Treatment of Animals—all of whom had something to say about materialism, the hole in the American dharma, the destruction of the rainforest, the clubbing of baby seals, and the ozone. (Some of the punks were voting yes.) One hemp society postulated that the hole was a giant seed about to sprout. Cannabis maximus. Eternal bliss, obviously.

Then there were the outspoken. The ex-Harvard professor who'd been living in the woods for six years, who was yelling at the top of his lungs about gravity, space and time travel. The Veterans of the CIA group who held that the Chinese had been working to create a race of giant crustaceans since 1946, and that the hole was an entrenchment of the abominations. The twelve-year-old girl who was adamant in the notion that the hole was, well, a wishing well.

An unstable fellow had this to scream—

"Brain staples, you all have them!"

A large lady in a *Star Trek* uniform, having set up a stand with diagrams and free pamphlets, offered proofs that the world was flat. "The world is flat!" she declared—

"It's us! It's us that's twisted!"

(This was a hypothesis that appealed to Thing, as the world-is-round proposal had always confused her. She'd never been able to reconcile herself to the formula that the Earth rotated on an axle as it revolved around the sun in a pumpernickel biscuit.)

And the teens, they voted on "Best Hole Explanation," and "Best Hole Music Video." (The music video options were, Jimmy Eat World, "The Middle," Patsy Kline, "Whole Lotta Love," Soundgarden, "Black Hole Sun," Outkast featuring Killer Mike, "The Whole World," and a late entry which related to the popular lobster alien theory, the B-52s, "Rock Lobster.")

The artists and celebrities had a great deal to contribute, as most, if not all of them, had realized that they had been psychically attuned to the phenomenon, as, in their music or films or whatever it was they were up to, they had been addressing the hole, in one way or another, in their latest project.

Throughout the morning, and then the afternoon, Thing had little to say (how could she improve on any of that?) except for, "The sacred cows have come home to roost with a vengeance!" and a gushing, "I couldn't put a price on all I've learned here today—it's really been of infinitesimal value."

In her final interview of the day, Thing came across an odd theory that Bobby Peterson had been adopted by the Petersons, and that he hadn't been born at all. He had been, as the theory was put forth (by a googly-eyed woman in a medical gown), grown from a fetus, in a jar. Furthermore, he was somehow the wholesale cause of the hole. Janice, as the woman called herself, elaborated on the government mastery of such fetus-growing technology, and went on to explain that, anyway, the government might have been helped by the aliens. *Or even*, thought Thing, unexpectedly, *the Black Rabbit!* And while she did not understand the reason for this thought, or what possible motivation the Black Rabbit could have for helping the government grow Bobby Peterson in a jar, her instinct led her to intuit that, regardless, eventually, she would.

Then came the news. The hole had enlarged, again. But this time, it was not at the site of the hole, but rather, at several seemingly unconnected sites around the globe. (*But was it a globe?*) Miniholes. In New York— Times Square, the Shakespeare in the Park Theater in Central Park, and a variety of restaurants and spa/healing/beauty-related businesses, which had been hardest hit. Charlie Rose, who had been taping when his studios were inhaled, had narrowly escaped with his life. In Roswell—the Best Western, all the tourist traps, a certain compound that belonged to a cult group called the Santa's Helpers, and a trailer park. Las Vegas—the Lady Luck Hotel and Casino, the Convention Center, the Mirage, several other casinos and hotels, and the bus station. The bus station had sunk in Salt Lake City, Utah too, as had the entire Temple on the Square area. The Temple, the Inn, even La Caille at Quail Run had been lost forever. Also, a local convenience store had been swallowed. Cleveland was mourning the fate of a television studio. In Washington, the White House dining room was totally destroyed, as was the White House parking lot. Los Angeles had dimples all over it. Hawaii and Maui also had a few. As did the United Kingdom—in Greenwich and London. India, Alaska, New Orleans and Mississippi were reporting depressions as well. Fate evidently had it in for the airports—as they were dropping into the ground far and wide.

Thing mentioned to some big-wig scientist type that she had recently, very recently as a matter of fact, been to each and every one of those locations, but he assured her there was no connection. Actually, said the scientist, who was in step with the scientific consensus of the world science community, this had been quite expected—and that was definitely, definitely the last of it. No more hole, no more holes—anywhere.

So, the news updates updated and the death tolls tolled.

As for the festivities at the site of the hole, one might think that such updating and tolling might droop the proceedings. But the aforesaid pall did not develop, and, to the contrary, the throngs were as elated and carefree as they were before, if not more so. The bands were playing. Guitars were singing and men were screaming—and the audience of the world, from South Pole to North, was enthralled. Thing, glowing among the multitudes like some miraculous party angel, floated and danced into the darkness of the desert night. Bodies undulated, and sweating flesh pressed sweating flesh, and eyes turned upwards to look at the stars and anticipate whatever it was they knew would happen.

Everyone was beautiful and divine—right down to the white and sometimes bleeding pimples in the middle of their foreheads!

At some point Thing's pink cocktail thermos ran dry, and she returned to her tent, hoping, not so much for another thermos, but for a frosty glass and the Black Rabbit, who she was keen to see. Despite everything, he was such a delight, that rabbit, and that's exactly what she was thinking when, upon entering her tent, she discovered that not only was there no rabbit, there was no new thermos either.

It was with a sense of profound neglect that Thing made ready for bed. It had been so long since she didn't have a pink cocktail in hand, that she was unable to imagine anything ahead but endless days of desponding. And worse yet, the nights. No nightcap. To creep into bed so unmoistened was nearly beyond the capacity of any human being to endure hardship. And she was not just any human being—her ability to endure hardship was extremely limited.

There was no comfort to be found in her cotton nightie. None either in the application of the rabbit-ear vibrator, which did its duty, but with a morose quality that left Thing, afterwards, in tears.

All she could think about was pink cocktails. But alas, there was nothing she could do. The bunny hadn't replenished her. She was alone, without even a recipe.

It had been such a long hard journey. The milestones had passed and she had pushed on. And now, having pushed far beyond the last milestone, the last pink cocktail, here she was—arrived at the terminus alone. No family, no friends, no Rabbit. She was just empty, and alone.

Thing rubbed her pimple. *I don't like being afraid—it scares me.*

Worse still, she wasn't afraid enough. Since she could remember, the only thing that held her back from suicide was the fear that she would die a nobody. No bereaving world. No lines to lay flowers on her grave. But she'd dulled being afraid for so long—all that time she was drinking those cocktails—that she realized she wasn't afraid anymore. Not even of dying nobody. And that's what was so scary. She was alone, and it was so hard to just cling to her fear.

Maybe she really was a nobody—some delusional person in some other place. Maybe she drank Hawaiian Punch with grain alcohol, and stared at her television. Maybe she watched construction men out the window, and listened to the radio, and nibbled on oatmeal raisin cookies. And she prayed for a moment that maybe it was true, because she needed to stay afraid.

She was alone, and she was afraid that she wasn't afraid enough. The world was full of billions of creeps and crazies and nobodies, and she needed them all, to help keep her afraid. And there was always music playing, but it didn't make any sense. And something was going on outside, but she didn't have the wherewithal to get out of bed.

> *There's something about a pink cocktail—*
> *A fizzle, a whizzle, a wow.*
> *A singing, stinging pink cocktail,*
> *I wish that I had one right now.*
> *There's something about a pink cocktail—*
> *And I think that I'm onto its secret.*
> *It ain't the froth, the lime or the kiwi.*
> *It's the inebriatin' ingredient.*

theWH●LE

She slept restlessly. The tent was warm. Sand blew against the stretched nylon.

She woke to a sponge on her body. Then she saw a long paw wielding a scalpel.

When she woke again, it was to the paw squeezing bloody water from the sponge into a bowl. She slept again. And again, she woke.

The pimple on her forehead was aching. Her eyes were closed. She furrowed her brow, to feel the pimple. Then, it was as if a lid lifted, and she could see through the pimple. Her two eyes remained closed. A figure stood at the far end of the tent. He was drinking a pink cocktail, thank heaven, and smoking a cigarette too.

"Third eye?" asked Thing.

"Yes," he said.

"Is the operation complete?"

"Yours is."

Thing noticed, then, that the figure was slumping somewhat.

"What's wrong?"

"Sometimes we all have our doubts, but I'm sure everything was for the best."

"I'm sure it was," agreed Thing, helpfully.

"You know," she suggested, "I see that you're drinking a pink cocktail, so you must know the Black Rabbit. And I would suggest, if you're having any difficulty about anything, that you talk it over with the Black Rabbit. He's an excellent conver, conversionalist, uh—"

"Conversationalist?"

"Yes, that, and there's nothing to be, uh, contaminated, uh, in-seminated, uh—"

john**reed**

"Intimidated?"

"Yes, there's nothing to be intimidated about, because it's not like he's wise, or anything, it's more like, well, he's otherwise."

"I'm afraid you don't understand," said the figure, who stepped out of the dark to reveal that he was a Red Alien (the Soft-Shell Lobster Alien!) with one eye in the middle of his forehead and two more eyes at the ends of long antennas which extended from either side of his enormous head—

"You see . . ."

And here, the Lobster Alien turned his back to Thing, and struggled with a latex mask he held in a grabber incongruously fuzzy and pawlike. Having at last managed to stretch and pull the item over his head, he faced her—

"I am the Black Rabbit."

And Thing could see that, indeed, he was. The Black Rabbit was a Lobster Alien from outer space. Yes, he'd always talked funny, but Thing had just assumed he was from England.

The Alien/Rabbit began the laborious process of removing the mask.

"Eyeball antennas, eh?" asked Thing.

"Yes, there is a bio-energy that surrounds every life-form, and horns are lovely (and we do worship cows), but, for the most part, ancient texts are referring, not to halos or horns, but eyeball antennas."

"Aha."

The prawnlike figure tugged at the rabbit ear that sheathed his alien eye.

"Well," exhaled Thing, resigned to the development, "it's about time you told me who you were."

"Yes," said the Red Alien, liberating his second antenna, "my apologies."

"After all we've been through," Thing shook her head.

"Really," agreed the Alien, yanking himself out of a pair of fuzzy latex gloves, and finally free of every fuzzy latex encumbrance, "you're absolutely right."

the**WH●LE**

And then Thing realized what it was they had been through. The abortion. Bobby Peterson growing in a jar. Thing knew that it was possible. She had been to Washington, and she distinctly remembered having heard something related to this very subject. "Life," someone had said, "begins at contraception." Yes, Thing knew, her aborted fetus had been birthed in someone else. (She couldn't guarantee it, but she thought she had even seen a story like that on the cover of a *National Examiner*.) Then, her child was adopted—becoming Bobby Peterson. Yes, what the psychic said made perfect sense. *Bobby, Peter, Sam. Bobby Peterson.* And yes, the psychic was right too in that, no, it wasn't "the one" that Thing was looking for. It was "the them," the father and child.

That had been her mission all along. To find "the them."

But who was the father?

Then she had a hankering. A hankering for the rabbit-ear vibrator. And then, she knew. The Black Rabbit, that is, the Red Alien formerly known as the Black Rabbit, he was the father. It must've been one of those drunken nights she didn't remember—*those pink cocktails*! And that's why he was always hanging around, and telling her about his investments—because he was the father of her child.

Yes, she knew, Bobby Peterson was the key. He had started it all. And now, it was her mission to reveal to the world that he was the future of the Earth, and that the Alien/Rabbit had done his part in contributing to that future, and that, most of all, she was the mother. The blessed mother.

"So, all along, my mission was to . . ."

"Yes," confirmed the Alien, "probably."

Thing sighed, first with exasperation, then forgiveness, as, even if the Black Rabbit was a Red Alien who had impregnated her while she was unconscious, she was quite pleased to see him—

"Well, anyway, I'm glad it's all cleared up."

The Alien offered her a cigarette, which she took. Then he sampled his cocktail, and she remembered—

"What happened to you? I needed a cocktail and you were nowhere to be found!" Her lip began to quiver—

"I felt so, uh, ab, ab, ab, uh, abandoned. Got it, ha!"

john**reed**

Notwithstanding the three-syllable word, Thing's faucets turned on. And the three-syllable word, which she was so proud of, repeatedly repeated itself through her lips—and all the while brought back the terrible memory of being alone, without a cocktail.

"Abandoned, abandoned, abandoned . . ."

"Oh," said the Red Alien, "I'm so sorry, please don't whimper. It was just that, we had to do this operation. We really couldn't wait any longer. And as you know, it's inadvisable to perform surgery upon a patient under the influence of, well . . ."

"A cocktail?"

"Yes."

"Like Marilyn Monroe? Pills and cocktails?"

"Precisely. Bad mix."

"I understand."

"I'm relieved that you do."

"But . . ."

"What?"

"Can I have one now?"

The Alien turned to a frosty glass that was already prepared—

"Fresh as a stripper at a ladies' garden society! I thought you might want one."

Thing drank thirstily, "Oh, I did."

"Don't hold back. We have more."

"Thank God."

"You're welcome."

Once Thing had regained her equilibrium, she thought to inquire after the Alien's investments—

"What's going on with your stock, um, No Worries Munitions?"

"Why, thank you for asking," said the Red Alien. "Actually, I think we're in for an upward turn. I had a major revelation, you see, and, having perceived the problem, I awakened several buyers to a principle that was somehow eluding them. However facile a concept to you or me, they had somehow failed to grasp that the cause of war is peace—that peacetime activities produce

the**WH●LE**

wartime results, that peacetime economics and social introversion produce wartime economics and conflicts, et cetera, and that furthermore, peace always precedes war, and war always follows upon peace, and so forth. And therefore, I explained to them—and this is where profitability was restored to me—that the military establishment must remain the chief industry, especially in times and places of peace, as a time of peace is when, and a place of peace is where, the threat (that is, the unknown threat, which is the most threatening threat) is most, well, threatening. And, beyond that, since the converse is also true, that is, that war is the cause of peace, I explained that if you want peace, well, you'll have to start a war—for which you'll need munitions. And, there it is, the peaceniks, the warmongers—all on board. So, yes, amen, my dear, there have been some industry sales, and the stock's performance is considerably improved, and I expect a marked upswing, oh . . . any minute."

"That's super!"

"Yes," the Alien sipped his cocktail, "most."

There was a rumbling through the tent. It rumbled outside too. The ground cracked. There was dust in the air. The signs were unmistakable. The hole was growing. Thing sat up—swung her feet into her shoes. But it wasn't just that the hole was growing, it was something else.

"Excuse me," she said, "um, I mean, uh . . ."

"You suddenly know what the hole is."

"Yes."

"Well, *naturellement.*"

"So I might—"

"Yes, by all means," said the Alien, excusing her, "you're excused."

Thing was out the flap of the tent, shouting for her crew—

"I know what the hole is! I know what the hole is!"

And then she saw that her crewman, Otto, was now an otter, and that her crewman, Roth, was now a sloth, and that her producer, Matthew, was now a musk shrew. And each of them had third eyes. And not a one of them was at all uncomfortable being a furry mammal, or having a third eye, and each was alert and attentive, and standing upright with his chest thrust out, like a little

john**reed**

whiskered marine, ever-ready to do his job, despite a widespread lack of thumbs. And the three of them were calling back to her, in response to her excitement at having solved the riddle of the hole—

"We know you know!"

"We know!"

Otter was up beside her first, and Thing caught sight of herself on the monitor of his camera, and yet, she didn't wonder why she'd remained human, while Otto, Roth and Matthew were Otter, Sloth and Musk Shrew. No, there was no confusion, she understood that too. And, however intuitively, so did Otter, Sloth and Musk Shrew.

All around, everyone had been transformed into animals. Red River hogs and Shetland ponies.

White-tailed deer and Galapagos turtles.

There were even a few old boyfriends here and there. Danziger the duke was now a duck.

"A merganser!" he quacked happily as he passed. And Caesar, or Roy, he walked by, discoursing upon his incarnation as a Chihuahua, and his kennel classification as "Toy." And, that golden lion marmoset, and Lump-nosed bat—they looked awfully familiar!

And behind her, Thing saw the Alien, formerly the Black Rabbit, holding up a long claw, as if to say, *halt*—while his other claw was pointing, as if to say, *follow my pincer, there.*

The one human among the animals, Thing began to walk towards the hole. Otter, Sloth and Musk Shrew followed her. There were also, aside from the former Black Rabbit, other Red Aliens. They carried medical bags, and held scalpels in their hands. As the three-eyed animals and Thing walked, trancelike, to the hole, those who had not yet been transformed ran in the other direction, and desperately attempted to drag their critterized friends and loved ones, who they would momentarily recognize, away from the irresistible impulse. Then the humans, as they ran or struggled with their companions, were snagged by the aliens and laid upon the ground. There, the aliens lanced the pimple in the middle of each human's forehead, and, in so doing, unveiled a third eye. After inserting a small computer chip behind the third eye, the alien then cut away the human epidermis, and elaborated several procedures out of the alien medical bag, and the individual was shortly transforming into the animal that he or she had, by the logic of alien judgment, earned. The process of the transformation itself, once activated, lasted no more than a minute. If the animal were considerably larger or smaller than the human in question, however, the process took longer. A hundred-pound woman transformed into a ten-pound rabbit, for example, took several minutes—and left behind not only a pool of blood, but a ninety-pound pile of poop. A man transformed into a hippo, conversely, required a several-minute feeding—the Red Aliens provided a green mash, seemingly at will. To complete the process, in every animal/human, a new pair of lungs was implanted. (Yes, thought Thing, glancing down to her chest and the incision mark that was disappearing before her own three eyes— it really was easier to breathe.) Then the penguin or gorilla, or whatever kind of creature it was, walked to the hole (on hind legs, or fins) with Thing and all the other creatures. Of everyone, those of the Santa's Helpers sect enjoyed the easiest transformation. In their case, the aliens simply grabbed them by the scalp, and pulled sharply upwards, thereby separating the seams that ran down from the crown of their heads, and freeing them from their human skins like the coiled interiors of baseballs from their leather husks.

As for the security guards, police officers and soldiers—it seemed that they had all been previously transformed. Their weapons and now-misfitting clothes were strewn everywhere—as were a considerable number of poop piles. The protectors, mostly reborn as farm animals (the majority, roosters), having benefited from a slight lead, walked at the head of the pack. Some, trampling and skittering over the fences, were already pushing their way into the hole.

All this, while at the first amphitheater, on the edge of the hole, the band was still playing. The guitarist was a giant condor. The drummer—a large rat. The bass player and lead singer—both were Tasmanian devils. Brothers, possibly.

She goes forty feet below,
Where the ancient cities glow
Through everything I know.

john**reed**

Then the hole grew again. And the band was sucked in. The mustardlike mud covered their speakers—but still, they played.

Like a miner in an open field,
I've nowhere to go but down.

Then the mud covered them, and the music was gone.

And the aliens had done their work—everyone was a three-eyed animal. And everyone was getting sucked into the growing hole. The fences had collapsed, and bodies were pushing forth to the rim and sliding in—edged forward by those behind them. Like sheep. Like lemmings.

Airplanes and helicopters appeared overhead—then plunged into the mud.

And then, Thing found that she was at the rim of the hole. Not so much a discovery, it was just a fact. She had walked there, and now she had arrived, and was looking into an abyss so deep that the bottom could not be seen.

Then she looked up, and lifted her arms, because it seemed to her that the sky was calling. And she screamed. And all the other people around her, who were giraffes and rats and flamingos and crocodiles, they were all looking up too, and howling, moaning, squawking and hissing at the sky.

And the humans-turned-to-animals were everywhere. Koala bears clung to the rock faces of the hole wall. Blue herons circled and hawed at the stars. All looked with their third eye as far as they could—all screamed with their new lungs as loud as they might.

And for an instant, it was as if Thing's third eye could see from above, as if she were receiving transmissions from the alien broadcasting network. Yes, she could see through her third eye—down below, everyone was looking up, and everyone was screaming.

Otter was behind her, and as much as he too was looking up, into the sky, he pointed the camera at Thing as the mud under her feet fell away, and she dropped into the whirlpool that was engulfing the world. She had her microphone in her hand, and she was screaming into it—as if that were the report she were making. Musk Shrew and Sloth, too, were motoring as if on autopilot—Musk Shrew answering his cellular, and Sloth adjusting the dials on his sound box, as Thing slipped with her microphone, downwards. Then she was gone, into the mud, into the sludge. The cord of the microphone followed her. Then the plug pulled from Sloth's sound box, and the microphone cord trailed Thing into the hole.

Then, by the sight of her third eye, Thing saw all the places she had ever been get sucked into the hole. Entire cities—New York, Roswell, Las Vegas, Cleveland, Washington, Jigtown, New Orleans, Los Angeles. Whole islands—Manhattan, Hawaii, Maui. Cities abroad—London, Greenwich, Goa, Rishikesh and New Delhi. A swath of Alaska. Then, too, Aruba, Barbados. Texas, Cannes, Mexico, the Swiss Alps. Her hometown of Maplewood, New Jersey. Her childhood summer camp in Bangor, Maine. Her day school. Everything. Gone.

And Thing—microphone still in hand, as if still reporting to the world—she screamed. A silent scream into the mud. A scream of joy, of terror and of utterly nothing. She screamed, as it all went down.

The mud took her. She pushed. It pulled.

Through the crust of the Earth, she descended. Then, released, she fell through the air—into the bottomless crevasse. Mud clung to her—her body as if formed of clay.

She splashed into a pool. Otter, Sloth, Musk Shrew and her team followed. Though bodies fell endlessly into the pool, the water was clear and blue. She stood, clean.

And Thing knew—all that had happened, it was so the world could understand. And even if she never thought she'd write a book, now she had a book in her that would put an end to all books. Or, oh, maybe she'd just tape it. Maybe they'd just take a few broadcast minutes for her to explain—to expose every secret global conspiracy that everyone was aware of. Thing consulted her producer, Musk Shrew, who was there, preening and punching numbers into his cell phone. Approved ("Yass'm!") Thing made her live broadcast to the world. Everything would be elucidated. And everyone would understand.

The brain staples, she said, were coming out.

She advanced through the pool—Otter captured the plash of water on her thighs. She shook her blonde hair. Her nipples tested the stretch capacity of her cow-print bikini. And she embarked on the report that would wow the world. They would fall to their knees and worship her. And, if they were animals that didn't have knees, well, for example, they would lower themselves to their flippers.

"You may wonder," Thing began, "why you're an animal," as she was aware that this question might eventually arise to every person on Earth, as, she was also somehow aware, every person on Earth was currently an animal.

Otter gathered the footage. Muddy figures fell from above into the crisp water of the blue pool. They arose, clean and wondering—elks, wild boars and wombats. A few of the transformed, porpoises and fish and such, swam downstream towards what Thing implicitly knew was an underground inlet that fed into, according to one's preference, a freshwater river, a stream, a lake, a bay, a coral reef or the open sea. Thing narrated—

"All of nature is reflected in humanity. When the Red Aliens first came to Earth, many millennium ago, they updated our DNA not only with their own DNA, but with an equal sampling of all the Earth species that existed at the time. Now, all those species, whether or not they've since become extinct, are represented by the human, as in, former human race. The animals that we are span the gamut of the natural world. And, by thus representing the animals, by being animals, we may fully realize our animal connection—individually, in the animals that we have become, and communally, by our equitable interaction with each other. The PETA people, that is, the People for the Ethical Treatment of Animals people who were formerly people, will be pleased to find that all the world's dogs and cats and rabbits, and so on, are henceforth as articulate as they are. Probably, those newly articulating creatures will make excellent contributors to the effort of finding, for the PETA organization, a new name and purpose—as it's a forgone conclusion that there'll be no more animal testing."

From there, Thing answered the question—why wasn't she an animal too? Well, there were several reasons. Number one—as the crowning achievement of human cultural and evolutionary development, she had been singled out to represent humanity as, not only what it had been, but what it should have been. Now herself, plus, she had been improved not just physically, but mentally. It was as if, in addition to the attendance of a plastic surgeon in heaven, she'd had a program upgrade too. Though everyone had been hardwired a computer chip, hers was, comparatively, a superchip.

"Admittedly, my literary gymnastics were always brilliant, and as vigorous as an excited fish on a trampoline—but, from this moment on, I won't be joking around quite as much. And, even if I never really made any mistakes, well, if I did they were largely due to a slight undiagnosed hearing impairment that has since been corrected by my superchip, and, in any case, those mistakes I wasn't making, well, I won't be making them any longer."

the**WH●LE**

What's more, it had been as the pinnacle of humanity that she had been chosen by the Red Aliens to fulfill a *special* human role—the comprehensiveness of which would soon be appreciated. Suffice it to say, as the new Madonna (not the rock star, but the mother of the messiah), the human form would be most appropriate and "universal," at least in terms of Earth, because, of all former humans-turned-to-animals, the single form they had in common was the one they lost, which was the human form, which she had.

"And lastly, I'm just not like the rest of you," she said, kindly, "and the difference between me and you is, well, what was formerly the difference between humans and animals."

Then Thing and her crew began to walk. They were followed by the others. Their direction was the center of the hole. Thing smirked, enlightened—

"They're here, you're here, to witness—to be, not just my disciples, but my converted flock."

A few of the sheep baa-ed—

"We love you."

"I mean," Thing made it clear, "the future is now. I mean, the future, it's over. It was, like, yesterday. We're at the beginning. The end. Peace. War. It's a simpler time, but more complex. And it's out there. And it's here."

Thing went on to lay bare all the theories about the cause of the hole. In terms of the environment—yes, the aliens were changing a few things, and human beings, on their own, were changing a few things. But actually, the things that people were changing that looked like changes for the worse were changes for the better, because, in conjunction with the changes the aliens were making, and the changes that the aliens were making to humans themselves (such as enhanced lungs), the sum total of all changes would result in a world that was a much pleasanter, healthier place (for humans and aliens). It was, as Thing said, all to the good. In terms of the various disease ideas—the herpes, the smallpox and the like—yes, the hole might be looked on as a planetary or societal disease, but it was also an inoculation against more potent forms of disease that the aliens, albeit unintentionally, would invariably bring to Earthlings and the Earth. And the politics? Well, in the same way as the disease stuff, the current political difficulties—local, global—while on the face of them terrible and insurmountable, were, on closer analysis, completely minor, and major only in the sense that they would be the final pesky obstacles to hurdle, kick out of the way or sidestep at the threshold to paradise and prosperity, et al. The great variety of military testing that had gone on in the secret installation beneath the site of the hole had, likewise, aided in the multifaceted conditions required to create the hole, and, thereby, were also due their credit for the God-bless-us-every-one-of-us, blissful denouement to everything. Yes, and the aliens, as well, should be in no ways forgotten for their contributions in bringing the hole about.

The Olympic Committee was also owed a debt of gratitude, for all their support. And Thing, taking this opportunity to thank the thankworthy, felt duty-bound to single out the 7-Eleven in Roswell that had sold her and her crew the Olympic flip-flops, as, had it not been for those, and the tiny needles therein outfitted with receptivity drugs ("a good thing"), she never would have put it all together. Oh, and she had to thank Mitch and Ponte, as, without them, she might never have know what an important role the Olympic Committee had played.

Also, Thing acknowledged the government and future government, among others, for making her immortal, and she explained how every ten years she would be returned to the past, and the age of twenty-four, and that as good as things were going to get now, well, with her wisdom ever-increasing, future futures would have even more to thank her for. Way more, incidentally, than anything she had to thank anyone else for. But, regardless, for all that, she was deeply thankful.

"So," summarized Thing, "I'm finally going to get to be immortal—and not immortal like Lady Di, but live immortal!—and the world is going to have everlasting Eden, and goodwill among men and whatnot. Excellent news, you say—but how does it all relate?"

And with that, Thing pointed, and Otter redirected the camera at a boy in the distance—the distant center of the hole. He was digging. With a red, plastic shovel.

"For those of you who've been following from the beginning, you know that even nothing means something. And so, if you know that, you probably realized that this cow-print thong bikini that I'm wearing also has a meaning. First, just by looking at me, you know I'm a Bovinity (which, as you can see, was no simple-minded pun, but a prophetic insight). What you may not have known, however, is that this cow print signifies a sacred animal to the aliens (who are here for our own good). To them, the cow is a source of organs for organ transplants, and, in my case, I represent the sacred animal in the form of—transplanted mother. The mother of Bobby Peterson, who's there in the distance. And, of course, I'm just generally sacred too."

Otter turned the camera back to Thing, and then, suddenly, the entire world could see what his lens saw—but without a television. The entire world could see through Otter's lens by way of their third eye!

"The hole, and the whole enchilada," reported Thing—

"It was all about me. I'm the new Madonna. Madonna with alien child. That's why I not only followed the hole, but it followed me. New York, Las Vegas—everywhere I went, the hole went, because I am the source of the hole."

Then, as it was relevant, Thing spoke of Tina and Tim, and her recent marriage and separation and probable divorce (if she ever went to Mexico, which was more likely than ever, now that she knew she wasn't heading there for hell), and of her subsequent conversation with a phone psychic, who foresaw that ultimate fulfillment for Thing came in the form of "the one," who was a them. And yes, the psychic had also been right in predicting that Thing would discover she had a long-lost child, even though she had thought she only had a nearly forgotten abortion. And so, the one had turned out to be two—that is, her son, and the father of her son. And, in yet another sense, the one had been not only her son and the father of her son, but all the world, as Thing, by way of discovering her fulfillment, was bringing fulfillment to everyone on Earth. Indeed, Thing noted in an aside, Myrtle the psychic had been right about everything, including not lending her some money.

"I mean," said Thing, "there's no reason to lend money to the future Madonna—who would ask her to pay?"

Otter laughed. Sloth laughed. Musk Shrew laughed. "Surely no one!" they said, adding that, because she would never have to pay anyone, her income as a Lawimi princess would rapidly accrue into a vast fortune.

("Ah yes," sighed Thing, taking it all in stride.)

She then went on to explain about the Rabbit, and how Bobby was her and the Rabbit's son, and how the Black Rabbit was a friend of hers who was really a Red Alien who had impregnated her when she was unconscious as a result of drinking one of those cocktails that he mixed, which were suspicious, but legal. The child she had conceived with the Red Alien/Black Rabbit would realize every ancient and modern prophecy, she further elucidated, and would bring all the world together, and all people of the world together.

"For example," she said, as, in the background, Bobby Peterson peeled off his latex mask and gloves to reveal that he was not a brown-haired human but a half-red half-alien who, with his lobster skin and exotic features, looked as much like an ancient Aryan as he did an ancient Egyptian, "my son is not only the white messiah, but the black messiah, and the Asian messiah, and the Indian messiah and every other messiah, as the Red Alien is the parent species (and genetic manipulator) of all humans."

Thing turned to address Otter's third-eye camera—

" 'Genetic manipulator.' You didn't think I'd get that, did you?"

Thing resumed—

"Certainly, the Lawimi are also right. They were the original Homo sapiens servants engineered by the Red Aliens, who were the original Atlanteans. You may know that there are dozens of theories as to the location of Atlantis, and, it just so happens, all of them are correct, as, in the language of the Red Alien, the word for *city* or *compound,* is, *Atlantis.* In myths and legend, the Lawimi remember the Atlantis, i.e., city, that was located at this site—the site of the hole. But, while far and away the largest Red Alien Atlantis, the Lawimi Atlantis is only one of many Red Alien Atlantises that once dotted the planet. Hence, the deepenings that have occurred in various other locations (rediscovered by dint of my all-encompassing investigation), where other Atlantises will be raised."

Thing's squad slid down a last muddy slope towards the former Bobby Peterson, now the Red Alien/Homo sapiens messiah. He was still digging as Thing scooped him up in her arms. And throughout the Earth's entire former-human population, there was not a single dry third eye. All wept. Thing wept. The boy/alien/messiah wept. And Thing, instinctually knowing that he was thirsty, tore off her bikini top and offered him her breast—or, well, breasts. The five-year-old chose one, and knew what to do. The suckling was successful, apparently, and milk dribbled down her chest.

"They work!" Thing exclaimed.

The hole rumbled, and the eternal drain (ever-clearing) sucked everyone and everything in, again. The mud, the gravity. But this time, not even a feathery flutter of fear. The hole was a dark cool place where you could sleep forever. Thing felt the soft-shell lobster skin of the former Bobby Peterson pressing pleasantly against her torso. His lobster lips gently clawed her nipple.

Then came a deeper rumbling, as if up through the bowels of the Earth, and Thing, with her child in her arms, felt the mud rushing past her— pulling her hair down her back—while she was rising. Rising with such velocity that she strained to hold Bobby to her breast. Rising with such velocity that she released the child, and ascended with her arms and legs akimbo—a willing doll. Her bikini top was stripped from her grasp. Her bikini bottom was stripped from her body.

And then, she was in the air—shooting skyward. With a sucking exhalation, the mud had released her into the atmosphere.

The fast wind snatched gobs of muck from her flesh—and soon she was muckless, and pink, and her hair was ruffled and half-dry, and Otter, shooting up beneath her (with Bobby and the crew, and the innumerable others beneath them), pointed his camera and finally answered that question the world had always wanted answered.

Yes, she was a true blonde.

(One of the ways she'd been improved.)

And the gold alien shuttlecraft that swooped to the rescue (first her rescue, then that of Musk Shrew, Otter, Sloth and her crew—the others below got beige shuttles) was not at all surprising, as she had seen it before. The ship was identical to the alien shuttlecraft that had been rendered by the ancient Colombian, solid-gold relic she had seen displayed at the Roswell UFO Museum. But while the real ship was shiny like gold, it was obviously constructed of something rarer, and *plus cher*. The interior was luxuriously appointed with fully reclining Corinthian leather seats, electric everything and plenty of legroom. The hieroglyph control panels were generous and easy to read (and Thing could read them, as she recollected the symbols from one of a plentitude of past lives of which she was now cognizant. Why, no wonder her handwriting was so flamboyant—untamable—in the dull print of English!) The pilot was outfitted in white cowboy boots, a white flyer suit and a white space helmet. He lifted his face visor. It was the Red Alien/Black Rabbit. He handed Thing a robe. She hesitated—

"Silk?"

"What else?"

"How could I have doubted you?" she asked, and took the kimono.

"Ewww," she rustled in the garb, "nice."

"Pink cocktail?" inquired the Red Alien/Black Rabbit.

"What else?" asked Thing.

She took the cocktail, and introduced the Red Alien to her crew and the world.

"Might I—"

The Alien approved—

"A capital idea, pink cocktails for the world."

"On you—you Lobster Aliens?"

"Yes, as always, the pink cocktails are on us—although, not meaning to offend, we prefer to be called the Star Race. Lobsters are fine creatures, to be sure, and I cast no aspersions, as many a fine human being is now a fine lobster—but, well, lobsters are only red when they've been cooked, and we Red Aliens have had our own trouble over the millennia, as we too have a delicate white flesh, and, alas . . ."

"Star it is."

"Thank you."

Cocktails were distributed to Thing's crew, and, Thing could see by her third eye, to former humans worldwide. Thing, taking stock of the resplendent shuttle, sipped thoughtfully—

the**WH●LE**

"I guess your investments picked up?"

"Yes," confirmed the Alien of the spacecraft, "it's a Mercedes," and he pointed to the hood ornament.

"Oh, so I see," said Thing, taking the Red Alien by the arm. He removed the white helmet of his white space suit.

"My white knight," Thing reported to Otter's ready camera, "the Red Alien."

The Red Alien/Black Rabbit then directed the team to look downward, which, through a downward-oriented window, they did. And they saw every type of alien craft that Earth had ever recounted or even just imagined. And at the helms of the ships, as well as on the ground below, there were not just representatives of the Star Race, but as many species of aliens as there were types of beings in mythology, religion, folklore, legend, fable and hallucination.

Then, through the preparation of this intergalactic delegation of aliens, the ground below shook, and the apex of a dome appeared—the yellow mud clearing from its surface in a swirling akin to that of a soap bubble. Then, the glowing city of Atlantis. Inside the dome, white surfaces were polished by diligent aliens with eight arms, or, legs. With more rumbling, the colossus lifted from the ground—freed. And the city rose silently.

And Thing lifted her hands together, gesturing in prayer and nodding, that yes, all things were whole.

johnreed

So, Thing got her pullover award for investigative journalism, a sweater which she frequently wore, which was called a Howitzer. Also, later that year, she got her Nobu Prize. (The official names of the honors were changed from Pulitzer and Nobel to the Pullover, Howitzer and the Nobu Prize, as it went without saying that Thing was the one who'd had it right.) Shortly after that, having gone as far as she could possibly go in the field of journalism, Thing officially retired from the profession. So, officially, that would be the end of our story. But, as we began somewhat before the beginning, tracking Thing's history prior to the onset of the hole, let us now end somewhat after the end.

The world adored her, et cetera. Adulation, and so forth. All loved Thing. And most importantly, America most of all. It was not as if she was loved on some weird tour in Europe or Scandinavia or Japan, but America. New York and L.A. They made "Thing" everything, from shampoos to motorbikes. Whole magazines were dedicated to the "Superstar Supersavior," as she was dubbed. Indeed, she was presented with three of her own third-eye channels. And they weren't hard-to-find channels either, they were stations 2, 4 and 5. Worldwide. Channel 2 for *Great Performances*. Channel 4 for *The Forefront*. And Channel 5 for home shopping. For those of a philosophical bent, Thing had allowed the humanism professor that she had met in Las Vegas (he'd turned wallaby) to dedicate himself to a series of picture books that explained her beliefs. Subjects that went unaddressed due to the time restraints of broadcasting would be taken up by the professor. Volumes one through twelve resolved such questions as the missing link, the disappearance of the dinosaurs, and crop circles. Entirely voluntarily, the world had offered up all other (now-outdated) books to a recycling program that would supply everyone (ex-humans and sentient animals lived in perfect harmony) with the option of receiving the materials. Moreover, everyone was afforded the opportunity to receive a full-size poster and

john**reed**

eight-page photo album of the former VJ's omniscient self—an opportunity that every last earthly soul seized upon.

Of her numerous, numerous accomplishments, she was most proud of her role as the world's model mother. Since being reunited with her progeny, she had continued to lactate. (Her breast implants had, miraculously, disappeared, while her breasts had, equally miraculously, enlarged and lifted.) She was always nursing her child, the former Bobby Peterson, and, in that, she had made nursing in public not only acceptable, but doggone trendy. She was a planetary hero for bringing down the absurd social inhibition, and freely availed herself to her son, absolutely whenever and wherever he wanted—and paying no mind at all to the minor detail that the boy was pushing seven. No, it was not unseemly at all, it was universally agreed. No not at all. Not ever. No, never unseemly, ever, at all. Thing, having advanced far beyond her previous incarnation as "Thing," took the name Yum Chen Mo, which, in Tibetan, meant, "the Great Mother," which, it turned out, she was, to everyone. Everyone on Earth.

Of course, it didn't hurt that everyone else had been transformed into an animal—a talking, thinking animal, but an animal, nevertheless. Yum Chen Mo, being the last "human being," as such, commanded a certain level of attention, and respect. (Even her son was not human—rather, he was half-alien.) And she was—the best way to say it would be—divine. She was far more perfectly human than anyone had ever been—and not just in perception, but in actuality. She was, in everything, vibrant and pure—even her temperaments. Indeed, she was of such strong character that she uncomplainingly bore the limitations of all the squirrels, Komodo dragons, kangaroos and buffoons that surrounded her.

"She was," to quote *The New York Times*, which was one of the many newspapers available to one's third eye, "so beautiful that the sun marveled every time it shone on her face." She'd but the faintest memory of makeup, as she was so in tune with her body that she could just naturally retint her complexion to suit any broadcast or lighting contingency. She was in perfect harmony with, well, the whole shebang. Even so, she had a stylist to dote over her. An attractive armadillo by the name of Sue with a very pretty third eye. And her wardrobe was personally attended, daily, by any designer she desired, be that Ostrich Delorenta, Calvin Swine, Isaac Mahi-Mahi, Donna Courlan, Lippizaner Versace or Emu Miu. (Apropos of her fashion preeminence, Yum Chen Mo also chose the designer variations of the red and green sweatsuits that were available, or, make that *preferred* by everyone else.)

Tonight, on her WE (World Eye) hour, which was broadcast to all third eyes, worldwide, live, Thing was awarding General (Giant) Schnauzer the Goddess Gives You a Kiss on the Brow Award. The weekly hour was not so much a show, as a visit to the Yum Chen Mo temple, which was sort of like a Tibetan temple, but made of a substance so light and white as snow.

The aliens, having restored order, had departed Earth, and left Yum Chen Mo the Lawimi city of Atlantis (which was the biggest and best of the former Red Alien cities). She was served by ten thousand faithful adherents (she could only take so many), and spent her time, primarily, at the temple atop it all, where today, upon her throne, she was receiving General Schnauzer. Careful not to tip her intravenous supply of pink cocktails, she leaned over her perch—the highest point on Earth—to look through the pristine crystal window, to see the hole, far below. For third-eye viewers the world over, Otter, camera-mammal, turned his third-eye lens to the site, way down there, which was getting filled in with a substance that could only be described by the untutored as fairy dust. Two massive, flexible pipes wound down from the circumference and pumped in the powder, while a line of open trucks, No Worries Munitions trucks, drove directly off the perimeter into the shining heap.

General Schnauzer was a fine animal—robust and sinewy, and immediately imparting, to any companion or third-eye viewer, not only his high spirits, but his extreme reliability. He wore an exquisitely tailored Giorgio Armadillo red sweatsuit, and, on his hind paws, a pair of Reeboks.

Having been so honored as to lick the hand of Yum Chen Mo (her charm bracelet rattled charmingly), he took his place on a pillow at her feet. (A filled-to-the-rim, pink-cocktail dog bowl had been provided.) Surrounding them, in a gazebo, terrarium-type architecture, were scores of plants and small living things—which was plainly quite enjoyable to the General, who was known to be disposed to plants and small living things, such as caterpillars, worms and beetles.

"These are some nice larvae you have here, Yum Chen Mo."

"Thank you, General Schnauzer. Now, let me ask you, how does it feel to be a hero?"

"Well I wouldn't call myself a hero, Yum Chen Mo, I'm just trying to do my job, no different than any one of a great many of the great citizens of this great nation."

"Why diamond dust?"

"As you know, Yum Chen Mo, diamond dust is uniquely suited to this purpose. Our nation, as the world's lifeguard, employs diamonds in the building of our bombs, as diamonds make excellent shrapnel. Needless to say, they are treated so as to revert to coal after impact, as will the diamond dust we're employing in this scenario—after about a year or two."

"What other uses do you have for diamond dust?"

"Well, since we began using it as shrapnel, our scientists have found that by grinding large diamonds into a fine powder, we have an excellent filler for general purpose sandbags. And with the surplus we had of diamonds, it became a legitimate replacement for gold dust—for, like gold dust, it doesn't corrode and is extremely heavy."

"Couldn't you, in a case like this, use sand to fill the hole?"

"Sand?" Schnauzer pshawed, "Why, Yum Chen Mo, this is the Lawimi Nation! We can't use an inferior material because of the cost. Our military represents all of us. And in times of crisis, when we call upon the military for assistance, we must have confidence that we are to have the very best. It can't be a question of," and he said this disdainfully—

"Money!"

Yum Chen Mo, sensible, agreed, then asked her next question—

"Why is diamond dust better than sand?"

And the General was well prepared with his answer—

"Sand can be highly irregular, and may clog, or just not flow with the same fluidity as diamond dust, which, having been ground down from larger stones, is of a quintessential uniformity. Now, you're perfectly correct to suggest that a civilian might wonder why we don't use sand from the thousands of miles of desert that border the site, but, for a military-grade standard, sand is so irregular, and so riddled with organic matter, that it represents a totally unreliable, unstable element—one distinctly ill-suited to our purpose. But the diamond dust, not only was it an ideal material, but we had a considerable amount of it on hand, at two bases within pumping range, and one within truck range."

"General, might we talk about that for a minute?"

The General perked his ears, glad to oblige. Yum Chen Mo turned to Otter, "Otter, show the clip." This, Otter did, while Yum Chen Mo explained to the third-eye audience what it was seeing—

"As I understand it, General Schnauzer, two pipelines are pumping diamond dust into the hole, while from a third location, trucks are caravanning loads from an undisclosed military installation. Now, though it might appear odd to some viewers that the trucks aren't dumping the diamond dust, but driving headlong into the abyss, I believe there's a sound rationale."

The third-eye clip illustrated just this—two gargantuan tubes pumping diamond dust, and a caravan of No Worries Munitions trucks driving headlong into the abyss.

"Why yes," answered the General, indulgent of Yum Chen Mo's viewers, "that's an affirmative on that sound rationale, Yum Chen Mo. You see, it's not within the design specifications of that particular dump truck to dump anything."

"And," Yum Chen Mo widened her worried eyes, "are the drivers all right?"

"Oh yes," answered the honorable, jovial General, "there are no live drivers in those trucks, they run on guidance systems similar to those of our smart missiles."

Yum Chen Mo nodded, captivated, and moved on to a more serious note—

"What if the hole gets bigger?"

But the General didn't seem too worried. He shrugged it off with, well, as he didn't have shoulders, a roll of his back, and a self-congratulatory wink of his third eye. The impression he gave, indeed, was that if patting one's own back were possible, patting his own back would have been precisely what he was doing.

johnreed

"Since the geological curtain has been lifted—meaning to say, since the illusion that the world is round is no longer being imposed on our consciousness—the military has been permitted to declassify this critical bit of data, and the civilian science community has been able to update numerous equations and entire fields of study. Meteorology, for example—now the daily weather report is accurate to the minute. By the same token, the field of geodynamics has advanced to the most exact of the exact sciences. Having said as much, geologists, both military and civilian, assure us that the hole won't be getting bigger. But we'll be monitoring it closely, just the same, and even if it does get a little bigger," the General chuckled—

"There are always plenty of diamonds!"

Yum Chen Mo turned to Otter, "Otter, is the other clip cued up?" It was, and Yum Chen Mo nodded to the General, who rubbed his third eye in preparation. And then, wearing her I'm-the-Queen-of-the-Earth smile, she viewed the clip through her own oh-so-lovely third eye.

Far below, children, that is, young animals—mules and oxen and Siamese cats—were gliding through the slopes of the hole on bright red sleds. And all around, they frolicked and cavorted in "Duh Whole," a theme park that transitioned seamlessly into the cities and suburbs beyond, which stretched, as if forever, across the expanse of the flat Earth.